It Started with You

Melissa Alexander

It Started with You

EISBN: 978-0-9973094-0-9
ISBN: 978-0-9973094-1-6

Cover Art Sig Evensen, Inkubus Design

Table of Contents

For my husband, Shane. Thank you for supporting me while I wrote this book (and reading it!). You did not even laugh when I told you my crazy idea to write, or complain when I took hours on the weekend to write while you played with our kids. You have been my biggest encourager and champion. I love and appreciate you more than you know!

I never knew how many people it can take to create a book. Thank you to Sig at Incubus Design for this fabulous cover. You captured my book and my vision completely. Lisa R., you read this book and I know you do not like to read. I owe you and Jeff dinner for the nights you spent on this. I appreciate your honest feedback and I never got angry at you for showing me my mistakes. And to the rest of my family, you all have been so supportive when I told you my crazy idea. Last, but not least, all of my beta readers. I took all of your comments and suggestions to heart, you may notice a few changes from the version you read many months ago.

Chapter 1

The party started out like every other boring work function, plenty of schmoozing, fakeness and alcohol. For Alexandria McNeil, it is painful to stand there with a smile on her face, glass of wine in her hand and making small talk, but it is her business.

Looking around the room at all the rich, powerful, famous faces should make me ecstatic. We have pulled off a fabulous event for Senator Gregg's re-election campaign, but being the party planner for him is exhausting. I wonder how many reporters got into the event as guests to get some dirt on him and his wife. My guess is we will be busy tomorrow with media inquiries. At least the Senator's wife showed up and stayed sober enough not to create a scene. Unlike the last donor event which resulted in a wine glass being thrown. I guess I should be happy that incident was the straw that broke the camel's back, which resulted in my firm being hired to plan all of the events and manage his wife.

The Senator just wrapped up his speech and made his plea for more campaign donations; dinner has been served. All that is left is watching him walk around the room trying to get more money while everyone gets stinking drunk on the free booze. I hope his wife will not be one of those getting stinking drunk. I made sure that the staff knew to give her a splash of alcohol in each of her drinks.

I wonder how long this donor dinner will continue so I can leave without being noticed. It is surprising I have made it this far into the evening without being cornered by anyone asking how my father has been. As the only daughter of the current Vice-President of the United States, who is well known for his voting records and his constant outspokenness on all things political makes my life interesting. Besides dealing with that press, my socialite mother and her frequent attempts to keep me in the spotlight makes my life stressful. All I want to do is work hard and be successful without my parent's interference. So far so good, and the evening looks like it is getting better since Senator Gregg is coming over, maybe the evening is done.

"Alexandria, this was perfect. You were right when you suggested using this venue. And thank you for making sure the wait staff put a splash of vodka in Linda's drinks," says the Senator.

"It was no problem. I hope this evening was successful for your campaign. Your speech had the right amount of passion. We will make sure that several of the news networks get copies to run for airtime," I reply.

"Call me tomorrow and we will review the next few events to confirm the details. Your father was right when he told me to call you and have your firm plan our events for us after that last donor dinner," he says as he is leaving.

Wow...am I ever going to get out from underneath my father's name and interference. I can't help getting frustrated. I hope my work speaks for why anyone would want to hire my firm, not my father. Well, as one of my friend's always says "don't look a gift horse in the mouth, it will pay for a new handbag."

"Thank you Senator Gregg. I will call you tomorrow morning so we can complete the schedule of events for the next few weeks. Have a good evening," I tell him. I am more than happy getting those words out of my mouth since that means I can call it a night as well.

This has been the worst day of my life. The last thing I want to do is stand here and make nice with people. I want to go home and have another glass or bottle of wine. As I finally figure out how to slip out unnoticed, my co-worker and best friend, Catherine Knight, shows up with another glass of wine for us. "Stop looking so miserable Alex. The Senator is gone and the party was a success. Drink up," says Catherine. "Plus, Peter was a douchebag. I know it hurts that you caught him sleeping with someone else, but he was a total bore and you said the sex wasn't great."

Like usual, Catherine was right. My mind is still reeling from learning that someone I spent the last three years of my life with is a scumbag cheater. I should be happy our relationship is over. Now I can focus on me and stop listening to his nitpicky, micromanaging way of life.

"I'm not thinking about Peter," I state hoping Catherine can't tell I am lying. "I just hate these types of functions. There is too much fakeness in one room."

"Alex, this is our business and a part of your life. How can someone so successful in the party planning industry hate this part of the job?" Catherine is right, yet again, this is why I love her.

"Okay, you win. It has nothing to do with the party. I am thinking about Peter. You know he called me a cold fish, and said I was a lousy lay. Which is why he was sleeping with other people! He said he still loves me and I should forgive him."

"Well, that is just b.s. Now I know I have no experience with you in the bedroom, but I know you can't be a cold fish," says Catherine with a laugh. "Plus, I have seen you dance and flirt when you have too much to drink on girl's night. There is no way you are a prude and you have your vibrator to finish what Peter could never do."

Catherine can make me laugh and stop feeling sorry for myself. Maybe this evening can be salvaged. "Catherine, you have an amazing way with words," I tell her laughing. "By the way, is everything ready for your birthday party this weekend?"

"You know it is. My house will be packed, but I am excited to see everyone. All my brothers will be there. Most of my brothers and their friends will be happy to know you are back on the market," she says with a huge grin on her face. "Maybe we should try to set you up with one of them or at least get a good orgasm from one of them."

I start laughing my head off at her outrageous statement. "You know I am not that kind of girl. Maybe I should give it a try though, one night and no strings. That may be what I need to bring a change in my life," I say as I clink my wine glass to hers still laughing away.

I love Catherine's family since they have an ease about their love and life that is unfamiliar to me and the way I was raised. They are close and her brothers are some of the most attractive men anyone has laid eyes on. One in particular has always been an object of many daydreams of mine, and if I admit it masturbation dreams with my vibrator as well. Catherine is the baby of the bunch and the only girl, so her brothers are always trying to be protective. In all honesty, they are like that with our close circle of girlfriends. I guess I should have seen the warning flags about Peter when none of them really cared for him after I introduced him to her family at her birthday party a few years ago.

"I am sure none of your brothers or their friends could even care about me being single now. Darcy is the one they all drool over." You should see our friend Darcy, she is 5'7 and has the body and looks of a model. She is your essential blonde hair, blue-eyed girl while I am maybe 5'3 with black hair and blue eyes. Even

Catherine has an exoticness about her with her Italian heritage shining through with her tan skin, dark hair and eyes. When I stand next to those two, I am invisible.

"You are so full of shit. I swear your mother did a number on you and your self-esteem. You have no clue that when you walk into a room everyone always looks at you. Do you even see yourself in a mirror?" exclaims Catherine.

I do understand what Catherine is talking about. I know I am pretty, not show stopping like Catherine just described. With parents who are always in the press, I think I have grown up trying to stay in the background so I could live my life. I am tired of having every thing I do show up in pictures and articles. Even tonight while most women went for low cut or short cocktail dresses, I stuck with the very easy, always great looking little black dress.

"Plus, my brothers do ask about you all the time. Especially since we went into business together. Carson is always wanting to know what we are doing on the weekends, during the week, who we are seeing, asking if you are still with Peter," she says.

"What?! Carson asks about me?" My mind is blown...Catherine just said that her drop dead gorgeous brother Carson, my long-time crush, has asked about me. Every time I see him I become an idiot who can barely string two sentences together.

He all but runs out of the room. I swear it's like he cannot get away from me fast enough. This is an interesting tidbit to learn!

Catherine just starts laughing and finishes off her wine, "Really, you seem interested in the fact that I said Carson's name. Do you have a crush on my brother?" She makes kissing noises at me. I respond by sticking my tongue out at her.

"Ok, we have to grow up or we are going to be the ones who make a scene," I say laughing and finishing my wine. I wonder if Catherine noticed that I hedged about Carson. If she did, she's being nice and not calling me out on it.

I put my wine glass down on the table and look over to Catherine who is just staring at me with her mouth wide open, this can't be good. "Oh no, did we make a scene? Is there a reporter behind me who just got that entire conversation? Please tell me that it's not a gossip columnist who is going to write about me saying that I am going to give a one night stand a try or print the orgasm comment," I say nervously.

"Well, don't look now but the d-bag just walked in the room and is headed this way."

Please no, this day cannot get any worse. All laughing aside, I look over my shoulder and sure enough Peter just walked into the room. Of course a few women are eyeing him like a steak. Those women can have him. He may look like filet mignon but he is more like chopped liver. Spoiled and will give you a stomach ache.

This is the excuse for me to get out of here. "Can you handle representing our firm since this party is winding down? I am leaving before he causes a big scene, and we end being the news story versus Senator Gregg," I ask Catherine.

"I'm on it and will keep you updated." I give her a hug and I am all but running towards the door.

As I quickly exit the ballroom of the hotel, I glance over my shoulder and see that Catherine is introducing Peter to an actor that we know. Peter being the fame hog that he is, he's loving every minute of it. At least this will give me the time I need to get out of the hotel and back to my condo.

It is funny how things will fall into perspective when you are no longer in a relationship. I am amazed at how blind I was to the real Peter King. I remember when we first met, he was so sweet and attentive. Slowly our relationship changed to him being critical and trying to manage my life. I should have known that he was only interested in me because of my name. I could kill my mother for introducing us at that benefit gala three years ago. His pedigree is just what my mother was hoping for. I have been nothing but a disappointment to her since I was not pushing for an engagement. Of course, it's not my mother's fault that I started dating him. Peter was very attractive and the first year seemed perfect but then things slowly changed.

And all it took was me leaving my Louboutins I wanted to wear tonight at his place, and swinging by this morning to grab them before work. Wow…that was something to walk into. Seeing Peter come flying out of his bedroom wondering why I was there. Then I noticed the purse on the table and we all know what happens next. Well, not everyone comes face-to-face with a girl named Candi, but that was the girl that I met this morning in his bed. I grabbed my shoes and got out of there as quick as I could. Obviously not quick enough since the screaming match that took place outside of his townhouse was ugly. At least I learned that I was frigid and apparently really bad in bed. Talk about killing a girl's self-esteem more. Something my mother could not even do. Maybe I don't need to do the one-night stand thing after all.

Once I am outside the hotel I begin slowly walking the four blocks to my condo. I adore this area of Atlanta, it has great shopping, restaurants and bars, and has the hip vibe of the 20-30 year olds. I love feeling like I am finally growing up. Doing everything on my own without the help of my family's money. Well, I can tell myself that but who am I kidding. At least my dad is being sweet and trying to secretly send work my way. You can't be angry at a father who wants to help. I also realize as much as my mother drives me crazy, she does it because she loves me. She loves her life of charity work and social events and wants the same thing for me. She is happy for me and my career, but I know she does not understand it.

I notice flashing lights and see there are a few police cars in front of my building. That is weird, I wonder what is going on. Probably a neighbor having a party that got too loud and someone complained.

Now there is something that everyone who really knows me, knows is true. I cannot walk in a straight line. Seriously, even stone-cold sober I will walk diagonally. If you are on the left side of me, sorry I am walking into you. It is something in my DNA. As I am walking down the hallway towards the elevators, I begin to look for my keys in my massive purse. I bump into a super handsome guy. This guy is amazing looking but seems to be really pissed off at me for bumping into him.

"I am so sorry. I tend to not walk in a straight line if I am not paying attention," I say with a laugh. The guy just stares at me, like crazy stares at me. His eyes remind me of black pits with no emotion behind them. As I am looking at him, I recognize that he is the same guy who has been visiting my neighbor, Allison. "Hey, aren't you seeing my neighbor, Allison," I ask him as we are standing there awkwardly.

"No," he replies rudely as he continues to stare at me.

I realize he is giving me the kind of look that really, really crazy pyschos give you before they kidnap you and make you their play toy. I need to get into the elevator, like now. "Um, again, sorry and enjoy your night." I finally found my keys and walk to the elevator.

I glance over my shoulder and see the guy is still standing in the foyer staring at me. Then he turns to walk towards me. Crap, this is making me nervous. Thankfully, the elevator doors open and I walk in, press my floor and hit the close door button before he can get on with me.

I realize I have overreacted. Why would a gorgeous guy freak me out? Well, the way he stared was a little more than freaky. Wow, wait until I tell the girls about this at girl's night. That guy had a very distinctive chiseled face that makes Brad Pitt look ugly in comparison. I also need to ask Allison about her boyfriend and his weird behavior.

At least now I can get out of these dreaded shoes that changed my life. I get off the elevator and as I am walking towards my door I notice there are policemen everywhere. "I am sorry but you cannot come any closer," a policeman tells me.

I glance at his name on his uniform. "I live right there, Officer Hoffman. Why can't I go into my house," I ask him.

"We have an active crime scene investigation right now. You will have to wait."

"What happened?" I try to look around him to see what is going on.

"I am not at liberty to say."

What a great way to end my day. My phone beeps and I glance down and see that Peter is texting me. Ugh, I am ignoring that. "But I have been at work all day, my feet hurt and I want to go into my place and go to bed," I tell him knowing that I am whining. I am pretty sure I may have stomped my foot as I said that.

I glance around him and my mouth falls open. I recognize a man who has stepped into the hallway to make a phone call. "Adam, is that you?" The police officer who stopped me gives me a dirty look for yelling down the hallway.

He glances my way. "Alex, what are you doing here?"

"Well, I am trying to get into my condo but this guy won't let me thru and my feet hurt."

"Those look like some killer shoes. You live on this floor? Carson mentioned you lived in the building but never said which number," Adam says as he walks over to give me a hug.

He is standing in front me and I can tell he is thinking about what to do. "Ok. Eric, can you walk Alex to her condo? Stay with her until we come over. Alex, I know this sounds weird but I can only let you come down here if you promise you are not going to look inside your neighbor's place."

"Sure, is everything ok," I ask him nervously. "Carson and I will come over when we are done. I know it is late but wait up for us," he tells me as he heads back towards my neighbor's place.

"Sure and thank you," I reply as the officer lets me under the police tape. "Sorry for being a pain," I tell him with a smile.

"No worries. My feet would hurt if I was wearing those shoes."

I am making sure that I follow Adam's instructions and look at my side of the hallway. I wonder what the hell is going on.

Chapter 2

The police officer who accompanied me back to my place is looking around and stops at a photo of me and my dad and then he put two and two together, "You are Alexandria McNeil."

"Yep, that's me," I reply as I open my refrigerator to pull out a bottle of wine. Maybe a glass of wine will help calm down my nerves.

"Your dad is the Vice-President," he says with awe. I can tell that this police officer has a total man crush on my dad. Thankfully there is a knock at the door that saves me from being embarrassed. The young officer opens the door and apparently his day gets better.

"Hey, Detective Knight. Her neighbor is over in her kitchen. Not sure if you are aware of who she is, but it's the Vice-President's daughter," says the officer who seems excited to see know who I am.

I am trying to open a bottle of wine and when I hear the officer announce the detective I turn around in shock. While his day is getting better and better, mine just got a whole lot worse. This cannot be happening. Carson Knight is in my condo. Carson Knight who happens to be the very same brother of Catherine's, subject of my many fantasies for the past eight years, and the same person who ignores me whenever I am around. When I turn, I hit the side of my counter and the wine bottle shatters into a million pieces. "Crap!" I squeal as wine and glass spill all over me and the floor.

Here he is, standing in my foyer, all six foot three inches, dark hair and even in his dress shirt you can tell his abs look like they are chiseled out of granite. All I can think about is how striking he looks in his suit this late at night. And how much I like the scruffy, unshaven look he is sporting now. I am covered in wine and look like an idiot. I wonder if he was out on a date since it is so late, and who the heck wears a suit this late?

"Alex, stay still so you do not cut yourself. Adam and I will come help you," Carson states from the door. "I know who she is. She happens to be my little sister's best friend," he adds to the officer.

Walking in behind him is his partner, Adam Miles. Adam is always the jokester and seems to be in a constant state of contentment while Carson is always serious and uptight. "Good to see you are still a klutz Alex," Adam says trying not to laugh at the mess I have made.

"Thank you for keeping an eye on her while we were finishing up next door. We have it from this point, Eric," states Carson in his serious tone. The poor policeman, Eric, now that I know what his name is, leaves pretty quickly under Carson's intense stare. Of course, that intense stare is now turned on me.

"Are you ok Alex?" Carson asks as he walks over. I swallow and realize that my throat feels like a desert.

I clear my throat, "Yes, I am fine. Minus being covered in wine and glass. In the grand scheme of things, I should not be complaining." Carson is standing in front of me looking me up and down. Without warning he leans over and sweeps me off my feet.

"Hey, what are you doing?" I exclaim trying to make sure my dress is covering my butt.

Carson drops me on the counter, "You are barefoot and there is glass everywhere. I was making sure you did not cut yourself." I watch as he begins grabbing paper towels to wipe up the wine.

"Where do you keep your broom?" Adam asks as he is walking around to join us.

"It is in the pantry. You guys know that I am a big girl and can clean up my own messes."

"Calm down kitten. We are trying to help you out since you have been wearing those god awful shoes all night," Adam replies.

"I am sorry, thank you both. Were you guys both working or out on dates?" I ask trying ease my nerves.

"Why do you ask?" Adam replies.

"It's after midnight and Carson is in a suit. You are always in jeans and a button down shirt, so it's hard to tell," I reply with a shrug as I am swinging my legs against the counter. When I am nervous I get fidgety.

Adam smiles at me. "Nah kitten. We were both working on our case when we got this call."

I glance down at Carson and see that he has finished wiping up the floor, but is staring straight ahead. I glance down and realize with the way I am swinging my legs he has an excellent view up my dress. I quickly cross my legs hoping he did not see my panties. His eyes meet mine and I am awestruck by the heat that I can see in his eyes. From that look, I assume he did get a good look up my dress.

"We need to ask you a few questions. Are you up to it?" Adam asks.

His question startles me and I break the eye contact with Carson. "Of course. But what's going on next door?" Then my manners finally kick in (my mother would kill me), "Do you guys want anything to drink, coffee, water, wine?"

Both of them reply, "Water."

Simple enough, I can handle making three glasses of water. My phone beeps again with a text message from Peter. I glance down to read it, 'You have to talk to me. Stop avoiding me. This is all your fault and I am willing to forgive you.' Holy shit, that asshole. I cannot believe he sent me that text message. I am not even going to reply.

I reach for the glasses and again my hands are shaking so badly because of that text message. I am furious, tired and want this day to be over. I almost drop one of the glasses. Next thing I realize, Carson is by my side and taking the glasses out of my hands. He touches my hand for a little longer than necessary. All I can think about is how his hand feels rough but soft at the same time. I start thinking about how I would like to feel those hands all the time and OMG…I must be crazy. They are here to talk about something that happened with my neighbor, and I am acting like a thirteen-year-old schoolgirl who has touched a boy for the first time. I look up at him and the look in his brown eyes says he is dangerous to me. Like he is pissed he is having to help me.

"Let me make the water for us. Go sit down on the couch before you break something else." I am more than happy to give him the space he needs after that look. Adam has made himself at home on the couch so I go sit down by him.

"Adam, can I ask you a question?" I say as I am getting comfortable on my couch.

"Sure," he replies with ease.

"Why do you always call me kitten?" This has been driving me crazy for years, Adam started using that nickname but never told me why. He starts laughing at my question.

"When I first met you, I told Carson that you reminded me of a sweet kitten. I could tell that you are very loving. I may have added in a lewd comment about how you would purr if someone scratched the right places." He can tell that he has caught me off guard and is loving every minute of it.

"I guess I get that for asking." I am trying hard to not laugh at him.

*****

Dear lord, I am a dirty old pervert. I am ten years older than Alex, and can barely keep it together when I look at her. I cannot believe she just caught me looking up her dress. Watching her gorgeous legs swinging by me was such a distraction. I could not help but stare at them. Then I was distracted by the glimpse of red lace. I can tell I scared her with my look, but the feel of her and the look on her face was tempting me to take her and kiss the living daylights out of her.

How can I be thinking of something like this when we have a serial killer on the loose who struck so close to her home? I should also be lucky that she did not ask how I knew where she lived since I have never been here.

Alex looks amazing even though she is paler than usual. She is wearing a simple black dress but it is clinging to all the right places. I have a hard time figuring out where to look because this dress is highlighting all of the parts of her body that I should be avoiding looking at. Her breasts, butt and legs. Not to mention her hair. She has a mane of rich, dark, coffee colored hair that she has curled tonight and I would love to see it spread out across my pillow. Great, now my other brain has decided to spring up and take notice of her. I cannot believe after all these years I still act like a sixteen-year-old-boy around her.

Looking around her place and taking in the soft greys, pinks and purple, it screams femininity but in an appealing way to me. Add in her smell of flowers and whatever else in god's name that she puts on her body, I could stand here all day breathing in the scents. I will probably never get these smells out of my brain.

I glance over to Adam and the smirk on his face tells me nothing has gotten past him on this. Adam has been my partner long enough to witness how I keep Alex at arms length, and he has called me out on it. Adam thinks I am insane for not asking her out but given the idiot she has been seeing for the past few years, and the age difference, I just stay away from her.

"Are we ready to get this going Carson?" asks Adam. I am walking over and give him a dirty look which he just rolls his eyes. "Of course," I reply sarcastically. I hope he is not planning on being the smart ass that he usually is. The last thing Alex needs to hear is our locker room banter.

*****

"Alex, can you tell us anything about your neighbor, Allison?" Carson asks gently.

"I do not know much. We lived across from each other for the past two years and she was friendly. We would chat if we were in the elevator together. Why, what happened?"

Carson clears his throat and looks uncomfortable. "She was murdered tonight."

"What? That is awful. Who did it?" I am shocked. How could something like this happen in our building?

"That is what we are trying to figure out. Did you see anyone or anything when you were walking into the building tonight that may stick out?" Adam asks.

That's when I remembered the guy downstairs. "Yes. When I was walking into the building, I bumped into this guy. I am pretty sure he is the same guy Allison has been seeing for the past few weeks. When I asked him if he was seeing her, he said he was not. Also, when I apologized to him, he stared at me like he was really pissed off that I ran into him."

"Did you get a good look at him?" asks Carson.

"Well, yeah, I did. He was extremely good looking. I couldn't help but stare at him. When I looked at his eyes they seemed kind of emotionless. It freaked me out so I walked away quickly." I look at Carson and then at Adam. Both of them are just staring at me with these dumbfounded expressions. "What's wrong?"

"Do you know the boyfriend's name or anything about him?" Carson continues while they both ignore my question.

"I'm pretty sure she said it was Philip or something like that" I am trying to remember what she told me about him. "All I can remember is that she said he was really good looking and would send her sweet notes and flowers. She thought it was very romantic," I add.

"Thanks Alex, that is helpful. Can you come down and work with the sketch artist on the guy you bumped into? He may be a lead," Adam asks.

"Alex, since we are talking to you about this and it will make the news we have to ask you to not discuss any of the details that you saw. The scene is very similar to several other cases that we are working on. We think the guy you bumped into may be a viable suspect," Carson says.

"How can you guys be sure that this guy I saw is the same person?" I ask them.

"Based on Allison's body temp and the call we received from the killer telling us where to find his victim, she had only been dead for fifteen- twenty minutes. Which is why we want to talk to this guy you saw. He could be a viable lead," Adam says.

This is staggering, how on earth did Allison end up dead? "Do you guys know how he is targeting his victims?"

"We think he is dating the victims for awhile and when he is done with them, he does what he does," replies Adam.

"Adam, enough with sharing information with her. She does not need to know all the details," Carson says sharply.

I look at Carson. Seriously, who does he think I am? Someone who is going to share with the media the details of the investigation. I am getting ready to let him have it when he asks, "Speaking of dating. Where is your boyfriend? If you were at function doesn't he usually attend?"

This conversation is going sideways real fast. The last thing I want to share with Carson and Adam are the details of why Peter and I broke up. "We broke up this morning. So no, he was not my guest even though he showed up near the end of the event."

"Why did you guys break up?" asks Adam. I can hear the curiosity in his voice. I am sure they both want to know what happened since they have met Peter before.

And here we go, down the path that I have no desire to go with these two. "Well, to be honest, it's not any of your business and has nothing to do with why you are here." I really hope this shuts down the conversation.

Adam has a smirk on his face and I realize he is not giving up. "Humor me kitten. Inquiring minds want to know. Plus, I view myself and Carson as your friends in addition to being the lead detectives on this case."

Ugh...I am such a pushover for a nice smile and sense of humor. Fine, I will tell them truth and maybe make them feel uncomfortable for asking. "Fine, you want to know. I went over to his place this morning to grab the shoes that I wanted to wear tonight since I left them at his place last week. I walked in and found him in bed with another woman. Needless to say, we are done."

"Your hot. Why on earth would anyone ever cheat on you?!" says Adam.

"Well, thank you for that but apparently in Peter's words, 'I am an ice princess and lousy in bed but he still loves me and wants us to be together'," I say turning bright red and praying that this conversation is done.

Well, that statement sure stopped Carson and Adam in their tracks. Both of them have stunned looks on their faces. I glance back at Carson and his eyes have gotten dark again and look hard and angry. "Peter was an idiot and never good enough for you, good riddance. I'm sorry he cheated on you, but you deserve better," states Carson.

"Ok, we are done here for tonight. Alex, you have both of our numbers so call us if you need anything and come down tomorrow morning to work with the sketch artist," says Adam as he is getting up to leave.

"Are you going to be fine here tonight?" asks Carson.

"I should be fine. I have an alarm and locks. I figure you guys will be across the hall for a while longer."

"Have a good night," both of them reply as I walk them to the door. Carson takes one last look around and then looks directly into my eyes and says, "You deserve so much more than Peter. Don't lose any sleep over him. That's horseshit what he said about you and you know it." With that statement, Carson closes the door and I am just standing there with my mouth hanging wide open.

WTF...did Carson mean what he said? How can he say that with so much conviction when he has no clue how I am intimately? If only he would give me the time of day, but what is the point of dreaming since it is obvious he is not interested in me. Other than being Catherine's best friend.

Chapter 3

"Dude, it is your lucky day!" Adam exclaims the moment we hear the lock turn on Alex's door.

I just look at him and raise my eyebrows. "How exactly is this my lucky day? First, we have another missing eyeball murder. Which means the mayor and probably the governor will be breathing down our necks. Second, our only witness is the VP's daughter which means we may have the Secret Service get involved. Third, what the hell are you talking about?".

Adam just grins at me like he does not have a care in the world. "Your secret long-time love, crush, whatever you want to call it, is single. You should ask her out or at least make a move. If you don't, maybe I should because she has the look of someone who could use a good- "

"Don't even finish that sentence or I will punch you in the mouth. She's my little sister's best friend you are talking about doing something to." Sometimes I want to strangle Adam. We have been partners for so long you would think I would be used to his joking.

"Noted. Then I take that as you call dibs. Plus, what kind of jackass is Peter to not know how to pleasure Alex in bed? You can look at her and tell if you hit the right buttons she will take off like a wonderful big-breasted rocket ship."

I look at him and see his grin. He has gotten me just where he wanted me, worked up over Alex. I just shrug my shoulders and reply, "Let's get back to this. Alex is safe and we need to solve this."

I am so full of it. All I can think about it is Alex across the hall getting ready for bed. A bed I would love nothing more than to be in with her. What the hell was that loser Peter thinking when he cheated on her? The guy has to be insane to not be able to see all the passion behind her formal, quiet façade.

I need to focus on this case and stop thinking about Alex and her bed. The crime scene techs are still working on gathering all the evidence. This scene is like the others, nothing is out of place. There is a bottle of wine on the coffee table with two glasses. This still goes with our theory that the killer is dating or knows his victims well enough to let him in their homes. There is also no sign of a struggle so the victims trust him enough that they do not realize he is about to slit their throats then remove their eyes and write on the wall with their blood.

"Hey Carson, come look at this." I walk down the hallway to what appears the victim's office where Adam is standing over a desk. In one of the drawers are a ton of florist cards. We begin looking over them and at first them seem normal except instead of a name it is only signed 'with love- P', the usual notes you see. 'I had a great time', 'Your eyes are amazing', 'Your eyes are beautiful'. Then they take a turn, 'You think you are so beautiful but I see you',

'You look thru me but I see you', 'I am coming to see you' and the final one 'I will take your eyes so I can see you always'.

"I believe these are from the killer," states Adam.

"No shit Sherlock." We have believed he was dating these women then killing them since there was never any sign of a struggle. This is the first time we have found evidence of this. "I wonder why he didn't take these with him," I murmur to myself.

"Maybe he had no clue she saved them. Most people just throw the cards away with the flowers. She seems to be a saver."

"Maybe he gave her more gifts. I am going to look in her bedroom." Adam just grunts while he is still going through her desk drawers. I walk thru the door that connects the bedroom to the office and look around. The room is very neat and organized which may make our job easier. I wonder if Alex's room is neat and girly like the rest of her place was. I hope she will be able to get some sleep. I need to stop thinking about her, especially since she is now involved in this case. I can add that to the list of reasons I should stay away from her.

You would think after eight years the list was long enough but nope. I am a glutton for punishment. I look forward each year to our family beach vacation knowing Catherine will bring Alex, and I will have a week of just watching her. She has a body to die for. While she is short, Alex is curvy in all the right places. Based off what I have seen of her in a bikini, her breasts are more than a handful. I shake my head as I realize how crazy and stalker-like I sound.

I open up the nightstand table and find of all things a vibrator. Dear lord, I should have let Adam search the bedroom. At that moment Adam walks in and starts laughing, "Man, if you could see your face. All women have one of those. I bet your sweet little Alex has one."

"Adam, I swear I will punch you in the face if you say anything else about Alex. Grow the fuck up!" The last thing I need on my mind is to picture Alex using a vibrator and pleasuring herself. "Well, Allison had an active sex life it looks like. She has condoms and more sex toys in her nightstand but nothing else," I state.

"Dude, this girl Allison may help us break the case. She saves everything. Look in this box on this shelf," says Adam. I walk over to Adam and in the box is her diary. Seriously, women in their late twenties still keep a diary. I shake my head.

"We will have more to start looking into tomorrow. We need to get the surveillance videos from the building. Alex is going to work with the sketch artist so we will have that to work with. The crime scene techs should finish up here tonight. Get the techs to dust the diary so we can start reading it tomorrow to see if we can get a name of this mystery man who sent all those flowers."

It is going to be a long night for me. I know when I try to fall asleep for a few hours Alex will be in my dreams. Why on earth did she have to stumble into this case?

Chapter 4

I wake up exhausted. It was not a good night for sleep for me. All I kept seeing was Peter yelling at me then changing into Carson who was kissing me. I decide I need to run down to the gym to get my brain back in order and to de-stress from last night. As I am getting ready, I grab my phone and take a look at my calendar since I know I have to go down to the police station. I will call Senator Gregg at 7:30am while I am getting my coffee. Confirm his schedule then head over to the police station. I should make it to the office by 10:30-11am, which isn't too bad.

It is only 5:30am, but I know that Catherine should be awake. I need to let her know what happened, and to find out how the rest of the party went. As I am lacing up my gym shoes, I put on my headset and call Catherine. I get her groggy voice, "Alex, you are killing me with your morning gym routine. I am up and getting ready for the gym."

"Good morning Sunshine. You are never going to believe what happened last night. I came home and I couldn't get into my condo because the police were investigating a murder. It was my neighbor, Allison."

Silence, then "Oh my gosh. Are you kidding?"

"No, your brother, Carson and Adam are the lead detectives. They took my statement. I have to go down to the police station and work with a sketch artist because they think I bumped into someone who may be a lead."

"Ok, well I will see you in the office later. Wow, I am in shock. What a way to end the night. By the way, Peter was trying to tell me that you had everything wrong, and he did not sleep with Candi. Seriously her name is Candi? He said she is a co-worker who drank too much and they shared his bed. I told him he was full shit and he needs to stay the hell away from you and all of us. Did you know he said he was going to propose to you," Catherine tells me in one quick breath.

"Ugh, I am so glad he did not because I would not have said yes. I can't believe I did not grow a spine before now. Why was I ever with him and why did I put up with the way he treated me? Ok, enough of my pity party. I am going to the gym. I will call Senator Gregg to confirm his schedule, and then when I am in the office we can review all of our work."

"Are you still up for my birthday party tonight after what you have been through?" she asks. "Of course. I need to let loose, and maybe I will get a wild hare up my ass and take someone home," I say laughing.

I need to have a good time and let my hair down for once. I am free and I need to enjoy it. "Sounds good. See you later this morning. Also, did my brother look good when he came over? Were you drooling all over him?"

So I can see this is not going to be forgotten. "Shut up Catherine. Carson looked like Carson and he was doing his job. See you later," I say ending the call. The last thing I want is more teasing about her brother.

I take the elevator down to the gym and figure the next hour is all about me. I work out regularly to keep in shape and to keep my figure firm so I can enjoy eating. I am not a size two nor do I want to be, but I want to keep my jiggle to a minimum. The best part about working out at 6am is there is never anyone in the gym with me so I can have space and time.

Heaven… is how I feel after a good workout. Now my brain starts going a hundred miles per hour. I need to shower, get dressed, get coffee, etc….. And the day begins at breakneck speed. While I am getting dressed, I keep an eye on the news shows. I am happy to see the emails Catherine sent to the news channels with the Senator's speech are being aired, and he is getting good reviews. That will make work easier. There was no mention about his wife being a spectacle. Again high five to us!

As I finish doing my happy dance my phone rings and it is Senator Gregg. He is such an easy client. We never have to chase him down and usually he calls us before our scheduled time to call him. "Good Morning Senator Gregg."

"Good Morning Alexandria. Great job, the press is loving the event last night." I appreciate how direct he is and this call should be quick. "We have five more donor events like the one last night over the next two weeks. Let's switch up areas in the city that we host these events. I will have my staff email you the information. I expect that you and your partner, Catherine, will be at each of these events. Please feel free to bring a guest if you would like. Also, the Vice-President will be attending the event next Wednesday night so we will need to coordinate with Secret Service for his security, which I am sure you can handle," he adds.

"This is perfect. Catherine and I will work with your staff and the venues for these events. Also, it will be nice to see my father and I am glad to see that he working with your team on your re-election."

"Speak to you soon Alexandria and again, thank you. The press is eating out of your hand!" Again, another quick happy dance. Senator Gregg is a nice man and has been friends with my father since college. I am happy to see that I am helping his campaign since these events can make or break someone.

I do not have any meetings with clients face-to-face so I pull on my favorite pair of skinny jeans, a black blouse and boots. I am a minimalist when it comes to make up. A quick swipe of tinted moisturizer, mascara and lipstick and I am ready to go out the door. I disable my alarm and walk out the door and bam, I have stumbled into someone. Again.

When I look up it is Peter with flowers in his hands. The police officer standing by Allison's door says, "Are you ok Ms. McNeil?".

I smile at him and remember his name, "Eric, I am fine. I have a habit of running people over and please call me Alex." I look at Peter and as he is opening his mouth to speak when I cut him off, "Peter, I have no desire to see or speak to you. You made it very clear yesterday morning that our relationship is over. Take your flowers and give them to Candi or some other girl that may be interested in you. I am done."

I turn to start walking away and Peter reaches out and grabs my arm to stop me. I stop and look at him. "I am so sorry Alex. You have to forgive me. I love you and want to be with you. I want to marry you."

"Let go of me," I say as a I jerk my arm out of his grip. "I don't have to forgive you, and you are insane if you think I want to marry you." I try to walk past him, but he grabs my arm again with such force that I drop my purse and coat. I am stunned for a moment because Peter has never been aggressive before. He pushes me up against the wall with such force that my head hits the wall and gets close to my face, "I am never letting go of you. I have put to much time and effort into our relationship to let you walk away."

"Sir, remove your hands from Ms. McNeil now. She has made it apparent that you are not welcomed," states Eric with his hand resting on his gun. At this point I am so happy to see this young police officer who is trying to help me. "Yes, Peter. Listen to the Officer and let go of me and leave," I firmly state.

Peter throws the flowers down and as he stalks off, he turns back and yells, "Alex, this is not over between us."

I stand there in the hallway waiting for him to get on the elevator. There is no way I am getting on the same elevator with him. As I am waiting I begin to realize this may not be over by a long shot. I pick up the flowers and look over at the policeman who just may be my favorite person. "Eric, do you have anyone special in your life you want to give these flowers to? I don't want them."

He smiles and takes the flowers. "My girlfriend would like them. Thank you." Eric looks down at my shirt and points, "Um, you may need to go in a change your shirt. There is rip on the arm." I had no clue that Peter had grab and pulled me hard enough to rip my shirt.

Crap. I run back into my condo, grab a white, fitted dress shirt. I take a quick look, not a bad outfit and run back out the door. It is only 8am and so far my day has started out with a bang. I hope it can only get better from here. I take the elevator down to the parking garage in my building and jump into my car. As I am cranking up my car I notice a card on my window. Ugh, really another advertisement. How on earth do they get into the building parking garage to leave these things on our cars?

I jump out and remove it from under the windshield wiper and glance at it. It wasn't an ad for a company, it was a card that says 'You are beautiful' signed with a P. That's weird. I bet Peter left this stupid note. I am not going to be able to deal with him doing these kinds of stunts. As I get back in the car I throw the note into my purse and finally get myself on the road to the police station.

She is beautiful and she took the note. This one will be fun to play with, I can already tell. Who would have thought I could have just bumped into my next girl right after I finished with my last one? This one seems special, I will have to continue to watch her before I approach her. She has beautiful eyes and I think she actually saw me unlike the others.

I finally find parking near the police station and it is freezing outside. Thankfully I had grabbed my coat before I left this morning. When I walk into the police station, I realize I have no clue where to go. I walk over to the desk to a busy police officer who answering phones and wait for him to finish. "Do you know where I can find Carson Knight or Adam Miles?" I ask him.

The officer glances up while the phone starts ringing again. "Go up to the second floor, turn left and that is the homicide division. They should be in there."

"Thank you," I reply and head off to the stairs. I should have really thought about my shoes. I love shoes and since I am short, I tend to only wear heels so I can pretend to be tall. Going up stairs in these four inch heels was not smart. When I turn the corner I immediately see Carson standing there laughing at something Adam said. He is amazing to look at when he is smiling and laughing. It is like there is sunshine shining over his face. Look at me with the poetry, I shake my head and need to get moving.

As I am walking towards them, Carson glances in my direction and then he does a double take. Adam gives me a whistle and says, "Well aren't you looking good, Alex. I like the jeans and boots look on you. Did you go to a special school to teach you how to walk in those heels?"

"You are such a flirt and full of crap," I say laughing at him. "I wasn't sure where I was supposed to go this morning for the sketch artist so I figured one of you could tell me."

Carson started to open his mouth to speak but his phone started ringing. "Knight," he says as he walks down the hallway from us.

"Is that a Guns N Roses ring tone he has?" I ask Adam.

Adam smiles and nods his head, "Our uptight boy is not as uptight as he wants everyone to think he is." The things you learn about a person. "By the way, are you planning on letting loose at Catherine's party tonight since you are single?" Adam says while wiggling his eyebrows.

"Stop it and yes. I plan on having fun tonight."

At that moment Carson turns around and he looks like he is ready to murder someone. He walks towards us and there is a fire in his eyes that I have never seen. Obviously Adam has seen this look before because next thing I hear, "Dude what's up? You look like you could murder someone," states Adam.

Carson looks at me and points his finger at me, "What the hell happened outside your condo this morning Alex?". The way he makes that statement it sounds like I have done something wrong and my hackles get a little raised.

"Nothing. What the heck are you talking about?"

"What am I talking about? Are you out of your mind?" he says as he raises his voice at me.

Seriously, am I out of mind? I feel like I am in crazy town because I am being yelled at for something I have no clue about. Also, why does Carson think he can yell at me? "Stop raising your voice at me and quit acting like a jerk. Tell me what I supposedly did this morning." I yell back at him. I think I shocked him by raising my voice back at him but at least he shut his mouth.

I glance at Adam to find him standing there with a huge grin on his face and just watching this yelling match. He is no help.

"Apparently your ex-boyfriend shows up this morning. You guys get into a fight in the hallway in front of Officer Hoffman and Peter grabbed you and slammed you into the wall and ripped your shirt!"

Ohh… that is what he is talking about. Well at least I learned what Eric's last name was from all of this. "Oh…well that did happen and it wasn't a big deal. Peter came by and tried to apologize for what he did. He thought asking me to marry him was a brilliant move. By the way, I did not realize he had ripped my shirt until Eric pointed it out to me. Also, why did he call you and tell you about this? It has nothing to do with you. And I let him have the flowers to give to his girlfriend."

I hear a snort from Adam and look over. I can see he trying his best to not bust out laughing. I roll my eyes at him. "Where the hell do I need to go for the sketch artist? I have to get going this morning and did not come in here to get yelled at by you."

"Let's go kitten, I will take you over to the sketch artist and we can let Carson cool his temper," says Adam as he grabs my elbow to steer me away from Carson. I look over my shoulder and if looks could kill, I would be dead.

"What is Carson's problem with me anyways?"

Adam's lips twitch like he wants to laugh before he answers my question. "That's a hard question to answer, but I think you are the problem he is trying to work out in his head."

"What do you mean I am the problem? I have never done anything to him other than be nice." I know that I can stare at him and maybe Carson has picked up on the lust vibe that I send out when I am around him. I am mortified. I bet he is trying to figure out how to get me to stop lusting after him.

"Alex, you have not done anything to Carson. Let's just say that you may be a nice change of pace for him, and he does not know how to react around you."

"OK, you have really lost me with that. Tell Carson to stop being an ass. I'm a big girl and can handle Peter," I tell him as we are walking down another hallway. Adam stops at a door and knocks on it before walking in and introduces me to the sketch artist, Kate Kish.

"What's up Adam?" Kate says around blowing a bubble with her chewing gum.

"This is Alexandria McNeil. She is our witness and needs to describe a guy she bumped into last night."

"Cool. Have a seat Alexandria. Nice to meet you," she says and turns around to get everything she needs for this. "Where do you want me to take her when we are done?".

"She is good to go once you two are finished up." He turns before he closes the door and winks to us and says," Alex we will see you guys tonight at Catherine's. Be prepared because Carson may be in rare form after dealing with you this morning."

What the heck does that mean, "rare form"? I did nothing wrong today. In fact, I am helping them out by even doing this so he should be thanking me. I look over to Kate and she is just staring at me. Great, another stare. "So what do I need to do to in order help you?" I ask her.

She pops one more bubble, "Come over here and let's get started. Give me any details about the guy and then we can clean it up once you are done." She motions for me to come over closer. As I sit down she asks," So how close are you to Adam?".

I look over at her and smile, "He's Carson's partner and I am best friends with Carson's little sister. We know each other from going to family events of the Knights." I can tell that she is happy with that response. That is interesting, I wonder if anything is going on there. Maybe I can get the scoop on her after Adam has had a few drinks tonight.

Once we start working on the sketch, it takes longer than I expect. Once we are done, I feel like I really am helping with finding Allison's murderer. Kate was surprised by the detail I remembered and she agreed with me the guy was a total hottie minus the dead-looking eyes. When I get back into my car, I glance up again there is another card under the windshield. Again, I am hoping this is an ad for some fast food restaurant and not another note from Peter.

I retrieve the card. In order to keep up with how my day and week has been going it is another note, 'You are even more beautiful than I remembered, I can't wait to see you.' Peter has got to be kidding me, we are not getting back together. I slam my car door closed, throw the card back into my purse and headed over to the office.

She is magnificent. I can tell she has a spirit about her that will be hard to tame but will give me such pleasure to master her. She will be hardest subject yet since she does not seem to be flattered by the notes. I will have to figure out how we meet so we can begin this dance.

Chapter 5

I have to get myself together when I am dealing with Alex. I cannot believe she just blew off the entire incident with her ex like it was no big deal. I know I mishandled the situation with her. When Eric told me what happened I could not think straight. How dare that asshole put his hands on her like that? Based off what Eric was telling me, she handled the situation without it getting out of control. I also think Eric is now infatuated with her.

"Dude, you need to ease up on Alex. The poor girl asked me what your problem was with her," Adam states as he walks around to his desk. "I just dropped her off with Kate and she will bring the sketch up when they are done." I nod over my computer. This is not a discussion I really want to have with Adam.

"So what's your issue with her? You can't blame her for you calling it quits with Sarah?" I look up and give him a look that should tell him to drop it, but he still doesn't get the hint. "By the way, be nice tonight. Try to have a good time and hit on her," he says with smile.

"I have no issue with her. She is ten years younger than me, my little sister's best friend and oh the Vice-President's only daughter," I say rolling my eyes. "That pretty much makes her untouchable in so many ways."

My real issue with her is ever since I laid eyes on her when she was twenty, I have been fighting a major case of lust. I also was engaged to a girl I spent five years with. After meeting Alex and experiencing that type of mind-numbing lust for her, I knew I could not get married to Sarah. It was a painful year, breaking off the engagement and not sharing with anyone the reason why.

Adam is the only person who knows the truth behind it. It amazes me that eight years later I still have the same reaction around Alex. I am also surprised she has never realized how I feel about her.

"You are wrong and could miss out on a good thing. She's into you. Maybe I should make sure Alex gets stinking drunk so you end up taking her home safely, and you can get an up close and personal view of her bedroom. Plus, I am a little concerned about Peter showing up again. It seems like he doesn't want to give up on her. He could become a problem she doesn't need."

I do agree with Adam on that statement. The incident this morning and then finding out from Catherine how Peter showed up last night at their work event is making me realize this asshole is not going to go away quietly. Even though he apparently cheated on her.

"By the way, the florist is a dead end," I update Adam on the calls I have been making all morning. "Each of them were paid in cash and no surveillance videos in any of those businesses."

"Well crap. This guy seems to cover all of his tracks. I was hoping we would catch a break on that lead since it's the first real break we have had. Hopefully, Alex's sketch can turn up a suspect."

"Why don't you get started on reading the victim's diary and see if it can give us a clue about this guy? We need to give an update to the team later today and I would like to actually have something to update them on instead of another pile of nothing."

"Hey, Carson, Adam! You are not going to believe the memory on that girl," exclaims Kate running into the room. "Look at this sketch. I am not sure if Alex realizes it but she has a killer memory and we should get some leads on this."

I take a look at the sketch and there is nothing that stands out other than his eyes are freaky looking. They look like black, soulless pits. I can see why Alex would get away from him.

"So this guy is a hottie if you overlook the eyes. I am hoping we can get some other women who may recognize him once we share this with the media," states Kate. "By the way, Alex is a pretty cool girl. I thought she would be high maintenance and pain to work with, but she was pretty funny."

Adam takes a look at the sketch and says, "Wow, this is a pretty good sketch. How much did you guide her versus she told you the details. I mean is this your fantasy guy?"

"Hey jackass, this was all Alex. I only had to ask the basic questions before she took to describing him."

"Chill guys, this is good and we need to get it approved and get it out to the media," I state interrupting what is about to become a fighting match. "Kate, good work. Adam, let's go meet with the Chief and get this approved to release to the media with a statement."

We walk down the hallway to Chief Anderson's office. He is a grizzly old man but has a heart of gold and a genius of a mind. Nothing ever gets by him and Adam and I are both lucky to be on his team.

We knock on his office door, "It's open," yells out Chief Anderson. When we walk in he asks, "Have you two jerks solved the case so I can stop this ulcer from growing out of control?"

Adam replies with a smile, "Not yet Chief but we have a solid lead with Alexandra McNeil."

"Take a look at this sketch that Alex and Kate did. We would like to get this out to the media and see if this will flush out any new leads," I tell him. "Speaking of Ms. McNeil, we need to call the Secret Service and her father and make him aware of this situation," states Chief Anderson. "Don't you have his phone number Carson?"

"Yes sir. We may want to call the Secret Service first then have the conversation with the Vice-President."

"Well, let's get this train wreck going," he says as he is dialing the Secret Service. He will take the lead on this call while Adam and I just sit back and listen.

This is the last call I want to be involved in. Vice-President McNeil is an intelligent man, and he is not going to be happy to find out his daughter is our only witness on a serial murder case. At least I know him well enough so maybe the Secret Service will stay out of this investigation. I know they routinely do security sweeps of Alex's condo and office and keep a light detail on her without her noticing. It was one of things they arranged when she decided to live far away from DC and she wanted her privacy. Plus, Adam and I are close friends with one of the agents who is assigned to watch the Vice-President. Between those two connections, we should be able to keep the lead on this investigation.

"Ok, good. We will hold while you get the Vice-President on the line. I will have you on speaker so he can ask the lead detectives any questions," states Chief Anderson as he finishes updating the Director of the Secret Service on our case.

After a few minutes of waiting Vice-President McNeil is on the line, "Chief Anderson, it's a pleasure to speak with you again. I appreciate you keeping regular patrols going by Alexandria's building and office."

"Of course Mr. Vice-President. It has never been a problem for our officers. We do have a situation that we want you to be aware of involving Ms. McNeil and a crime that took place in her building." The Vice-President may be a nice man, but this is his only daughter and child we are talking about so things may get dicey.

"What happened? Is Alexandria ok? I haven't heard from her today."

"She is perfectly fine. In fact, she may be the one person who is going to help us a solve a serial murder that we have been investigating over the past six months. Her neighbor was murdered last night. We believe that Ms. McNeil bumped into a person of interest as he was leaving the scene. She was able to provide us with a very detailed sketch that will be released to the media today."

"I don't know what to say. Who are the detectives handling this case? Do they need any help? Is Alexandria in any danger?" the Vice-President stammers out quickly. "I can get the Secret Service down there immediately to help."

I can hear in his voice how upset he is. Time to step in before we have too many people involved in this investigation. "Vice-President McNeil, this is Carson Knight, Catherine's older brother. I am one of the lead detectives on the case, and will personally make sure that Alex is kept safe. I will not let anything happen to her or put her in any danger."

"Carson, it is great to hear your voice. I have told you to call me Ryan. Are you sure that you don't need any help?"

"Adam and I, with the help our team, have this investigation under control. If we need anything, we will let you know."

"Ok, I expect you to update me daily. You have my cell number. I also expect you to keep Max abreast of the investigation. He will be heading down to Atlanta prior to my arrival in a few days. And know this Carson, if we so much as think Alexandria is in danger, I will pull her out of Atlanta and back to D.C to keep her safe," the Vice-President states forcefully.

"Sir, we understand and either myself or Adam will call you each day with an update," I tell him hoping that I can keep his team on the fringes of the investigation.

"Thank you Carson. I know that Alexandria trusts you, and I hope I get a chance to thank you in person when I am in town for Senator Gregg's fundraising gala. Chief Anderson, you have a great team. I trust you guys will solve this quickly," the Vice-President says as we end the call.

"Well that went over better than expected. Get this picture out with the approved statement from the communications team to all media outlets," states Chief Anderson.

"Adam, can you run this over to the communications team? I'm going to swing by Alex's office and make sure she is good," I tell him as we are walking down the hallway.

"Sure you are going to make sure she is good," Adam says wiggling his eyebrows and making kissing sounds.

"Shut up. You know the issues with her ex and I want to make sure that he's not bothering her today," I state as I grab my jacket and heads toward the door.

Chapter 6

I cannot believe how late it is! I figured I would have been back to my office by 10am, but now it's pushing 11:30am. At least no one had parked in my spot in our garage. As I step out of the elevator on the tenth floor, I can't help but smile. This has been mine and Catherine's baby since we thought of going into business back in college. It is amazing that we are both twenty-eight years old and own our business and it's successful.

"Hello Shannon. How are you today?" I ask our receptionist as I enter our lobby.

"Hi Alex. Today is Friday and it's a crazy one but good," she replies with her bubbly personality. "By the way, your voicemail is full so I have been taking messages and leaving them on your desk. It looks like the donor dinner was a success and you guys are getting great press."

"That is great to hear. Sorry I'm in late and have not been available to take calls."

"That's my job. I am happy to help. Also there are a few other surprises in your office."

I turn to start walking down the hallway and wonder what other surprises are waiting in my office. As I am walking my phone starts ringing and of course, it's Peter. Like I have anything to say him. I send the call directly to voicemail. I look up and see Catherine standing outside of her office and wave to her.

"How's today going?" I ask her.

"We are on fire but in a good way! There has been nothing negative about the event last night. We are getting a ton of calls asking for the dates and details of the Senator's next events so he is going to be getting great press."

"What about any questions about his wife?" This is what I really want to know about, did we handle that piece since she could damage his entire campaign.

"Not a word. The only things that have been printed are pictures. Everyone is saying how stunning and composed she looked. I think the wine throwing incident may be behind us."

"That is great news. Want to come and chat in my office? I want to tell you about what happened this morning with Peter. And then what are the plans for tonight?"

As we turn to walk into my office the first thing I am greeted by is a ton of flowers. Seriously, my office looks like a florist shop. "What the heck is all of this? Who put all these flowers in here, is this a joke?"

"Nope. Looks like Peter is trying to win you back," Catherine says with a smirk on her face. "I was nosy and looked at some of the cards."

"Well, that's not going to happen. I told him the same thing this morning when he showed up at my place with flowers."

"He showed up at your condo?"

"Yes. I was running out the door and ran right into him. We had a little bit of a heated exchange, he ripped my shirt and the police officer in the hall had to step in."

"Wow, that's pretty serious. Peter sounds like he's not giving up."

"I know but he is the one who cheated on me and called me an ice princess. Why would he want to waste his time with me if he feels that way? Ok, enough about that. Let me look at the cards and we can move on to more exciting things to talk about like your birthday", I state with a smile on my face. I really want this day to be done so we can go out and have fun.

On my desk is a huge vase with two dozen red roses, I read the card out loud, "Please forgive me Alex. You are the love of my life and I will spend the remainder of my life trying to show you how much you mean to me. Love Peter".

Is he serious? How does someone say the things he said to me then think sending me flowers with this crap written on the card would change anything? Catherine is just standing there laughing at my facial expression. She knows me so well.

On my small, round conference table are three large mixed bouquet arrangements in massive vases. I take a look at that card and it says, 'Just seeing your magnificent eyes makes me want you even more. P' Next to that bouquet is another vase of mixed flowers with a card that says, 'When I look into your eyes, I know you can see the real me. P' The final card says, 'Once we meet, I know your eyes will be only for me. I will continue to shower you with gifts to show my affection for you. P'.

"Catherine, did you read all these?" These are bizarre notes and I am not sure what to think about them and where Peter's head is. This is giving me the creeps like a psycho stalker is about to kidnap me and never let me go.

"Yes, I read them. I think Peter's a little crazy in the head. Which is why I'm glad my brothers will be at the party tonight since I know Peter was originally going to come with you. I want to make sure we have a great time without a crazy ex getting too close."

"This really doesn't make any sense to me," I tell her shaking my head. "I forgot to mention, in addition to these flowers, the incident this morning outside my condo. Peter has been leaving these types of notes on my car windshield!"

"That is really crazy behavior. You should call Carson and tell him."

"Why would I tell Carson? He hardly speaks to me whenever he sees me. Why would he be interested in this or want to be involved in it?"

"Duh...Carson is working that murder investigation that you are the witness in. Don't you think he should know if someone is acting like a stalker?"

As Catherine is making that last statement there is a knock on the open door and Carson is standing there. I must have really pissed someone off to keep having these things happen to me. He looks a little irritated standing there. "Who's acting like a stalker?" Carson asks. "By the way, what's with all the flowers?"

"Peter is acting like a stalker and all of these flowers are from him. He wants her back," says Catherine. "I was just telling her to call you and she said that you would have no interest in knowing about it."

"It's not a big deal. I can handle this," I tell them both. "He just needs some time to realize us breaking up is the best thing that could have happened. We were miserable together."

"This is a big deal Alex," Carson firmly states as his eyes harden and look like black coal. "This asshole has showed up to your place, assaulted you, is now sending you flowers. I do have an interest in this."

"I'm done talking about this," I sharply say to both of them. "Plus, I need to get to work so I can get home to change and be ready for your birthday party."

I know that this will get Catherine off Peter the stalker topic. Hopefully Carson will get bored and leave. I glance over at him and he is still leaning on the door frame looking like a Greek god. I wonder if I could pay him to stand there and let me stare at him all day. It should be illegal for a man to look so gorgeous in a suit. I would love nothing more than to walk over to him and grab his tie and jerk his head down to my level so I can kiss the ever-loving daylights out of him. What the heck is wrong with me? I should not be thinking about him like that right now, I am sure there is drool all over my chin.

"Are you ok?" Catherine asks me. I try to stop myself from blushing but I can feel that I am turning red from head to toe.

I clear my throat, "I am fine. I was just distracted and thinking about other things."

"Yeah," smirks Catherine. "Make sure you are at my house by 8pm." I can tell that Catherine has an idea about what was distracting me.

"That sounds like a plan."

"By the way, the reason I came by, was to say thank you and let you know the sketch you did was phenomenal. We are about to begin airing it so it may be just the break we need," Carson says with a speculative look in his eye.

"Oh, that's good to hear. I really hope it helps."

"Also, back to the Peter thing. This is beginning to look like an issue. Do you want Adam and I to talk to him?"

"No. I think he should back off after he realizes that I am not interested in getting back together with him. It should be fine. But thank you for the offer."

"So Carson, why don't you take me to lunch while Alex finally gets some work done today?" Catherine say with a laugh.

"Sure thing little sis," Carson says as he slings his arm around Catherine shoulders and they leave my office.

As they are leaving, all I can think about it is how nice and firm his butt looks in those pants. This is why I need to stay away from him, I can't think about anything but his body. He probably can tell that I am ogling him and it grosses him out. I need to get to work and stop thinking about Carson.

Chapter 7

After cramming eight hours of work into four hours, Catherine and I managed to leave the office at 4pm. It is Friday and we are ready to begin the weekend and celebrate her birthday and a great week for our firm. "See you tonight!" I tell her.

"Make sure to wear something low cut or super sexy tonight. You are single and we need to make sure you find a man!" Catherine responds laughing.

"I will see what I can do." I get into my car and head over to my condo. A warm, long bath sounds heavenly to me. I should have plenty of time to relax and get ready before I head over to Catherine's. My ten-minute commute home seems to only take five minutes before I was pulling into my parking space and jumping out to hit the elevator.

As I am riding in the elevator I start thinking about Allison and I hope the sketch will help Carson and Adam catch her killer. I did not realize how much this bothers me until I glance down and realize that my hands are shaking. As I step off the elevator, I go ahead and get my keys out of my purse. That way I can get in quickly and not worry about Peter or anyone else bothering me. Speaking of Peter, I am almost to the point of turning my phone off if he continues to call every ten minutes. I have not even listened to the fifty voicemails he has left me.

As I walk into my condo, I turn off my alarm, throw my keys and purse on the table and kick off my shoes. Finally, time to relax. When I moved into this place I had it renovated to how I always envisioned my own place would look and I love it. My kitchen, dining and living room are an open-concept, and I had my contractor take my three bedrooms to two bedrooms so I could have a massive master bedroom, closet and bathroom.

I walk into the bathroom and start the water since it takes a few minutes to fill up the tub. I go and grab a glass of wine and bring it back to the tub. After I undress, I have to take those critical few minutes to look at my body. But realize I look pretty good. Maybe I will sex it up a little tonight with what I wear. After all, Carson will be there and I wonder if I can get a reaction out of him.

Ah…. the water is so warm, my wine is a smooth and buttery chardonnay and I feel all the tension leaving me from this week. My mind keeps going back to Carson. He has made it clear that he views me as Catherine's best friend and nothing more. So why do I even torture myself with fantasies about him, but I can't help it. Plus, Adam eluded that Carson may be into me but seems to have an issue with that. Add to that the few times I have caught him looking at me and those weren't the usual disgusted looks. I may not be very smart when it comes to picking out boyfriends, but I do recognize looks of lust. I swear that is what I have seen in his eyes.

My phone starts ringing again, well at least that pulls me out of daydreams and I realize I need to get moving if I am going to be ready and at Catherine's by 8pm. I am standing in my closet and after much debate figure out I want to wear a black top that dips in a V and ties behind my neck with skinny jeans and knee high boots. Now to find the right bra and panties to wear underneath this outfit.

I love, love, love lingerie and have an entire dresser in my closet dedicated to my love affair. I lay out some bras to try to make sure the straps do not show with this top. I glance at the clock and know if I do not hurry, I will be late and never hear the end of it from Catherine. I throw everything on quickly and take a glance in the mirror, not too bad so this should work.

I am switching out my large purse for a small clutch when my phone beeps with a text message. I glance down to see that the text is from Peter, 'You invited me to Catherine's party so I am showing up to talk to you.'

Ugh, why is he so difficult? I text him back, 'You are no longer invited. You were my date and we are no longer dating. Do not show up. We have nothing to talk to about.' So much for relaxing tonight. I set my alarm, grab my coat and I am out the door.

I go ahead and hit the auto-start for my car since it is freezing tonight. As I am walking over to my car I hear a noise behind. I turn around and look to see what it is and notice a man going into the building. He doesn't look familiar but I think nothing of it. As I am getting into my car I see another card on my windshield and I see red. I am so pissed off at Peter over the way he is acting. If he had cared so much about me to begin with then why was he a prick and why did he cheat on me? I glance at the note and roll my eyes, 'Your eyes are lovely and I can't wait to see you and have you see me. P', who is he kidding with this crap. I will have to show this to Catherine.

Luckily, the drive over to her house was short and uneventful. I get there right before 8pm and I can hear the music from the driveway. Catherine does know how to throw a great party. As I am getting ready to get out of my car another car pulls up beside me, it is a pretty little BMW coupe. As the people get out of their car, I realize it is Adam and Carson and my heart starts beating quickly. Adam smiles over at me and opens my door, "Hey kitten," he says with a smile as he moves out of the way so I can get out.

"Hi guys. Nice car Carson."

"Thanks," Carson replies tersely. Ok...so he is back to being his normal, not wanting anything to do with me self.

I glance over to the door to see Catherine standing there waving to us. "Happy Birthday!" I exclaim as I give her a big hug and hand her a present.

"You shouldn't have gotten me anything Alex." I watch her begin digging around the tissue paper trying to see what it is.

"Do you think you guys think we can move and do this inside since it's freaking cold out here?" Carson grumbles at us.

"Ok, sourpuss. We will move inside," Catherine replies as she sticks her tongue out at her brother.

Once we are inside, Carson is standing behind me and leans over, "Let me help you with your coat," he says as he begins to remove it for me. I am blown away by the manners that all of Catherine's brothers have. They are constantly opening doors and helping women with everything. I need to remember to thank Mrs. Knight for the manners she taught her boys. As Carson is removing my coat, his fingers graze the back of my neck. I fight back the urge to moan as the sensation from this one, little action generates is enough to make my nipples tighten. Maybe I do need to get laid if this little bit of contact is affecting me this way.

"Thank you," I tell him and walk over to Catherine who is digging through the tissue paper of gift.

"Shut up! You did not get me this!" she screams. Adam and Carson walk over to see what the fuss is about. I am just standing there with a huge grin on my face.

"What are you talking about?" I ask her innocently. Catherine has been eyeing this beautiful St. Laurent handbag and I bought it for her.

Catherine is hugging the purse and jumping up and down. "Wow, so I guess my bottle of wine is going to look silly next to that reaction to a purse," Adam says sarcastically.

"It's a purse, what's the big deal?" Carson asks.

"It's the purses of all purses and my new baby," Catherine tells them giving them a frown for not understanding her excitement. She is hugging her new purse closely to her chest.

Catherine gives me a big hug and when she steps back, "Wow, Alex, you look great tonight!". Now that my coat is off she can see my top and I glance over to Adam and Carson and notice that they both are staring. Carson in particular is staring intently at my cleavage and I smile at them.

"Thanks, I try sometimes," I tell her laughing as we walk away.

"Dude, did you see what Alex is wearing?" Adam says to Carson.

"Yes, I did and she looks amazing."

"Lets go get some drinks and see who else is here," Adam says pulling Carson with him.

Catherine hands me a glass of wine while I say hello and give hugs to rest of her family and our friends. I am getting a lot of questions about Peter and I breaking up since everyone has heard about it thru the rumor mill. I glance across the room and notice Carson is looking intently in my direction and it feels like he is undressing me with his eyes.

I glance to my right when I feel someone tug on my arm and it's my friend Chelsi, "Hey, how are you tonight?" I ask her.

She glances over to where I had been looking, "Good, but it looks like Carson can't keep his eyes off you tonight. I guess he and Kristy broke up," she replies.

I had no idea that Carson was seeing anyone. I mean I should not be surprised given how hot he is that he would have a girlfriend. "I did not realize he was seeing anyone."

"She teaches spin class at my gym and was going on about him since she knew I was friends with Catherine. It wasn't serious at least for him, I think she was hoping for more but he has been blowing her off from the looks of it."

Before I can continue to get the gossip on Carson and his girlfriend, Catherine and our friend Darcy are at my side, "You aren't going to believe this Alex," Darcy says.

"What?"

"Peter just walked in and is looking for you," she replies.

Uh oh…this is not going to be good. Just what I need is a scene at Catherine's party especially since everyone was asking what happened and I made it sound like it was nothing. "I told him he was not invited and not to show up. Where is he so I can get him out of here before he causes a scene?"

We walk over to the foyer and sure enough there is Peter standing there talking with Harrison, Darcy's boyfriend. "I will have to yell at Harrison about being a traitor," Darcy whispers to me as she gives her boyfriend a dirty look.

They both glance over at the three of us and I step over to them, "Peter, what are you doing here? I told you that you were not invited anymore."

He grabs my arm to pull me closer to him. "I just want to talk to you and you haven't been returning my calls and you won't see me. I figured if I showed up here you would have to hear me out." I can smell the alcohol on his breath and realize this is not going to be good. I glance over my shoulder and see a few people are beginning to watch us. Carson and Adam have walked over and are standing by Catherine and Darcy.

Peter is looking me up and down and states, "What the hell are you wearing? You look like a slut with your tits showing like that."

"What did you just say?" Carson asks as he walks towards Peter.

"Peter, shut up. I am done with your awful criticisms of my body, everything about me. You are a jackass." I am so embarrassed by this scenario; I pull my arm back out of his grasp. "Please leave, there is nothing we have to say to each other. You cheated, you said hateful things to me. We honestly don't love each other so we need to go our separate ways."

Peter's eyes turn a stormy blue with anger at my statement, "I have not wasted three years of my life on you to have you push me away," he hisses at me.

"Uh…yeah you did. I am done. I have no desire to see you, speak to you or sleep with you ever again."

"You bitch. You think just because of who your daddy is, you are so fucking special!" Peter yells at me as he pushes me against the wall.

"Stop making a scene and leave Peter." I am at a loss on how to diffuse this situation, but I can tell it is spiraling out of control. "You are drunk and getting out of control. Please leave and stop harassing me," I tell him as I try to move away from him.

He blocks me with one arm and I look up to see the fury in his face. I can tell he is past the point of no return. "How dare you think you can walk away from me!" as he raises his hand to hit me.

At that moment you can feel how volatile the air is in the foyer and then everything happens at once. Carson is in front of me pushing me closer up against the wall with his back. The next thing I know he has punched Peter in the face and knocked him down on the floor.

"Don't you even think about touching her like that," Carson growls out. "If you ever try to touch her, speak to her, look at her in the wrong or make her upset, I will rearrange that pretty-boy face of yours."

Peter begins to stand up while blood is pouring out of his nose and there is fire shooting out of his eyes at Carson and at me. "Fine, I see what is going on here," he sputters at us. Peter glares at Carson, "Don't think we all haven't noticed how you have always had the hots for Alex. If you want to try to fuck the ice princess, then have it. She's awful in bed."

"Go fuck yourself," Carson spats back at him.

"Leave Peter. Stop calling, texting and leaving me those weird notes on my car and in my office," I tell him calmly.

"Enjoy slumming it Alex. You two deserve each other. And I don't know what the fuck you are talking about notes on your car and office. I haven't been near either in weeks," Peter yells as he storms out the door.

"Catherine, I am so sorry that this just happened," I tell her with tears filling my eyes. It has been a rough week and I think I am going to break down in front of everyone.

She comes over and gives me a hug, "You have nothing to apologize for, Peter is at fault here."

"Hey, at least I think he gets the point and will leave you alone now. Let me go get everyone a drink so we can enjoy this party," Adam says trying to alleviate the tension in the room.

I smile over to him, "Thank you Adam." Everyone goes with Adam to help bring back drinks for all us leaving Carson and I standing alone.

I glance up at Carson who still has dangerous look in eye and I am at a loss for words. He got into the middle of this fight and was protecting me. "I can't begin to thank you enough Carson. You did not have to get into the middle of the argument between Peter and I, but you did and I have no clue how to repay you for that."

Carson puts his hand under my chin to tilt my face up to his and I shiver from the contact. "It was nothing Alex. You don't have to worry about anything. You are too special to end up with someone like him."

We are both staring at each other and a different kind of tension fills the air. We continue to look at each other and I begin to see flames of desire shooting in his eyes when Adam comes around the corner. "Here you go guys, drinks all around," he yells breaking the sexual tension that was forming around Carson and I.

Chapter 8

I am glad that Alexandria went out tonight. I have been eager to get inside of her place since I have started doing research on her. Her security system was a little higher tech than I expected, but that is why I spent so much money on the alarm decoder so I can get into these places without people knowing. Alexandria McNeil will be a delight to begin seeing and taking her life, the Vice-President's daughter. Who knew I would be so lucky when I bumped into her.

As I am looking around, I hear someone putting a key into the front door and realize that I need to hide. I hope Alex is not coming home. I move into the living room and step behind the curtains as the door opens. I can hear someone rustling around and heading to her bedroom. I move around so I can see better and it is the guy that keeps showing up here. He is mumbling to himself, "That bitch. If she thinks she is going to leave me to be with that asshole, I will hide the camera so I can get video and ruin the both of them. How dare she think she can do better than me."

I watch him place a small camera on her dresser by a vase and he turns to leave. This is interesting, I may be able to use this guy to my advantage. I finish placing my hidden cameras throughout her condo so I can watch her and learn her habits. I take a quick look at the device that guy left and smile since it will be easy for me to hack. I already have a plan to introduce myself to her with a new look so she does not recognize me and place a tracker on her coat. The next few weeks are going to be thrilling.

I am trying to have a good time at Catherine's, but it is almost impossible to keep smiling and pretend everything is ok. Adam and Carson have barely left my side since Peter left. I am pretty sure Adam is trying to get me drunk, "Do you want another glass?" Adam asks again for the fiftieth time.

"No. I am pretty sure I have had a full bottle myself to drink." People are finally starting to leave, and since it's close to 1am all I want to do is go home and get into bed and pass out.

Catherine plops down on the couch next to me and hands me a shot. I am already shaking my head no at her. "Come on Alex. One shot, it's my birthday and I am using that as the reason so you have to take it," she says laughing and slurring her words.

"But I have to drive home, and I have already had four glasses of wine tonight," I whine at her.

"I can drive you home Alex," Carson says quietly.

"See. Problem solved, so take that shot!" Catherine exclaims.

We take the shot and I grimace. I am not much of a shot drinker and this was tequila so I am making a pretty ugly face at it. Adam starts laughing and Catherine gives me a big hug and moves on to harass other people.

"Ugh…I can't stand that," I tell them and take another sip of my wine. "Are you sure you don't mind getting me home?"

Carson smiles at me and my breath catches in my throat. "If I minded then I would not have offered. Plus, Adam can drive your car back to your place and you can ride with me so then you have your car in the morning."

All I can do is smile at him. "You are such a sweetheart. Let me go say good-bye to everyone and we can leave," I say to him and get up to go begin saying bye to everyone. As I am walking off I hear Adam say, "You are such a sweetheart. If only she knew what you really wanted to do with her she would not say that." I look over my shoulder and see Carson lean over and punch Adam in the arm while Adam is laughing at him.

I wonder what he wants to do with me. Hmmm…if its anything like I want to do with Carson then that would be fine by me. I can tell I have had too much to drink given my thoughts. I need to get home and into bed. After wishing Catherine happy birthday again and giving hugs and kisses to everyone, we are finally getting ready to leave. Carson helps me with my coat and I am still dazed at how these little things that Carson does effect me. A simple move like pulling back my hair from my coat makes me aroused.

I give Adam my car keys and laugh as I watch him try to get into my car. Adam is six feet tall and he can't even get in because the seat is so close to the wheel. "Stop complaining. My Mercedes has plenty of room. I just have to sit close to the steering wheel since I am short, and it's not nice to make fun of short people."

Carson is standing beside me shaking his head, "Adam, figure it out. It's cold and I want to get Alex into my car."

Adam glances over at us and smiles, "Sure you want to get her into your car Carson."

"Here Alex, get in and warm up," Carson tells me as he shuts the door. Adam has already started pulling away and headed towards my place. "Are you ok after everything that happened tonight?" he asks me as he is putting the car into reverse.

"I am fine. This has been an awful week. The funny thing is, Peter and I hardly spent anytime with each other over the past eight months so I am not really sure why he is being possessive now."

"Really? If you were my girlfriend, I would want to spend all my free time with you."

I know I must be drunk because I would never say what I am about to if I was sober. "Speaking of girlfriends, are you seeing anyone special?"

"No one special," he replies elusively.

"Are you seeing anyone not special?" I ask him again since he is being vague.

"What is with these questions?" he replies sharply.

It looks like I am hitting a nerve with the questions. I start laughing at him, "Calm down. I was just wondering since you are so cute if you were seeing anyone."

"You think I am cute?"

"Seriously, you have a mirror and should know the answer to that. Are you looking for an ego-boost?"

Carson begins laughing and I have never seen anything as beautiful as him when he is smiling and truly enjoying himself like he is now. "Ok, my turn to ask you all the questions," he says to me.

"Fine, ask away, I am an open book."

"If Peter was not spending time with you, then what were you guys doing?" This takes me a minute to answer because I really need to think about it since I have no idea why we stayed together for as long as we did.

"To be honest, we went to social events and he would drink so much and be so mean to me that it was exhausting to be around him for more than a few hours. He would drop me off at my place. I am assuming he would go over to one of the women who he cheated on me with or they came over to his place."

"Has he ever hit you before?" Carson asks quietly. I can tell that he nervous to hear the answer.

"No. Tonight was the first time he ever came close to hitting me. He was always critical, but the past few days has brought out a side of him I did not know existed."

"You need to be careful around him Alex. He seems like he is becoming unhinged. You have to promise me that you will call me or Adam immediately if you see him."

"I will. I am hoping that tonight was the last of it."

We pull into my garage and Adam has parked my car in my space and is waiting for us. Carson turns his car off and gets out to open my door but Adam beats him to it. "Hey kitten, let us walk you up to your door and make sure you get in."

"My two knights in shining armor," I say batting my eyelashes at them. Adam throws my keys over my head to Carson and we start heading into my building.

As we exit the elevator my phone beeps and I start digging into my purse to find it and stumble into Carson. "I'm so sorry. See this is just what I did yesterday to the guy who you think killed Allison."

Carson just shakes his head and smiles. "Everyone has a fault, Alex," Adam says with grin.

Carson is putting the key into the lock and asks, "What's your alarm code?"

"It's 0413," I reply. We walk in and the first thing I notice is there is a light on in my bedroom that I did not leave on. I stop dead in my tracks.

"What's wrong?" Carson asks me.

"I did not leave any lights on in my bedroom when I left earlier tonight."

"Are you sure?" asks Adam.

"Yes, I'm sure. I always turn everything off except for the light in the foyer." They both exchange a look and pull out their guns from beneath their jackets. Whoa, it never crossed my mind they both had their weapons on them tonight.

"Stay here Alex while we search your place," Carson says as they move to look around. I do not think I could have moved if I wanted to. What is going on in this building? First, Allison and now someone has been in my place. It seems like an eternity while they look around but no one but the three of us are in my condo.

"Take a look around and see if anything is missing or not where it should be," instructs Adam. I begin walking around with Carson close behind me. I cannot tell if anything has been moved but nothing seems to be missing.

"I think it is fine. Thank you for walking me up and checking out my place."

Carson stands in front of me and looks at me like he wants to say something, he clears his throat, "I will call you tomorrow Alex to see how you are doing."

Adam is standing by the door, "You have our numbers in case you need anything." I walk them both to the door and tell them good night.

Once the door is shut, I turn on my alarm and get ready for bed. I am feeling a little nervous since I know someone has been in here. It feels like someone is watching me, but I am not going to be a baby and call for Carson or Adam. My alarm is set, they checked my place, I am safe. I walk through to my bathroom to begin what my friends call my twenty-minute bedtime routine. I believe in always washing off your makeup and moisturizing every night no matter how drunk you are. Once I am done and have a clean face I slip into my into bed. Thankfully I fall fast asleep.

*****

"Something doesn't feel right in her place," I tell Adam.

"Yeah, I get that tingly feeling too, and it's not from seeing all those bras on the floor of her closet," he says with a smile. I swear sometimes I want to plant fist into his mouth but the guy loves to get a rise out of me when it comes to Alex.

"It may just be because of everything that happened tonight. I wanted to shoot Peter when I realized he was about to hit her."

"I have never seen you move that fast. I thought all hell was going to break loose but she handled herself pretty well given what shit he was throwing her way."

"I asked her in the car if he ever hit her," I murmur. This is getting pretty close to admitting that I really care for Alex and not just as my little sister's friend.

"Really? What did she say or do I want to know?"

"She said nothing physical. She said since they broke up he is getting more physical but while they were dating it was verbal."

"Well at least they aren't together and judging from the way she looks at you, she may like you more than she likes me," Adam says with a laugh.

"I'm taking you home. We still have a ton to do tomorrow with all the leads coming in from the sketch. I think tonight was the last free night we may have for a while," I tell him as we leave Alex's building.

Chapter 9

I wake up and surprisingly, do not feel awful. What I do need is some coffee and lots of it. I go into my kitchen and look for my coffee and I am stunned to see that I am out of coffee. How the heck did I let that happen? I may not cook a lot but I always keep coffee on hand. The good news is there is a coffees shop right around the block from me. I brush my teeth, throw my hair up in a messy bun and put on some yoga pants, t-shirt and running shoes and head to get my much needed caffeine fix.

It is a chilly morning but not too bad for a brisk walk. Plus, I can count this as exercise. I walk into the coffee shop and order my drink of choice (soy caramel macchiato). While I am waiting a man bumps into me. The impact pushes me forward a little bit and he grabs my arm to help steady me. "I am so sorry. I was too busy looking at my phone," he says to me.

I glance over to him and he is beautiful with glasses, not strikingly gorgeous like Carson, but pretty damn hot. "It's no problem. That happens to me all the time," I say with a smile.

"Can I buy you a coffee to make up for it? I hit you pretty hard."

"No. I've already ordered mine and I am fine, thanks though."

"My name is David. It's nice to meet you," he says holding out his hand.

"Hi, I am Alexandria," I say reaching to shake his hand. He holds my hand a little longer than necessary but I am saved from the awkwardness by the barista calling my name. "Well, that is me. It was nice to meet you David," I say with a wave.

"Wait, I usually don't do this. This may seem weird and uncomfortable but would you like to meet for coffee or lunch sometime?"

This takes me by surprise because the last thing I am ready to do is to jump back into the dating pool but a coffee or lunch seems harmless.

There is something that is making me feel slightly uneasy but it could be the situation. "Um, sure I guess. Let me give you my work number." I always give out my work number until I get to know someone. This has been drilled into me by my parents since they always worry about someone leaching on to me because of my family name.

"Great. I will call you Monday morning. Maybe we can meet for a quick coffee later in the morning."

"Talk to you then," I say as I turn to leave the coffee shop. I know it's early but I call Catherine to tell her what just happened.

"Hello. Who is calling this early?" she grumbles into the phone. I smile at the phone because she sounds so awful on the phone. "Hi sunshine, it's your favorite friend and you are never going to guess what just happened to me," I say to her. "A hot guy just asked me for my number at the coffee shop."

"What? Are you ready to jump back into the dating pond so soon? Plus, I was kind of hoping that you would jump on Carson and make him relax."

I start laughing. "First, it is just a coffee and I gave him my office number. Second, Carson is seeing someone."

"Well I know he sleeps with a few different women, but he doesn't really care about them," she begins explaining.

I interrupt her before she can even finish her thought, "I don't need to know that he is sleeping with a bunch of women. Your brother is not interested in me like that. I thought you would be proud of me for giving my number to a stranger and a good-looking one at that."

"I am. Now let me go back to sleep. I'm so hung-over," Catherine says as she hangs up on me.

I get back to my building and as I am walking in I glance across the street and do a double take. Is that Peter standing in the doorway of the bagel shop? I quickly walk into my building instead of walking over to see if it is him. I know Carson wants me to call him if I see Peter, but I am not 100% sure that was him. The last thing I want is Carson to think I am running to him for constant help.

Alexandria is simply marvelous. Her dark hair, those deep, soul-searching blue eyes and her porcelain skin. It was genius for me to take her coffee and spend the past few hours waiting for her to show up at this coffee shop. She was out late; I am happy to see she is an early riser.

She reminds me of a cautious animal, I was not sure she was going to give me her phone number or agree to see me again. I could see the wariness in her eyes, those incredible eyes. I am not sure I will be able to keep my excitement from shining through when I am with her. Our dance has begun and she seems to be open to taking the next step. This one is not desperate for attention like the others so she may be more challenging.

As I am walking into my condo, my phone begins ringing. I dig it out of my purse and when I see who is calling a huge smile appears on my face. My dad! I realize it is our Saturday morning weekly call. One thing we have understood with my dad is with his line of work, we have to schedule our regular call time or else I may never see or hear from him.

"Hi daddy. How are you?"

"I am good honey, but I hear from the police you are involved in a pretty serious murder case."

"No, I just provided a sketch. They aren't even sure if it's the guy. More of a person of interest." I tell him hoping that he is not about to tell me that my security detail is being reinstated.

"Well, I am not going to harp on you about this. I spoke with Carson and he promised me that he would keep you safe and out of harms way."

"I heard you were coming into town for the donor gala for Senator Gregg," I say to him to change the subject.

"Yes, your mother and I will both be there. I was hoping that you would accompany us and do my introduction at the gala."

My parents understand and respect my decision to stay out of the national spotlight, but I will introduce my father at speaking engagements to show solidarity with our family. "Of course, I will be more than happy to introduce you."

"By the way, your mother and I heard that you and Peter have hit a rough patch so I am assuming he will not be the event this week." Really, a rough patch and how in the world did my dad hear that.

"Daddy, it's not really a rough patch but more like a no-more patch. We broke up." All I hear is silence on the other end as my dad processes this information.

"What happened?"

I know my mother adored Peter, but I always got the sense my dad did not care for him. "I caught him cheating on me. I realized over the past eight months we have been growing apart and I want to be alone and focus on me. Maybe meet someone I have fireworks with versus a tiny little spark," I tell him honestly.

"Alexandria, you know your heart and to be frank with you, I never cared for Peter. He was not good enough for you. I want to see you with someone who can stand up to the pressure of being associated with the McNeil's. Someone who can be their own person versus someone who wants to become one of us."

I love my dad so much and I am happy to hear he supports my decision. "Your mother agrees with me as well. She liked Peter on the surface but did not think he cherished you enough. Those are her words, not mine. She is standing right here listening to our conversation," he says with a laugh. My parents were high school sweethearts. I want to have a relationship with someone like they have. It is a true partnership. I know they have had their ups and downs but they always work through them.

"I am going to warn you daddy, this break up is getting a little messy. Peter is showing up at places he's not invited to. He is leaving notes on my car and sending flowers to my office. I hope this doesn't leak to the press and hurt you in any way."

"Don't worry about me, Alexandria. We will be fine and can handle any situation that may arise from Peter. By the way, you know who I think would be good for you? Catherine's older brother, Carson. I spoke to him yesterday and he is the type of man you should be with. Someone who is in charge and knows who he is."

What, now my dad is jumping on the Carson train? What is with everyone? Did I somehow email all of my friends and family and tell them my deep and darkest fantasies revolved around Carson? "Carson is seeing someone else Daddy, but thank you for the love advice. I love you and tell mom I love her," I say to him as we end the call.

I decide it's time to get my butt in gear and get my errands done for the weekend which first starts with a shower and getting myself presentable. As I am getting out of the shower, I hear my doorbell ring. Who can that be? It's only 9:30am on a Saturday. I throw my robe on and go out to see who is here. I look out the peephole and I am stunned to see Carson standing outside my door.

I open the door, "What are you doing here?"

"Well, good morning to you." Carson looks at me with a raised eyebrow at my greeting and grin.

"Sorry, you just surprised me I was getting dressed. Come on in."

"I figured you may need some caffeine after last night and stopped by and got you your normal drink."

Whoa, Carson knows how I like my coffee. "Thanks, I am going to be jittery since this will be my second for today," I reply with a smile. "So why did you really come by, not to just give me coffee?"

Carson pauses for a minute before answering. "I get these weird feelings and in the cop world we are taught not to ignore those feelings. So I wanted to check and make sure you were good this morning."

"We can chat but do you mind doing it in my bathroom so I can finish getting dressed? My hair is dripping all over me."

Carson just stares at me for a minute. You would have thought I asked him if he would like to see me naked. He clears his throat, "Um, sure." he follows me into my bedroom and to the bathroom.

"I can't get over how big your bathroom is," he states as he walks in. "Do you really spend that much time in here?"

I start laughing and tell him, "More time than you realize." This feels so weird having him stand in my personal space and watch me put on make-up. I can see he's watching every little thing that I do. "So what did you want to know?" I probe trying to understand why is he really here.

"Have you seen Peter or anything else that is weird? Any strange bumps in the night?"

"Well, I thought I saw Peter standing in the window of the bagel shop across the street but I wasn't close enough to tell so I just came back up to my place."

"Anything else happen this morning?"

"No, not really."

"What does not really mean?"

"Not really means, I do not think it's weird or any of your business if a guy bumped into me at the coffee shop and asked for my number to meet for coffee or lunch."

That statement stops Carson in his tracks. He is silent as his eyes penetrate mine, "I wasn't trying to insinuate that you have to run everything by me, Alex," he says softly. "I'm just concerned about your safety and that is all." He clears his throat, "So what are your plans today?"

"I was going to go dress shopping. We have a gala coming up on Wednesday, and I need a nicer dress since I have to introduce my dad at the event." It feels pretty tense between us after I made that snarky remark so I try to lighten the mood by wiggling my eyebrows at him, "Are you up for some torture and want to come to help me pick something out?" I ask him jokingly.

Carson gives me an incredible smile and shakes his head, "You couldn't force me to do that but thanks for the offer."

I shrug my shoulders, "Suit yourself. By the way, my dad seems to be a big fan of yours based off the way he talking about you this morning."

"What was he saying?" Carson asks me sounding pretty surprised.

I start laughing while I walk into my closet and yell from in there, "I was telling him about Peter and I. After my dad did a quick Peter bashing, he suggested that I date you or someone like you. He says you can handle being beside a McNeil."

Carson goes completely silent at that comment. I finish throwing on a white V-neck t-shirt and jeans and walk back into the bathroom to see if he is ok. When I walk in, I glance at him and the look on his face is one of desire. He quickly masks it and has his signature, bland look of disinterest back in place. Interesting, one minute he looked like he was enjoying the suggestion and the next minute he could care less.

"So, what do you think? Should I shock my dad and bring you as my date to the gala?" I ask him. I am half joking, half serious to see if he is interested.

"Um...let me see about moving some things around. Sure, I can dust off my tux and go with you." Now it is my turn to be shocked into silence.

"Are you sure? I mean, I kind of just dumped this on you. If you have plans, don't change them on my account," I stammer out. I feel like I just jumped into the deep end of a pool that I am not sure I can swim in.

"It's no problem. I respect your dad. It will be nice to watch you and Catherine in action." He looks me up and down and smiles again, "Alex, I never noticed the height difference was so great between us. You barely come to my chest without your heels on."

I laugh as I slip on my pair of flats, "Yep, feisty, little, five foot three inches of me." I am not really sure what else to say since I just asked Carson out on a date and he accepted. Well sort of a date.

We walk back to the door and I ask one more time, "Are you sure you don't want to go dress shopping with me?"

"Nah, I am good. Thanks again for the offer," he says as he turns towards me one last time.

"Thank you for the coffee, I did need it.". There is that attraction simmering between us, waiting for us to acknowledge. But neither of us seem to know what to do with it. I am twenty-eight years-old. I should have the courage to make the first move with a guy I am interested in.

"Call me later and let me know that you got back home ok. Or call me if you need anything," he says as he leans over to kiss my cheek. "Bye Alex." and he is closing my door.

I did not even realize I had been holding my breath when he leaned over. Wow, what just happened here and what have I done? I pick up my phone to call Catherine, this is her brother after all. Catherine picks up on the second ring, "Hey Alex, sorry about earlier. I was exhausted but now I'm awake and have had coffee. What are you up to?"

"You are never going to believe what I just did."

"You ran around the neighborhood naked."

"What? No! I somehow invited Carson to be my date to the gala on Wednesday and he agreed," and I rush to tell her what just happened.

"Wow, that is amazing. I was hoping that he would grow a brain and realize you two together would be awesome."

"So you are ok with this? I mean this is your brother and what if we kiss and things get awkward between Carson and I. What if we end up hating each other, and this makes it weird for you and I? This was a huge mistake. I am going to call him now and cancel."

"Whoa, calm down Alex. You are getting yourself worked up over nothing. Hell yes, I am fine with you going to the gala with Carson. If it does not work out, then it does not work out. You and have been best friends for years. Plus, Peter was right about one thing, everyone in our family has always noticed how Carson acts around you and only you. Now are you dressed because you are coming over to pick me up and we are going to buy you a killer, sexy dress!"

Only Catherine would be cool with me potentially going on a non-date with her older brother and would want me to look sexy for it. I laugh, "Sure thing. I am leaving now and will be there in fifteen minutes."

I grab my keys, turn on the alarm and head down to my car. As I am leaving, I get the sensation that someone is watching me. I look around the garage but I do not see anyone. It must just be all this talk with Carson about Peter making me a little paranoid.

As I get in my car and turn it on, I glance up and son of a bitch, there is another card on my windshield. I angrily get out and grab it, 'I knew it would be mind-blowing when I saw you, your eyes are my soul and I cannot wait to have them looking at me. –P'. This note is seriously creepy. I put my car in reverse and head over to Catherine's. I will call Carson once I am at her place.

When Catherine opens the door to her townhouse, she takes one look at me, "What is wrong? You are as white a ghost."

"Peter left me another note on my car this morning and it kind of creepy."

"Do you mind if I call Carson or Adam and let them know? He told me to keep him and Adam updated if Peter was still pulling these stunts."

"I just got off the phone with Carson and they are at the station. Why don't we swing by there since it's down the street from Nordstrom?"

"Sounds like a plan," I respond as Catherine grabs her purse and we head over to the police station.

Luckily, there is a parking garage in between the police station and Nordstrom so we can just park and walk to where we want to go. It is November so it has finally gotten cold enough that we have to wear heavier coats. "I hate that I will end up lugging this coat around in Nordstrom," Catherine complains.

"I know, but I am too cold to go without. Plus, I am just wearing a t-shirt underneath this."

We walk into the police station and the policeman at the desk recognizes Catherine, "Hey Catherine, you going to see your brother? He seems to be in one of those serious moods again," the policeman says to her.

"Yep, we are heading up to see him and Adam," she replies with a wave as we begin walking up the steps to their floor.

I am surprised to see so many people working in the room on a Saturday. There are people answering phones, paper everywhere and just a lot of noise. We stop in the doorway to look around to see where Carson and Adam are. Just then someone calls my name. I look to my right and see Kate, the sketch artist, "Alex, this is all your doing. We are getting a ton of leads based off that sketch," she tells us with a big smile.

"That's great, I think. I feel bad that so many people are working on a weekend."

"Nah, don't feel bad. We are hoping this will be the break we need."

"There they are," Catherine interrupts us.

"Sorry, Kate we need to talk with Carson and Adam really quick," I tell her as we walk off. We are headed over to the desks where Carson and Adam are sitting.

Carson glances up and when he sees us, he immediately looks worried, "Alex, Catherine what are you doing here? What's wrong?"

"I'm so sorry to bother you guys, but Catherine thought it was easier to drop in instead of calling since we were headed over to Nordstrom," I begin trying to explain why we are there.

Catherine cuts in, "That idiot Peter left her another note on her car this morning and it's a little weird."

"Do you have the note?" Carson asks me.

"Actually, I think I have all the notes. This is my normal purse and I have been putting them in there and have not taken any of them out."

I begin digging through my purse. It's a massive bag so I start pulling out lipstick, ponytail holders, pens, my phone, keys and putting them on Carson's desk. Adam starts laughing, "How much crap do you have in there? Is there a sink in there?" I look up and roll my eyes and finally begin putting the cards on his desk.

"Here are the cards off my car and then the ones from the flowers," I tell them. Carson picks them up and begins reading them.

I am watching his reaction and realize this is not good. I notice a tick in his jaw like he is trying to not break his teeth from clenching them so hard.

"When did you start getting these?" he asks me quietly.

"I think I got the first one yesterday morning. The rest have been throughout the day whenever I go to my car."

"Adam, take a look at these." Adam begins reading each card and then laying them out on the desk.

"Holy shit," Adam breaths out. He turns around and walks over to a white board to unclip a bunch of things in plastic bags. When he returns, he lays the plastic bags which look like they have notes in them beside the cards that I have given them. Catherine and I are straining to look at what they are looking at.

"Ladies, I hate to do this but can you go sit over there for a few minutes why Adam and I talk?" Carson says. Catherine and I both glare at them and then walk over to another desk to sit in some chairs.

"What do you think they are doing?" I ask her hesitantly.

"It looks like those notes you have been receiving may have something to do with whatever they are working or at least that is what they think."

"So much for this being a quick stop," I mutter.

*****

"I'm assuming you see the same thing I see," Adam says murmurs to me.

"Yep, we need to call Anderson immediately. My gut is telling me somehow Alex has attracted this murderer or Peter is the prime suspect. Either way, she may be in danger. The girls are eyeballing us. I need to make that call privately so neither of them hears what this is about. Can you go over and keep them occupied?"

"On it."

I am seething with anger but I have no idea who I am angry at. Part of me wants to blame Alex for getting herself into this mess since she bumped into the person who we think may be killer. The other part wants to strangle Peter since he could potentially be the killer. Thinking back to what Alex told me last night, their relationship started going down hill and they spent less time together about eight months ago. The first murder was six months ago so that could fit into the timeline.

I dial Chief Anderson's cell as it is ringing I am trying to get my thoughts together on what to do. First, I need to get protective detail on Alex but I know she will not go for that.

"Anderson," the Chief answers abruptly.

"Hey Chief, it's Carson. We have a major issue on the case and I need to bring you up to speed."

"What's happened?"

"Alex just came in here because she has been receiving harassing notes from her ex-boyfriend. She showed Adam and I the notes. The problem is the notes are almost identical as the notes we found in Allison's apartment."

"Shit. This is the last thing we need and the last person we need in the line of fire. What do you propose we do?"

"I think we need to get a security detail on her. I know her well enough to know she's not going to want her full Secret Service detail involved but maybe we can have one or two of our guys stay with her until we know she is not in danger." I hope the Chief will agree to this.

"Fine. Figure out who can start watching her immediately. I will talk with the mayor to approve the formal detail. We can make a rotation schedule on Monday. Crap, Carson, I don't like the feel of this. You promised the Vice-President you would keep her safe. I don't want to piss that guy off."

I glance over to Alex and see her watching me and I smile at her. "I won't let anything happen to her. Let me make some calls to see who wants some extra hours," I tell him as I we end the call.

*****

Carson is walking over and he looks nervous which is something I have never seen on his face before. Adam glances up to him, "Are we good, do you have a plan?" he asks Carson. A plan, a plan for what, I wonder.

"Alex, you aren't going to like what we have to tell you," Carson says hesitantly. "The notes you have been receiving are very similar to some notes that we found in Allison's apartment."

My mouth drops open, "What?"

"We think that they may be from killer. These notes may or may not be from Peter. We are going to have to bring him in for questioning," Carson finishes.

"Seriously?" Catherine chimes in.

"This is crazy, I know Peter is acting a little pyscho, but there is no way he would have killed Allison," I stammer out.

"We need to make sure you are protected since you are receiving these notes so we have two options," Carson continues, ignoring what I said about Peter. "We can call in your Secret Service detail to stay with you or- "

"No, absolutely not. I am not losing my privacy and having the press speculate about what is going on or worrying my family about this. No to that," I say interrupting him.

"The second option is we can provide you with a plainclothes officer to stay with you 24/7 until we at least know you are out of harm's way,"

Carson finishes. I take a deep breath to calm myself down. I know I should be thankful that they want to help me and I need to take this seriously but it is too much to process.

"Who would be with me?"

"We are working on it but I can stay with you tonight and tomorrow. Then on Monday we will have schedule. You have two options Alex, but you have to pick one of the two. It's not negotiable," Carson says calmly.

That stops me short, Carson staying with me. I get a little excited at the thought of him being in close proximity to me. "Fine, option 2 then," I state.

"The only thing that is a problem is this afternoon. Adam and I really need to get some work done on this case."

"How about we grab Eric from downstairs and see if he can go with the girls while they shop? He seems to be in love with Alex after meeting her," Adam suggests.

I smile at the suggestion. I like Eric and the way he handled Peter in the hallway yesterday was great. "I am fine with that. Eric is a sweetheart," I reply.

"Plus, we need a man's point of view for the dress Alex needs to buy for your date on Wednesday," Catherine adds nodding towards Carson.

"Date, what date?" Adam asks grinning widely at Carson.

"He's doing me a huge favor and attending a gala on Wednesday with me. It's really a sympathy date," I say trying to lessen the focus on the date.

"It's not a sympathy date Alex. I told you that I was happy to go," Carson replies. "Let me get Eric up here and see if he is up for this," he says as he walks away from us. Meanwhile, Adam is just grinning away like a madman.

Chapter 10

Mmmm...I wonder what Alexandria is doing at the police station. I am glad I had the opportunity to place the tracking device on her coat this morning when I bumped into her. I need to watch and figure out how to approach her again so she will begin to trust me. Ah. Here she comes out of the station, I wonder who this guy is that is with them, laughing and smiling.

"Are you sure you don't mind going with us?" I ask Eric for the fiftieth time. I feel bad he is giving up free time with his girlfriend to babysit me.

"Stop worrying about it. It is fine. Just following you around and sitting and waiting is something I am used to when I shop with Madison."

"Too bad you have a girlfriend. You are someone that I could have fun with," Catherine tells him. She is a huge flirt and is not ashamed to let a guy know if he interests her.

"Um, I have no clue how to respond to you," Eric replies honestly. "Plus, your brother scares the hell out of me." Poor guy, he is blushing. I did notice him checking her out when Carson and Adam introduced him to her.

"Don't worry, I do not poach on guys who are dating someone else. I'm just playing with you. Anyways, we need to focus on finding Alex a very sexy dress for Wednesday night," Catherine tells him. Eric holds the door open for us to enter Nordstrom and we make a beeline for the dresses.

"Some ground rules, I am introducing my dad so it has to be tasteful. Nothing too short and not too much cleavage," I tell Catherine.

She starts laughing, "So you want to look like a grandma?"

I roll my eyes at her as we start looking through the dresses. My favorite color tends to be black but I will add a bright pink or purple into the mix. I glance over at Catherine and see she has already pulled five dresses for me to try on. All of them are bright colors and I have no desire to wear any of those colors. "Are you going to buy a new gown for Wednesday?"

"I am thinking about it. I figure I may try on a couple."

Eric has taken a seat so he can watch us but not stand directly over us. After about thirty minutes, I have managed to find a few black gowns that I think should work for this event. I am ready to head towards the dressing room. I am a very tactile person, if something does not feel good to my touch, I will not buy it. I also do not like spending a lot of time shopping for clothes. "Catherine, I have hit my limit for looking. Let's go try these dresses on."

"You are such a spoil sport. I am going to torture you longer if none of these dresses work for either of us."

"Hey Eric, we are moving into the dressing room if you want to take a seat in there," I say over my shoulder to him as Catherine and I are walking to try on these dresses.

"Cool, I am moving over."

"Are you ready for the fashion show?" Catherine says teasing him.

I begin trying on the dresses that Catherine selected and some of them are so low cut and ridiculous that I yell over to her, "I am not coming out in some of these. It's just tiny bits of material and there is no way I can show up with my dad in this." All I hear is laughter from her and then a snicker from Eric.

I finally put on a black gown that I picked out and I am sure this is the one. "Catherine, meet me outside I think I found the one," I yell at her. I step out of the dressing room and do a spin.

"Wow, that is gorgeous Alex," Catherine says as she looks me up and down.

"It does have the right amount of sexiness without trashiness." I look in the three-way mirror at the timeless black, V-neck gown. The front is stunning, it highlights my perky breasts and accentuates my skinny waist. When I turn around to look at the back, it has another low V down the entire back to the waist.

Eric lets out a low whistle, "Alex, you look wonderful. Madison would probably want to kill you for looking that good in that dress."

"I think this is the one that I am going to get," I tell them with a huge smile. "The only problem is now I need shoes," I say bursting out laughing.

"Any excuse to buy a new pair," Catherine says rolling her eyes at me.

"Did you find a dress?" I ask her as I slip back into the dressing room to change into my jeans and t-shirt.

"Yep, this little red number here has my name all over it." We both leave the dressing room with our gowns and walk over to pay for them.

After we make our purchases we head over to the shoe department. As we are walking, I hear someone say my name. I turn around to look because I do not really recognize the voice and I see a guy walking over from the men's cologne section.

"Alex, hey. I thought that was you when I glanced over." I look at him and recognize it is David from the coffee shop that I met earlier today.

"Oh, hi David," and I introduce him to Catherine and Eric. "What are you guys up to?" he asks us.

"Just shopping for a dress and shoes for an event that Catherine and I are attending on Wednesday." This is weird because we are just standing there and Catherine and Eric are just looking at us.

"It was nice seeing you again. We need to get over to the shoe section," I tell him with a smile.

"Sure thing, nice to meet you guys. Alex, I will call you on Monday about coffee or lunch," David says with a weird look in his eye. I glance over my shoulder as we are walking away, and I am surprised the angry look on David's face. He looks like he is ready to strangle someone.

I bump into Eric and start laughing, "Sorry, I walk into everyone when I am not paying attention."

"That was the guy I was telling you about from the coffee shop this morning," I say to Catherine.

"He is hot but he seems a little weird."

"I kind of got that vibe just now also. Almost like he was pissed that I did not keep talking to him or invite him with us."

I glance over at Eric who is listening to our conversation. "I don't think Carson is going to like hearing that you may have a date with someone else," he says to me.

"Why would Carson care? We are friends."

Catherine starts laughing, "Oh he is going to care because he is slowly coming around to realizing how bad he wants you."

I just look at the both of them and roll my eyes and walk over to the shoes. I immediately find a beautiful pair of black high heeled sandals that would go perfect with this dress. I try them on and I am in love.

"What do you think?" I ask Catherine and Eric.

"I think those are fuck me shoes," Catherine responds.

"Um. I have to agree with her on that," says Eric. I am turning bright red from that statement. I wonder if Carson would think the same thing if he saw me in these.

"Also, don't you already have a pair like them. You do know you are going to be the only person who has to do an addition to their closet due to your shoe fetish," Catherine adds.

I smile over at her and she starts laughing since she knows me so well. "I guess I am buying them."

As we are walking back to our car my phone starts ringing. I glance down and see that it is Carson calling and immediately start smiling. "Hi, how are you?"

"Good, are you guys done shopping?"

"Yes, we are walking back to the car now."

"Tell Eric that he can leave and I will meet you over at your place. I should be there by the time you get back from dropping off Catherine."

"Sure, see you back at my place," I say as I hang up. I turn to see Catherine eyeing me with a big grin. "Stop it," I say before she can even make a remark.

"Thank you Eric for spending the day with us. I owe you and Madison a night out," I tell him and give him a quick hug.

"Never a problem Alex. I will probably volunteer for some of the watch duty for you," he replies as he is walking away.

Catherine and I put our dresses and shoes in the trunk of the car and as we are getting in, I see another note on my windshield. "Catherine, look at my windshield."

"Oh shit, another note. Grab it and see what it says," she replies.

I get the note and read it, 'Your eyes are beautiful like the sky. I can't wait until I make them shine like the stars. We will be together soon. –P'. This is crazy, I cannot believe that I have some crazy stalker could-be killer after me. "Let me drop you off and I will give this to Carson when he comes over to my place."

I need to think about something else to get my mind off these notes and the fact that I now have a body guard. "What are you doing tonight?" I ask Catherine.

"I have a date with Tim. We are going to dinner and I am not sure what else," she says. Tim is a guy she sees on a regular basis. I am pretty sure she likes him, but isn't head over heels for him. He seems more like a fun guy to play around with. "What are you doing tonight?" she asks me in return.

"I have no idea since Carson has to babysit me. Maybe I will see if he wants to grab dinner and watch a movie at my place." I honestly have no clue what to suggest or if I should assume he would want to do anything with me.

"I bet he will enjoy snuggling up with you on the couch or in your bed."

"I am sure there will be no snuggling of any kind with him. He's not interested in me," I tell her firmly. Thankfully I pull into her driveway so this conversation is over. After I give her a hug, I am on my way to my place and to see Carson.

Chapter 11

I pull into my parking space and see Carson leaning against his car in my visitor spot with a bag sitting on the trunk. He is standing there looking so sexy with his scruffy, two-day unshaven face. He is wearing a hoodie, plain black t-shirt and jeans. I know my mouth drops open. I have never seen him wearing anything other than suits except at the beach. His t-shirt is hugging his body so you can see he has a six pack hidden under there. I am sure that I have never laid eyes on a man before who is oozing sex appeal like Carson.

I finally get out of my car and look up to meet his eyes and he has an eyebrow cocked up, "Is this ok? Like what you see?" he asks me with a grin.

"I. Um. I. Yes, you look incredible and wow. I have never really seen you not in a suit." I stammer out. Idiot... next time I should just say, 'You are hot; I want to lick you all the way down from your throat to your abs.'

I clear my throat and ask him, "How was your day?" I could get used to saying that to him as if he was someone who would be at my place every day after work.

I pop the trunk so I can get my gown and shoes out. Carson walks over and starts picking up the large bag with my gown in it. I grab my bag with my new shoes since he has his other hand full with his bag. "My day was fine. It looks like you found what you were looking for," he replies with a smile. I look up at his face and I am mesmerized by the way his smile can transform his entire face from serious stone to an unbelievable relaxed look. It takes all my might to not reach up and stroke his cheek.

I shake my head, "Yes, I found a new dress and some shoes. Poor Eric was bored out of his mind." We get onto the elevator and head up to my floor.

"He was not bored. He said he had a good time and the dress you bought was amazing. I can't wait to see it."

I feel my cheeks starting to heat up and I have no clue how to respond his comment. Fortunately, we are at my door so I can pretend to be distracted with unlocking my door and turning off my alarm.

"Where do you want your dress?" Carson asks.

"Oh, come with me. Let's put it in my closet." We walk into my closet and I show him where I keep my dresses. As we are walking out I stop suddenly as I remember that my supposed 'guest room' is really my office with a daybed. It will in no way be long enough for a man who is his height. This sudden stop causes Carson to walk smack into me, "Ouch," I exclaim.

"What the hell Alex? You stopped suddenly. Is everything ok?" I can hear the concern in his voice.

"Yes, except I know you said you were going to spend the night, but my guest room is really an office. It has a daybed that you are too tall for. I need to figure out where you are going to sleep this weekend."

"It's fine, I can sleep anywhere, the couch, a tiny daybed, wherever."

"Ok, well let's put your bag in the guest room and you can relax," I show him into the office and he throws his bag down and follows me out the door.

"Do you want anything to drink, a beer, wine, water, liquor? I was going to get a glass of wine," I tell him as I walk to the kitchen. It's almost 5pm and the wine may help me calm down from having him in my personal space.

"A water is fine." I glance over to see him standing in the living room just looking around. I grab my wine and his water and walk over and sit on the couch. "Sit down and relax, it's Saturday and you've been working all day," I tell him as I pat the couch for him to sit down next to me. I reach over and grab the remote off the coffee table to turn on the TV.

"Did you guys talk to Peter?" I ask him dreading his response.

"Yes. He has an alibi for the times that the murders took place," he says sharply. It takes me a minute, but I understand that his alibi's for these murders are at night are most likely other women.

"I see. It's ok. I am not upset. I mean my ego is bruised to know he was sleeping with other people, but we weren't good together."

Carson looks over at me and tucks a piece of hair behind my ear and says softly, "I'm sorry he hurt you. He has no idea how lucky he was to have you." That simmering chemistry has returned between us and I can tell by the look in his eye, Carson can feel it.

Just then I remembered the other note. "Oh, I got another note on my car," I tell him as I get up to grab my purse.

"Alex, why the hell did you wait so long to tell me that? And get a tissue before you grab it so we can check for any fingerprints!" he yells at me.

"Stop yelling at me. I forgot, Catherine and I were talking in the car and you distracted me when I pulled up so it got pushed to the back of my brain." I hand him my purse and a tissue so he can remove it.

"Do you have a plastic bag that I can put this in?" he asks as I go back into the kitchen to grab a bag for him. After he places the note into the bag, he makes a quick call so someone can come pick it up and take it back to the police station.

"What do you want to do tonight? We can go out to eat around the neighborhood and come back. Watch a movie, do nothing, I am not sure if you needed to work or what we do in this situation," I blurt out. Another problem with being around Carson is that I am full of nervous energy and it is coming out in the form of word vomit.

"I am fine with grabbing something to eat. Then coming back and watching a movie," he replies with a smile. I hand Carson the remote because I usually just watch the shows I have recorded on my DVR for the week. I figure he does not want to watch my mindless, trashy reality shows.

"Watch whatever, I am going to read for a bit," I tell him as I stand up to go get the book I have been reading from my nightstand. When I get back with my book and glasses, I get comfortable on the couch next to him. I look up since I feel him staring at me, "What?" I ask him.

"Nothing. I had no idea that you wore glasses," he murmurs and returns to watching ESPN. "Only when I read or spend a lot of time on my computer."

Carson glances back at me and smiles, "They look good on you."

I am saved from responding by my doorbell. "Stay put, I will go see who it is," he says calmly. I hear the door open and Carson greets someone with a laugh and a big smack, "Hey Frank, so you drew the short stick to drive over here and pick up this evidence."

"Not a problem Carson. When I got the call and was told what it was for. I said I would take care of it." Carson walks into the room with a tall, lanky man. "Alex, this is Frank. Frank this is Alexandria," Carson says as he introduces us.

I stand up to shake his hand and Frank freezes, "Holy crap, you're the Vice-President's daughter. My girlfriend loves you and is constantly trying to copy your wardrobe."

I smile at him and try to hide my embarrassment. "Well, don't tell her what I am wearing right now or she may be disappointed."

"Wait until I tell Cass that I not only did I meet you but I was inside of your place. She is going to be pissed I didn't swing by our house and pick her up."

"Thanks again Frank and call me if you get any prints other than Alex's," Carson tells him as he is walking him back to the door.

"It was nice meeting you," I yell behind them. Frank turns around and waves and is still shaking his head.

"You have quite the fan base don't you," Carson says as he is walking towards me.

"I know, it's weird. Being so far away from D.C, I am not photographed as much as I used to be." I am grateful that Carson can tell this subject is awkward for me so he drops it.

"How about that dinner we were talking about, I am starting to get hungry."

"There is a great Mexican restaurant around the corner that we can walk to. If you like Mexican." I love Mexican food; I swear I could eat it every night but try to limit myself to two-three times a week.

"I forgot about your love affair with Mexican food. I remember Catherine telling us in college that is all you guys would eat. That sounds good to me," Carson replies with a smile.

"Great, let me grab my coat and we can go," I tell him as we both start walking towards the door. Carson grabs my coat from me and holds it out so I can put it on. He helps me get my hair out of the way. When he touches the side of my neck, I hope he didn't feel me shudder from the pleasure of that little bit of contact. He is such a gentleman. Peter never did anything like that. I set the alarm and we walk out.

As we are walking down the hallway, I am messing in my purse when I walk sideways into Carson. "I am so sorry!", I say to him. "I do this all the time, if I am not concentrating, I cannot walk in a straight line,"

Carson starts laughing and says, "It's cute, don't worry about it. I have noticed before you tend to veer to the left when you walk."

"Peter used to complain about it all the time when we went out. He actually used to complain about everything when we went out."

"That guy is a jackass. You should have seen him today in the interview room. Adam made me the leave room since Peter kept goading me with comments about you and I."

"Really? I guess I shouldn't be surprised."

Carson holds the door open for me and we walk outside, it is chilly but still a nice evening. "This is a great area," he comments.

"Yeah, I love living here and being able to walk to restaurants, bars and shops," I tell him.

The sidewalk is a little congested with people which forces Carson and I to walk closer together. As we are walking over to the restaurant, his phone starts ringing and he glances down at the number, "Shit," he curses and glances at me.

I smile and raise my eyebrows, "Guns N Roses?" I am talking about his crazy ring tone.

He smiles at me and makes a face, "How do you know who that is? You were three when they were popular and I was at their concerts."

"Are you going to answer it?" To be honest, I am wondering who it is calling him to make him curse like that.

"Sorry, give me two seconds to take care of this," he says.

We move over so we are out of the way of people walking by and I hear him answer. "Hey Kristy, listen I left you a voicemail. Something has come up at work and I am not going to be available for a while." Ah. So it sounds like his girlfriend is pissed he broke a date with her. I am pretending to look in the window of this boutique we are standing in front but I am eavesdropping. I know it's childish but I am a little jealous of this girl who gets to have plans with him.

I hear Carson reply sharply to her, "No, I don't know when I am going to be free. I told you before this was nothing serious and if you were looking for a serious relationship, it was not with me." Whoa, that is harsh, I am not feeling so jealous of her now. "That's fine. I know I'm an asshole. I remember telling you something very similar to that before things progressed between us." I look over at Carson and find him staring at me, he gives me a slight smile and shakes his head. "I know I'm thirty-eight-year-old man who is never going to grow up. Yep, I am not going to beg you to stay with me."

At this point he glances down at his phone and puts it back in his pocket and I bust out laughing. "I am so sorry, it's not funny but it kind of is. We are in the same boat, aren't we?"

Carson slings his arm around my shoulder and pulls me into his side laughing, "Watch it little one." I snort at his comment.

"You know I want to hear all the sordid details during dinner," I tell him with a big grin. He gives me a pained look that tells me he really doesn't want to go there. I cannot wait to torture him over this.

We walk into the restaurant and the hostess takes us to a little corner booth. After the waiter takes our drink order we just stare at each other for a moment and then I bust out laughing.

"What?" Carson asks me.

It takes me a moment to stop laughing, "If you could have seen your face while you were on that call. It was priceless." Carson attempts to give me a scowl but I can tell he is not really upset.

"So, who is Kristy and how long have you guys been seeing each other?" I begin to quiz him.

"She is someone who I met a while back but it's not serious. I told her that from the beginning," he replies and based off his look, he would love for me to drop the subject.

"So how long have you been 'not serious' with her?" This question results in me getting an eye roll, this is so much fun.

"For about three months." I can hear the annoyance creeping into his voice.

"OK, one last question and I will drop it. What did you mean when you told her that you weren't someone to be serious with?"

Carson takes a deep breath, "My work has been my life and it is chaotic. It's hard for any woman to put up with the fact they aren't the center of my life. So I don't even try to have a serious relationship with any of them. If they can't handle it, and they want the wedding dress and white picket fence, I'm not the guy and they need to go find someone else." Wow, that's pretty blunt. I am not sure who would ever want to waste their time with him if he was that upfront about the relationship.

"You were engaged when I first met you, right?" Catherine never knew why the engagement was called off but she told me she thought Carson was the one to break it off. I look over at him and see that he has a weird look on his face.

"Um, yes, I was engaged," he murmurs.

"Is that why you guys did not get married? She wanted to be the center of your life?"

"I just knew based off the way that I felt about Sarah, it would not be fair to marry her," Carson replies uncomfortably.

"Why would you propose if you did not feel that you could marry her?" I am confused by his statement. Why would propose to someone you did not envision spending the rest of your life with.

"When I proposed to her, I thought I could marry her. Then I met someone I felt things with that I never felt with Sarah. So I called it off. Now this is a piece of my private life I have kept private, please do not share it."

"I will not tell anyone. Why did not you not marry the other girl then if you felt so strongly about her?" I wonder who this mystery woman is that could make Carson feel things that he called off his engagement and why is he not with her.

"I never told the girl how I felt or even asked her out on a date. We are done discussing this, Alex," Carson replies firmly. Wow, this is intense, he met someone he feels things for but never acted on them. That has to be miserable going through life not knowing if you are missing out on something.

I glance over at Carson while I am playing with my straw. I can see why women would try to change him. He is so captivating with his personality and his looks. "You don't have any desire to get married and have a family?" I inquire.

"Sure. I just haven't dated anyone who can live up to what I need or expect. Are we done with this topic?"

"Ok, I will drop it," I tell him and take a sip of my margarita and start eating some chips. "Yummy, this is my guilty pleasure," I state with a smile hoping to ease some of the tension that has developed between us from this conversation. "Is there anything you need to get done tomorrow? I feel bad that you are stuck on babysitting duty."

Carson looks at me with exasperation clearly showing in his eyes, "Alex, I don't consider this babysitting duty. If I did not want to be here with you, I would have someone else do it."

I smile at him, "OK, well is there anything you need to do that I can come along with so you don't fall behind in your life?"

"I wouldn't mind going to the gym to workout and then running to the grocery store. I took a look in your fridge and pantry and you are a little light on food."

"I don't really cook when it's just me. Usually I just grab take out from around here but we can do both of those." Maybe I can cook him a meal tomorrow night. What is wrong with me? I am trying to play house with someone who just said he has no interest in playing house. I am saved from more internal drama when the food arrives.

"This looks great," Carson says as he eyes his fajitas.

"That looks like it could feed half of the restaurant," I tell him shocked at the amount of food on his plate.

"At least it's food instead of whatever type of salad you got," he quips back. I just roll my eyes and dig into my chicken fajita salad.

"I am so full," I tell Carson as we walk out of the restaurant.

"I see why you like that restaurant, it was good." As we begin walking down the sidewalk Carson puts his arm around my shoulder again and pulls me closer into his side. I love the smell of his cologne and would enjoy wrapping myself around him and breathing in his scent.

"Do you realize this is the longest amount of time that we have spent together?" Carson glances down at me with a surprised look on his face.

"What are you talking about? We spend a week around each other at the beach every year." I frown at him and wonder if he really thinks spending a week under the same roof but nowhere near each other is his version of spending time together.

"Seriously, you spend the entire week trying not to be around Catherine and I. I am pretty sure you leave the area or room when we walk in." I recognize I am getting pretty close to crossing a line and letting him see that I may like him more than a friend.

"I guess I did avoid you guys, but that's my issue not anything to do with you." I can tell from his response this is a subject that we need to drop so as we enter my building I ask him, "What type of movie do you want to watch?" I decide to ease the tension, "I'm assuming you are a fan of love stories, right?"

That gets the response I was hoping for, Carson starts laughing pretty hard, "OK little one, you are really pushing my buttons tonight."

I try to pretend like I have no clue what he is talking about, "What? I really took you as a romantic comedy type of guy."

"Let's watch either an action or comedy but leave the romance out of it," he states as we walk off the elevator and walk towards my door.

This is not good. Not only is she with the lead detective trying to catch me but he looks extremely friendly with Alexandria. Who does he think he is putting his arm around her like that? This is frustrating not being able to get close to her like I want to, first the other guy and now this detective. I will need to hack into the hidden camera and see what I can use to help me figure out a way to distract him from her so I have my opportunity to develop our relationship.

Chapter 12

I turn off my alarm and throw my purse and keys on the table by the entrance. "I am glad to see you are diligent about your alarm," Carson comments.

I smile at him, "It wasn't an option with my dad. Part of our agreement to keep my Secret Service detail out of my personal space is I always arm it when I am gone and when I am here. He gets notified when it goes on and off."

I sit down on the couch and grab the remote to begin looking at what movies are on demand to order. I try to ignore the fact I can feel Carson's eyes on me or the sexual tension that seems to be growing between us. Carson and I finally agree on a movie to watch and we both get comfortable on the couch. I glance over at him when I hear his phone beep with a text message. He has a disgusted look on his face after he finishes reading it. "Everything ok?" I ask him.

"Yes, just a text from Kristy. Nothing for you to worry about," he says as he turns his phone on silent and keeps watching the movie.

I am trying to pay attention to the movie but I am exhausted after this past week. I finally give up trying to fight to stay awake and just go to sleep. My last thought is Carson can wake me when the movie is over.

She is adorable. I am not paying attention to the movie. All I can think about it is how close Alex is to me on this couch and how hard it is for me to keep from touching her. Having her close to my side on the walk home made me realize even though she is a foot shorter than me, she fits me perfectly. I glance over at Alex and smile when I see she is asleep. I can look at her without her knowing. Wow, what a stalker-like thought. This is a bad idea to spend time with her. I am already beginning to forget all the reasons I have stayed away from her. Tonight at dinner she made me realize that even though she is ten years younger than me, we have so much in common.

I am still shocked I shared so much information with her about the reason I called off my engagement. I am an idiot and the moment she begins to put the timeline together of Catherine introducing us and me calling off the engagement, Alex will realize she is the person I was talking about.

I pull out my phone out to see who is texting me now. It's Adam being a huge smart ass, 'Dude have you pulled your head out of your ass yet with Alex?'

I roll my eyes at his question and type out a reply, 'Stop it. By the way, Kristy is flying off the deep end when I told her I was out of pocket for the next few weeks and canceled on her tonight.'

'She was crazy to begin with. She thought she was going to be the one to turn you into marriage material. Too bad she isn't Alex because she is the only one that you are hung up on.', he types back.

Adam's last statement hits too close to home so I stop replying. Thankfully, the movie is almost over so I can wake up Alex and send her to bed. At least her couch is comfortable since there is no way I can sleep on her tiny daybed. Now her massive king sized bed looks like a place I would have no problem sleeping, except I would not do much sleeping with her in it.

I get up and move over to where Alex is sleeping and gently shake her. "Alex, the movie is over. Time to wake up. You need to go to bed."

She slowly opens her eyes and looks at me sleepily. "I guess I was tired and slept through the entire movie," she says, her voice husky from sleeping.

I look at her and immediately feel a surge of lust shoot through my body in response to how sexy she looks just waking up. To make matters worse I am watching as her hand reaches up towards my face and she strokes my cheek. "I have been dying to do this since yesterday. Your scruff is soft like I thought," she says sleepily.

My body is aching from that one little touch and I am shocked to hear she has been wanting to touch me. I clear my throat,

"Yeah but don't worry about missing the movie. I watched it and you didn't miss much," I tell her pretending I did not hear what she just said about my face.

I step back so she can stand up. "Let me get you some blankets and pillows. I'm sorry again you are sleeping on the couch." I can tell by her face there is something else she wants to ask me.

"What?" I am amazed when she starts blushing, I wonder what that is about.

"If you want, you can sleep in my bed. I mean it's huge and you may be more comfortable," Alex stammers out. Holy shit…my mind just went blank at the suggestion. Not to mention the lust surging through me a minute ago is about to knock my ass over since it is now roaring with a fury.

"No. The couch will be fine Alex. Don't worry about me, I have had to sleep in a car before on a stakeout, so the couch is an upgrade," I tell her as my dick is screaming at me for not agreeing to share a bed with her. "Well, let me go get you everything you need."

As she is walking away I sit down on the couch so she doesn't realize the affect she has me. I put my hands in my head and wonder how the hell did I get myself in this situation.

*****

Now that I am fully awake, I can't believe I just asked Carson to share my bed. What was I thinking? The look on his face was one I could not decipher. I thought he was excited by the suggestion but then he looked angry. I am grabbing him a few pillows, sheets and a comforter. I really have no clue what I am doing because I cannot stop thinking about him. He looked so handsome when he woke me up. I am mortified I stroked his cheek and told him I had been wanting to touch him. I am sure this is the last time I see him.

I walk back into the living room and see him sitting on the couch. I am going to pretend what just happened did not actually happen. "Here is everything I think you need. If you need anything, come get me or dig around my place."

"Thanks and sleep good," Carson says softly.

"You too and thank you again for tonight. I had fun even though I fell asleep on you," I tell him as I turn around to leave.

I leave my door cracked just in case he needs anything. I head to my bathroom to get ready for bed. After I wash my face, I go into my closet to pick out pajamas to wear. I usually sleep in just my panties. I decide since Carson is here to wear a simple, super soft, lace trimmed slip, nothing overtly sexy, but I am not sleeping in a paper bag either. I climb into bed, turn off my lights and I can hear Carson moving around in the living room. I am never getting to sleep with him in the next room I think to myself. Surprisingly I am asleep a few minutes later.

*****

I see the light go out in Alex's room and I try to get comfortable on this couch. I am so wound up I am not sure if I will be able to get any sleep, this is so embarrassing since I am thirty-eight years old. I finally get settled and drift off to sleep dreaming about her.

A few hours later I wake up with a start. I have heard a sound and it takes me a minute to realize it sounds like Alex crying out. I jump up and grab my gun off the coffee table and run towards her room. As I am standing by the door, I realize she is dreaming and it is not an intruder in her condo. I walk into her room and set my gun on her dresser and walk over to her side of the bed to wake her up. Alex must be having a nightmare because she is thrashing her legs and crying out for something or someone to stop.

"Alex, wake up honey. You are having a nightmare," I tell her softly as I lean over her. All of a sudden she rears up and her head collides with my nose as she is screaming. "Motherfucker that hurt! It's me, Carson, you were having a nightmare", I shout over her screaming while I am holding my nose. I am pretty sure it is bleeding.

Alex is finally awake enough to stop screaming and she turns on her lamp. "Oh my gosh, Carson. I am so sorry!", she exclaims getting out of bed and running over to me to try to help. She grabs me by the arm and pulls me into her bathroom and makes me sit on the edge of the tub. As my eyes are adjusting to the light I glance over at her and freeze.

This is not a good situation. First, I am only wearing my boxers. Second, she is wearing some flimsy, silky night gown that stops right above her butt cheeks. Third, I am beginning to get hard and there is no way to hide it. Alex bends over to get something out of a drawer and holy shit, she has a perfect ass. She also is wearing a very skimpy thong that leaves nothing to my imagination.

Alex turns around with a washcloth and walks over to the sink to wet it before heading over to me. "Carson, I am so sorry. You scared the living daylights out of me and I did not realize you were leaning so close to my head."

I hold up my other hand hoping to stop her, "Hey it was not your fault. I thought something was wrong and I came in. I should have realized that it would scare you when I woke you up," my voice is distorted and sounds like it does when I have a stuffy nose.

Alex steps in between my legs, "Move your hand so I can take a look," she says as she moves my hand away.

I move my hand and then I become conscious to the fact that my face is eye-level with her breasts. I begin to feel the hard pulse of my arousal and close my eyes hoping Alex will not notice. She begins to wipe the blood off my face and I look up and see the concern in her eyes. "It's fine Alex, you just gave me a bloody nose," I tell her and smile trying to ease her concern.

"I know but you are covered in blood now," she says sharply as she continues to clean my face. All of a sudden she freezes and I can see that she is staring at my chest. There are droplets of blood on my chest and she slowly begins to wipe them off. I am holding my breath because I am fighting to keep my self-control in check due to this sensual feeling. All I want to do is pull her against me and kiss her.

"There, you are all clean. You just need to wash your hands off," she says huskily. I glance at her face and I can see her eyes are clouded with desire and her nipples have hardened into taut pebbles. I can't let this situation spiral out of control.

"Thanks. I think I have it from here. Why don't you go back and get into bed?" I need her to leave because there is no way I can stand up without her seeing I have a baseball bat size erection in my boxers.

"Sure, I'm sorry again for hurting you," she says again as she turns to leave the bathroom.

I get up to wash my hands and splash some water on my face. I need to get myself and my body under control. I have to put some space between us and fast. I was an idiot thinking I could stay with her and stay objective. I shake my head in disgust as I turn around to go back to the couch.

As I walk back into her bedroom she is sitting in bed. "What was the nightmare about? it seemed pretty bad," I ask her before I leave.

She is sitting quietly and whispers, "It was about the guy who killed Allison and he was coming after me."

I walk over to her and sit on the side of the bed, "It's ok to be scared. I rather you be scared and take this seriously than think it is not a big deal and end up in danger."

"In my dream he was coming after me. I was trying to fight him off," she finishes while a shudder runs through her body. I lean over a give her a hug to offer some comfort. She feels so soft in my arms and like she belongs. Her lips move against my bare chest as she asks, "Will you lie down and stay with me? I would feel better knowing that you are close." I kiss the top of her head and while my brain is screaming go back to the couch, I can tell she is upset by the nightmare so I go to other side of the bed and climb in. Alex turns off her lamp and rolls over to face me.

Our eyes are adjusting to the darkness and she reaches over to stroke my cheek again and whispers, "Thank you and good night." That one tiny caress immediately sends another surge of lust pounding through my body. This is going to be a long night.

*****

I slowly wake up and I am feeling so warm on this chilly morning. I do not want to get out of bed. I snuggle a little closer to the warmth and then I realize I am up against something that is hard, very warm and smooth. I crack my eyes open and to my horror, I am sprawled out almost completely on top of Carson. My upper body is resting on his bare, handsome, to-die-for chest and my left thigh is on top of his throbbing erection. I can feel his heat pulsing under my thigh and all I want to do is shift and rub his heat against my now aching center.

This cannot be a normal reaction to someone. I just woke up and one glance at Carson's chest has me wanting to beg him for more. I think my sex drive has gone from zero to sixty in two days. I never felt this type of reaction towards Peter.

I need to figure out how to get off of him without waking him. I begin to slowly move when I feel Carson move underneath me. I glance up to see his eyes are open and on me. I smile, "Good morning. I am so sorry I am draped all over you. I was trying to figure out how to move without waking you, but I guess I woke you," I stammer out quickly. I am so embarrassed. I want to crawl under the blankets and hide. I am pretty sure he could feel against his hip I was getting aroused. Not to mention my nipples are standing tall like twin peaks.

"You are fine Alex. I was waking up anyways." I smile with relief because it looks like he is on the same page as me about pretending that neither of us are going to acknowledge what is going on with our bodies. I move off of him and get out of bed to grab my robe and go make some coffee.

As I am turning around, I glance over to see Carson getting up and my mouth goes dry at the sight of him in his boxers. He is all lean, hard muscles and the erection he is trying to adjust is showing just how endowed he is. I turn around quickly to put on my robe as he glances at me and he walks out the door. I hope he did not catch me staring at him but he is magnificent. I would love to have a look at him without anything on.

I give him a few minutes before I head into the kitchen to start making coffee. I glance over at him as he is buttoning his jeans and reaching for a t-shirt. "I was going to make coffee and some eggs and bacon for breakfast. Or would you rather go out for breakfast?" I ask him.

He glances over and smiles, "Coffee and breakfast here sounds fine. I am surprised you cook." I shoot him a dirty look and he starts laughing at me. "It's just that I have never seen you cook and I figured with the way you were raised you had people doing things like that for you," he replies.

I give him an even dirtier look. "Looks can be deceiving."

Carson walks around the kitchen island over to me to help get down the dishes I want, "Little one, I am just teasing. I know you can probably do a lot of things I have no idea about."

I decide to change the subject, "The coffee is done brewing and there is creamer and sugar on the counter." I begin working on frying up some bacon and whisking eggs.

"Do you want to go to the gym in a little a while?" I ask him.

"Sure. What do you want to do at the gym?"

I look up at him and say trying not to laugh, "Workout." This brings a bark of laughter out of Carson and one of those 1000-watt smiles that I am beginning to see more of. "I need to do upper body strength training and cardio," I tell him seriously.

"Sounds good." Carson sets a cup of coffee down beside me, "Here, I think this is made the way you like." I am stunned that he knows how I like my coffee. This is such a domestic scene going on right now. I take a sip and sure enough, it is made just like I would have made it.

"This is heaven, thank you," I tell him after I take a sip.

Finally, breakfast is ready and I place a massive plate of eggs and bacon in front of him. I am still floored by the amount of food he can put down, but with all those muscles he needs the fuel. "This is good Alex,", he says between bites.

Just then Carson's phone starts ringing and he glances down with a frown before he answers it. "Knight," is all he says as he answers the phone briskly. I am standing there watching his face and it slowly turns to stone with anger shining bright in his eyes. "Are you sure? That makes no sense," he says to whoever is on the phone. "Fine, let me get dressed and I will be over there."

Carson looks up at me and says, "Apparently there has been another murder so I need to get over to the scene." This must be part of the job his girlfriends have a hard time with.

"No problem, that is awful."

"Please don't go anywhere until I get back or until I send someone else over here to go places with you."

I smile over to him, "I have some work to get caught up on. There are towels in the guest bathroom so you can shower." He finishes up his breakfast and washes his plate off in the sink, Peter would never have done anything like. I cannot believe I put up with him for as long as I did.

I begin to clean up the kitchen and finish my coffee while he is showering. I turn around when I hear Carson walking out with his bag. He comes over to me and bends down and kisses my cheek. "Thank you for breakfast, it was delicious. Remember what I said about staying put."

"Talk to you later," I tell him since I do not know how to reply since he is going to a murder scene. Moments later he is out the door and I am standing there in my empty condo.

Chapter 13

What the hell is going on I wonder. Over the past six months this killer has stuck to a schedule as part of his MO. This is the first time he has deviated and I wonder what drove him to kill again so soon. The shrinks we have consulted with have all agreed he has a four-week cycle. This is part of his hunting and what makes him tick.

As I am getting into my car to leave Alex's, my phone starts ringing. I connect through my Bluetooth. "Knight"

"Dude, this is crazy," starts Adam with his typical California speak.

"I know; I was floored when I just got the call. I am leaving Alex's now so I should be over to the scene in about five to ten minutes." I wait for him to start busting my balls about Alex and sure enough, he does not waste any time.

"How was spending the night with Alex? Did you guys make out or anything?" Adam teases.

"We did anything but make out," I reply sarcastically.

It took all my strength this morning to not grab her when I woke up. The feel of her up against me was incredible. The sad thing was I had been feigning sleep for about thirty minutes before she actually woke up. I was relishing in the fact that her small, lush body was draped across mine.

She was driving me crazy when she woke up and I felt her body respond to mine when she realized where she was. I have to step back from her. I am not good for her and I know it. I could tell Alex was uncomfortable with the reason I was leaving. She deserves a guy who can spoil her, wait on her hand and foot and provide her with the lifestyle that she is accustomed to. I have my trust fund but I refuse to touch it. I make sure my lifestyle can be supported by my detective salary, minus my car, which is my guilty pleasure.

"Hey man, are you even listening to me?" Adam asks bringing me out of my thoughts.

"Uh, sorry, no I did not hear what you said."

"I was asking what are you doing about Alex's bodyguard duty now you are gone." Shit a brick. I can't leave her alone for long periods of time and I need to step away, way away from her because I am beginning to lose my head.

"Do you think you can spend the night over there with her tonight and so I can focus on the case?" I ask him hesitantly. Adam is about to call me out on my b.s. and I prepare myself for it.

"Are you insane?" he blurts out. Before he can even give me crap about this I interrupt him.

"I need to step away from her. I am losing my objectivity and not focusing on the case while I am over there," I tell him honestly. That admission stops Adam in his tracks.

After a few seconds of silence, he finally replies, "Sure thing, I have your back. I will swing by my house and grab a bag and go over there later today."

The thing with Adam is that no matter how much crap he gives me, he knows when I am being honest and always has my back. "Thanks man, I will see you in a few minutes."

I arrive at the crime scene and run into one of the crime scene techs. "Hey Knight, you better prepare yourself, this scene is different from all the previous ones. Which may be good for us," he tells me. I nod and keep walking and enter into a mess.

You can see and feel the rage the killer must have felt. Usually the scenes are clean except for the blood on the walls and the dead body. This place looks like a bomb went off. The couch has been slashed and ripped apart. The TV and all the paintings that were on the walls have been pulled down and smashed into pieces. The coffee table is overturned and there is debris everywhere. I step over a broken picture frame of the victim and what looks like her family. Then there is the writing on the wall, 'This happens when you don't let me see her eyes, if you continue to keep her away from me, I will continue to do this'.

Behind me I hear, "Holy fuck, look at this room. He was enraged," Adam states. I am looking all over the room in order to get a feel for what may have taken place.

"This is nothing like what he has been doing. It is off the schedule and there are signs of a struggle. Look at what he wrote on the wall. It is nothing like what he has written before," I say.

I begin walking around the room when everything clicks. "Adam, I think this is because we have started guarding Alex. Take that into context and look at the scene. He is frustrated that he can't get to her because we have had Eric with her and I was with her all night."

"Hmmm…that does make sense. There is no sense of wooing here. No wine, no romance. I think we don't find any notes," he agrees with me. "I bet this asshole did this to get us away from Alex and to distract us," I tell him.

At that moment the coroner walks over to us, "She was killed last night sometime between 12am-1am based off her body temp. I am going to assume cause of death will be the same as the others except this one fought him so maybe we can get DNA off her." I am hoping that will be the case, we need a break. I can tell we are pissing him off since Alex is clearly his next target.

"Adam, why don't you head over and grab your bag and go to Alex's? I don't like leaving her unattended, especially after this," I tell him.

"Sure, I will text you so you know I am there. What do you want me to say if she asks why I am there and not you?" Adam asks.

This stops me short, I have no clue what to tell Alex. "Just tell her I am busy with the case," I tell him and get back to examining the scene.

*****

It has been a boring day here by myself. At least I got caught up on cleaning and laundry. I wonder if Carson is going to get back soon so we can workout and go to the grocery store. I am contemplating doing some work so I can start the week off ahead of schedule when I hear my doorbell ring. I walk over and look out the peephole and see Adam standing there. "Hey kitten. It's Adam, open up," he says on the other side of the door.

I open the door and smile at him. "Hey, what are you doing over here?" I wonder where Carson is but I do not want to be rude or give Adam any ammo to tease me about Carson.

"Carson is busy with the case so you are stuck with me for the rest of the day and tonight."

Well that stinks, but I understand why Carson is not here. "Ok, well welcome to my home. Let me show you where you can put your bag. You will probably want to sleep on the couch since you are tall like Carson," I tell him as we start walking to my guestroom.

"Are there any errands you need to go out for?" Adam asks me.

"The only thing I need to do is go to the grocery store. While we are there, pick out what you want for dinner and I can cook for you."

"Nothing better than a good looking women cooking me dinner. This is going to be a fun night," Adam says with laugh.

"Why don't we go ahead and head to the store? Then I can workout and get some work done after that," I say.

I grab the grocery list I had made earlier and we head out the door. The nice thing about Adam is he can always keep the mood light. He is busy telling me about his date last night and it has me laughing all the way down to the garage. "I do not know if I really believe any of that happened," I tell him.

"What?! You don't think a woman would just jump into my arms and beg me to sleep with her after a fabulous dinner and want to invite her friend to join us," he says laughing. I just shake my head and hit the locks on my car so we can leave.

I am about to put the car in reverse when I see there is another note on my car. "Well crap, there is another note," I say out loud. "Stay put and let me grab it," Adam utters while he pulls out a plastic bag and gets out of the car.

After he has placed it in an evidence bag I ask him, "What does it say?" Adam glances at me while he is writing out a text to someone and hands it over.

"It's the same type of note that you have received before. Nothing for you to worry about." There is something in his voice that makes me want to question more.

"Adam, are you sure? I feel like you're keeping something from me."

"Kitten, it is nothing for you to worry about. Let Carson and our team handle everything." I still think he is full of crap and not telling me the truth.

"Let's go to the store and get back," I tell him as I throw the car into reverse. The drive to the store is uneventful and Adam is trying to cheer me up, but it is not working. I grab a cart and we begin strolling the aisles picking up food. As I am looking at the vegetables, I glance over at Adam and see that he is busy texting on his phone so I just start picking veggies I think he may like.

I am reaching for some potatoes when someone reaches over to grab one of those plastic bags but I am in the way. "I am sorry, let me move out of the way," I say as I glance over to the person who I was blocking. I smile when I recognize the face the hand belongs to. "Hi David, it is nice to see you again," I say to him.

David gives me a big smile, "Alexandria, we keep bumping into each other. It must be fate," he says with a laugh.

"I am assuming you must live in this part of town."

"Yes, I live on West Peachtree Street," he tells me.

"Oh, you are only a few blocks away from me."

At that moment I feel a hand on my shoulder and I glance over to see Adam standing there giving David the evil eye while looking him up and down. "Everything ok, Alex?" Adam asks me.

I can feel the tension immediately spike as these two males try to figure out who the alpha is. "Adam, this is David. David this is my friend, Adam," I say as I introduce them.

"How did you two meet?" Adam asks still eyeing David.

I laugh nervously since I will be telling Adam I gave a guy my phone number. "We actually bumped into each other at the coffee shop near my condo yesterday. We keep running into each other around the neighborhood," I explain to Adam.

Adam kind of grunts at the explanation and just stands there. David thankfully decides to be the one to back off, "I will give you a call tomorrow Alexandria and we can grab that coffee."

I wave to him as he is walking off, "Sure thing and enjoy the rest of your day."

I finish grabbing the potatoes so we can wrap up our shopping. Once we are in the car Adam clears his throat, "Alex, I'm not sure about that guy and you meeting anyone. It seems a little off with everything that is going on."

I am a little surprised to hear him say that. "He seems harmless plus I do not give out my cell number. I gave him my office number and only agreed to meet him for a coffee." I hope he picks up on my 'mind your own business' tone in the statement.

"I think Carson would agree with me and not want you to go." I take a deep breath. "Adam, I'm a big girl and I'm single so if I want to have coffee with someone, I really do not care what you and Carson think. You aren't my dad or my boyfriend," I snap at him.

"I get it Alex. I am just trying to look out for you."

I feel like crap for being so rude but at least I made my point. "I know. I am sorry I was snarky." We pull back into my garage and begin the fun of carrying up all the grocery bags.

When we are back in my condo, I begin putting up the groceries, "Adam, make yourself comfortable on the couch. The remote is on the coffee table and I am sure there is football or something on."

"I was going to do some yoga when I am done. Do you want to join?" I yell to Adam after I am done with putting up the groceries.

That gets a laugh out of him, "No, you have fun bending yourself into a pretzel. I am perfectly happy watching the Falcons play."

As I am changing into my yoga pants and sports bra, I hear my doorbell ring. What the heck is going on? Is my house grand central station today or what? "I will grab the door Alex. Don't worry about it," I hear Adam yell as I walk out of my closet.

"Alex, let us know when you are decent. The secret service is here to do their security sweep," Adam yells from the front door. I walk out and see Secret Service Agent Max Andrews standing in the kitchen talking to Adam.

"Max!" I squeal as I run over to give him a hug. Max has been on my dad's detail for years so it's like seeing my big brother.

"Hi Alex. Sorry to bother you, but you know the drill since your father and mother want to come see you at your place on Tuesday."

"Of course, I was going to do some yoga but I can wait until you are done."

"No, go ahead and do whatever you were planning to do." The problem is I know I will be only halfway through my yoga video when Max needs to sweep the guestroom.

"I will answer some emails and get caught up on work while you are doing your drill." I give him a quick hug and go off into my office.

*****

Max begins his sweep with all of the high tech devices in his kit. "So Alex has gotten herself into some trouble I hear," Max says. "Yes. She had two options, either call in her security detail or let us guard her. Needless to say, she chose us. So do you have any time off while you are here to grab a beer with Carson and I?"

"No, it is my two week's on. Plus, I think I just recovered from that hangover the last time I went out with you guys. And that chick from the bar you insisted I take back to my hotel is still calling me."

I start laughing. We did get Max hammered the last time he was in town. "Sorry. Sometimes those bar bunnies can be clingy. I think Carson is dealing with the same thing right now."

Max is moving a wand that picks up bugging devices in her coat closet by the door when the device begins emitting a sound. "Interesting," Max murmurs as he runs the wand over Alex's coat again and the device sounds again.

"What is it?"

"This device is designed to pick up any tracking tags, listening or camera devices that may be hidden. It is going crazy on Alex's coat," Max explains as he is pulling out the coat in question.

I let out a whistle, "This is not good," and I pick up my phone to call Carson. I am watching Max slowly examine her coat and he finally found what he was looking for. A small tiny transmitter, it is a slender as a needle and only 2 centimeters in length. He places the transmitter on the kitchen counter.

"I am going to leave this here for now until I finish with her sweep," Max says has he continues moving the wand over every square inch of the condo.

"Carson, get over to Alex's now. We have an issue," I tell him over the phone.

"Is she hurt?"

"No, she is fine but the secret service is doing a security sweep and they have found a tracking device in her coat."

"What the fuck is going on? We have this new murder and the new note. I will be over there in five minutes." I can tell Carson is close to his breaking point. The note on Alex's car was unlike the others. 'I get upset when I don't get to see your eyes every day. If you continue to hide from me, I will continue to hurt other women whose eyes remind me of yours. -P'. The killer has thrown down the gauntlet and we know Alex is the next target.

"Max, I don't want Alex to know we have found anything until you are done and we have a plan. Can you go ahead and sweep her office so she will be distracted doing yoga? That should give us about an hour before she is done.". I would prefer Alex to not realize what is going on and hopefully Carson will be here shortly.

"Sounds good. Let me hit that room."

After Max knocks on the door, I stand and watch him at work. I hope Alex does not pick up on the tension radiating from Max and I. "I'm just going to respond to a few emails and listen to my headphones if that works," Alex says to us.

"No problem Alex, I can do this around you so don't even move from your seat," Max tells her with a smile.

I glance over at Max when I hear his wand start beeping again up around the top of her drapes. I look over to Alex to make sure she is not paying attention while Max is slowly looking around the drapes to determine what is setting off his wand. I hear Max whistle and say in a low voice, "This is a problem."

Shit, like this can get any worse. I walk over to Max and smile at Alex while we try to pretend we are just shooting the shit. "What is it?" I ask. He moves the drape aside so I can see a small camera that looks like it has a full view of the room except for this spot we are standing in beneath it. "Leave it there for now."

My mind is going a thousand miles per minute trying to think of what to do. "Keep sweeping and leave everything where it is until we know how many cameras are in this place." Max looks at me like he is about to argue.

"Hey, I have no intention of leaving you secret service agents out of this mess. This may be a serial killer who is stalking Alex, and we need to handle this with care so we can catch him." That stops Max from arguing with me and he nods in agreement.

As we finish the room, Alex glances up and smiles at us. "Have fun guys. I am going to do some yoga now so let me know when you are done Max."

"Sure thing Alex, enjoy your yoga", Max tells her as we shut the door.

"You know the Vice-President is going to freak out once I tell him about this," Max says to me as we walk into the living room.

I rub my face with my hands and just shake my head, "I know."

"Do you have any clue who could have bugged her place like this?"

I think about that for a few minutes. "It could be her douchebag ex-boyfriend, Peter. But I'm not really sure it is him because why would he put a hidden camera in her office? It doesn't make sense."

Max is going around the living room and again the wand goes crazy by the drapes and he has found another camera hidden at the top of them. "I need to do her bedroom, that massive closet and bathroom of hers then I am done." Just then we hear a knock at the door. I get up and look out the peephole to see an extremely livid Carson standing there looking like he is about to kick the door down.

I open the door to let him in. "Hi honey. Welcome home," I tell him with a smile.

"What the fuck is going on here Adam?" Carson spits out at me.

He glances over my shoulder to see Max standing there. "Max, it's good to see you again," he says. Max walks over and gives Carson a hug and slaps his back.

"Hey man, Vice-President McNeil told me you promised to keep his girl safe, but it looks like you have a major problem on your hands. Let me finish my sweep and then we can talk." Carson nods at him before turning on me.

"Where is she?" he asks. I smile because I can tell that he is dying to see her.

"She's doing yoga in her office. We have about another forty-five minutes before she is done and we rock her world again."

Carson walks into her bedroom as Max is looking down at a vase. "What do you see?" Carson asks him.

"Well this is interesting, this camera is different from all the others. I know this make and it is not as sophisticated as the others. There must be a small DVR recorder close by recording everything." Max continues walking around and he finds two more cameras, one hidden in her closet and the other in her bathroom. There was a total of six cameras throughout her condo and the tracking transmitter in her coat.

*****

As soon as Max finishes his sweep the three of us are looking down at the tracking device and Max tells us, "This is pretty high tech, I am talking close to a CIA grade transmitter to be this thin and minuscule." My jaw is hurting from how hard I am clenching my teeth. I am surprised Max and Adam can't hear me grounding my molars.

Max continues telling us his thoughts, "So I can tell these cameras are video only so at least no one is listening to what is being said in her place. The thing that confuses me though is the one camera in her bedroom. It is not the same high tech grade and we need to go through her place and find the DVR recorder. We should be able to see what is on it and get an idea of when it was placed."

Alex is going to freak out the moment she knows someone invaded her privacy and has been spying on her. "Can we use the wand across the hall?" I ask Max.

Adam cocks his head to one side, "What are you thinking?".

Ever since Adam called me, I have been trying to figure out who or why anyone would want to put a tracking device on Alex. The first thing that pops to mind is some crazy terrorist who wants to kidnap her and use her for political leverage but that doesn't feel right. The second thing is based off the message the killer left us is he is watching her and knows she is not alone. He can't get close to her.

"I want to see if Allison's apartment was bugged like this. If it is then we have good reason to assume the killer has been inside of her apartment. If it is not, then we may be pulling Peter back in for questioning."

"Sure, you can use it. Let's go over there now and give it a sweep."

"How long before Alex is done with her yoga?" I ask.

Adam looks at his watch, "We have about fifteen minutes to do this before she is done."

I nod, "Stay here Adam. We will be back in a few minutes."

Max and I walk across the hall and I cut the tape and jimmy the lock open on the apartment. Since it is still a crime scene no one has been in there. We walk in and it smells awful, with blood on the wall and the floor from Thursday night. "Jesus, this is gross," Max says.

I glance over at him and smile sarcastically, "You fancy Secret service agents just wear your suits and attend fancy parties. Not used to the gore of the real world."

Max starts laughing, "Yeah, something like that," and he begins his sweep of the apartment.

Within a few minutes he has found a camera hidden in the drapes of Allison's condo. "Is it the same type?"

"Looks that way." This sucks but I think we can use it to our advantage.

"Ok, let's go back to Alex's and we can finish over here later."

Once we are back at Alex's, "Well?" asks Adam.

I nod my head and tell him, "We found one and it looks the same as what is in here. We can finish the rest of the sweep later since we need to find the recorder now.

"The first place I would put a recorder for a camera like this is either in the coat closet or under the kitchen sink," Max tells us.

I open up Alex's coat closet and begin moving a few coats aside looking in, "How many pairs of shoes should one woman have?" I say to myself.

That gets a laugh out of Max, "Man, you have no idea. You should have seen how many she had at her house before she moved down here. The girl has a serious shoe addiction problem."

I am moving a shoe rack over when I see a small black hard drive in the back of the closet, "Bingo, I am pretty sure this is it."

I stand back up and Max looks it over and agrees. "That is it. We should be able to hook it up to her TV and watch." I freeze when my brain comprehends when we watch this video, Adam and Max are going to see that I slept in her bed and witness my raging erection I woke up with. Not to mention the entire bloody nose incident.

"Let's wait on watching it. We need to let Alex know what is going on. Plus, she may not want all of us watching her and what she may be doing in her bedroom."

I glance over at Adam and he has his mischievous smile on his face, I know a smart-ass comment is coming. "You remember what you found in the nightstand across the hall. I bet you can see if Alex has something similar."

"Shut the fuck up Adam," I growl at him. Max is standing there watching us with confusion on his face. I walk over to the office door and open it.

I am taken aback by what I see. There in the room is Alex in her yoga pants and a tank top. The tank top is up around her neck because she is some crazy yoga pose that is exposing her beautiful, lush breasts in her skimpy sports bra. There is nothing left to the imagination and my body begins to respond to seeing her this way. Adam and Max have walked in behind me and all three of us are speechless. She is resting on her forearms but her entire body is almost bent over backwards. "Wow kitten, you are bent like a pretzel," Adam says to her.

"Hey, give me a minute to work my way back out of this pose," she says breathlessly as I watch a bead of sweat slip down her throat. To my amazement I get even stiffer as her body begins to move with such fluidity and gracefulness. I watch her arm muscles moving and I am amazed at how strong this tiny, little woman really is. After she completes what seems to be another ten moves, she stands up. Alex turns around and freezes when she sees all three of us staring at her.

Chapter 14

My arms are exhausted as I am slowly moving out of the scorpion yoga pose. I have spent over a year working towards being able to master this move. I am a hot, sweaty mess but at least I was able to put my life back into perspective. I can accept Carson is not going to acknowledge nor act on our shared attraction of each other since he has some mystery girl he is pining after. I turn around to grab my towel and see three pairs of eyes staring at me with varying degrees of astonishment on their faces.

"Hey guys. Carson when did you get here? What's wrong, you all look a little shell-shocked?" I say as I bend over to grab my towel. I begin to walk towards them, they all move aside so I can leave the room. "I'm going to shower since I am a little sweaty."

All of a sudden they come out of their stupor and yell almost at the same time, "No, don't take a shower!"

I turn around and now it is my turn to look surprised. "Would you care to explain to me why I can't take a shower in my own home?"

"Alex, sweetheart, we need to talk to you about the security sweep Max just completed," Carson says gently.

"Why don't we all sit in the living room?" Max suggests.

"Fine," I say but take a detour to grab a glass of water before I sit down.

"Alex, will you please sit over in that chair?" Carson asks me but it is not really a request, but more of a statement. If today is like the past few days, then I know they are about to tell me something that I am not going to like.

I watch the three of them take a seat on my sectional with their grim looks. "Alex, you know how I or another agent from our team will bring a wand that can detect listening devices, hidden cameras and other types of surveillance equipment in every two weeks and do the routine sweep of your place? We have never found anything unusual except for today," Max states.

"Max found a tracking device inside of your pink coat you wear all the time. Someone wants to know where and when you are going places," Adam adds.

Max nods in agreement, "It was pretty sophisticated. So we are dealing with someone who wanted to go undetected. They did not realize you have these security sweeps so it was placed on your coat sometime in the past two weeks." I am stunned and sit there and nod my head. Someone has been watching my movements, which is super weird and beyond creepy.

Carson clears his throat and I glance over at him. "Alex, there is more we need to tell you but I need you to promise me that you are not going to freak out or make any sudden movements. I want you to try to stay calm. Can you do that?"

I nod my head yes but I can feel my hands start to shake. What the hell is on going on in my home? "Max found six different cameras hidden throughout your place. They are hidden mostly at the top of your drapes here in the living room, office and then we found one by your vase of flowers on your dresser in your bedroom, in your closet and your bathroom," Carson tells me.

I begin to feel lightheaded as what Carson just told me is sinking into my brain. There are cameras all over my place and someone has been watching me. "Take a deep breath little one, you look like you are about to pass out," Carson says.

I slowly focus on my breathing, think about how you breathe moves during yoga, I tell myself. "I am fine," I tell him.

"That's why we don't want you to shower. Whoever who has placed these cameras has probably seen enough of your delightful body," Adam begins trying to make me feel better. "Adam, cut the crap. The last thing she needs is you being a smartass," Carson snaps at him.

"Alex, there are a few more things we need to talk about," Max says interrupting Carson and Adam's verbal sparing. "The camera in your room is different from the others. It's not as high grade and there was a DVR recorder placed in your closet by the door. We want to watch it. But it is video of your room and we do not know how long it has been recording or how long it stores what it records."

"So you guys want my permission to watch what goes on in my bedroom?" I say sarcastically. I turn beet red because they are going to see me in varying stages of undress and shit they are going to see what happened this morning with Carson and I. I glance over at Carson and can tell that he is thinking the same thing.

"It's fine Alex. We are all professionals and get there may be things that are embarrassing on the DVR but it just us and we will keep everything quiet," Carson he says tenderly. I know he is giving me permission to let Max and Adam watch the DVR with him.

"Fine, watch the DVR." This is going to be so embarrassing, I want to cry but I know I cannot show any signs of distress. "By the way, how and when are you guys getting these cameras out of my place?" I watch as Carson, Adam and Max all exchange silent looks.

"Alex, we aren't sure. I want to leave them up. If this is Allison's murderer who put these up, then we may be able to use it to our advantage," Carson explains.

I am shaking my head no from the moment he started speaking. "No, no, no, that is not acceptable. You can't expect me to sleep or get dressed or shower knowing that some pervert is getting his rocks off watching me!", I yell at him.

"Alex, what if we 'find' the cameras in your bedroom, closet and bathroom out of commission but leave the rest active. Would you be open to that?" Max asks me gently.

I think about it for a moment and know I should try to help them catch this guy and this is a compromise. "I think I can live with that solution."

"How are you going to do that without raising any suspension?" Adam asks.

"Well, whoever placed these cameras has probably seen me doing the sweep so I will go back again into those room and make a production of finding those," Max explains. "So either way this may help catch him."

"That sounds good, let's see what is on the camera in the bedroom and then you can create the discovery of those other cameras," Carson says. I nod in agreement and prepare myself to be extremely embarrassed as I think back to some of things that have happened in my bedroom over the past two weeks. I really hope the camera has not been there too long.

Max connects the DVR to my TV and they turn it on. Immediately you tell it was at night when whoever hid this camera was in my condo because they turned on my lamp that sits on the dresser. Whoever is installing the camera is staying where you can't see anything other than their hand and arm moving in front as they position the camera so I would not notice it. Which I never did notice. They must have gotten it set up the way they wanted it because there is no more movement of the camera.

We are just sitting there when something clicks in my head. "Oh my gosh, I think I know when whoever hid that camera was here! It was Friday night, remember when you both came up and I said I never leave my lamp on in my room. See, I never leave my lamp on in my room." If this is the case, then it means it has only been a few days since it was hidden.

"Let's keep watching and see how much video has recorded. I hope you are right Alex," Carson responds. We continue to watch the video when all of sudden the camera moves again and then it is set down back in the position it had been in.

"Uh, that's weird," Adam comments.

"I agree, given the camera in the bedroom is different from the rest of them, maybe we have two different people sneaking around this place," Max states.

This is bizarre and I cannot believe I have somehow attracted two psychos who are attempting to be voyeurs. "God, I must have the world's worst luck," I say out loud.

"What do you mean?" Adam asks me.

"Who the heck ends up with two people hiding cameras in her place?" I say rhetorically. That gets a chuckle from Adam and Max, Carson just looks pissed off.

We continue to watch the video and then you see Carson, Adam and I. "See I was right, this was on Friday!", I say, very proud of the fact I guessed it before the detectives did.

"At least we now have a timeframe of when this camera was installed," Carson murmurs.

"So we can turn it off now, right?" I ask.

I figure now we know when it was placed and you cannot see anything, so there is no reason to continue to watch. Especially since I know I will be walking around in nothing but my thong. Then there is the me waking up on top of Carson scene that as much as I love replaying it in my head, I do not want to replay it in front of Adam and Max.

"No, we need to keep watching to see if this guy has been back inside of here while you have been gone," Carson states.

I blow out a huff and cross my arms. "Well just to give you a spoiler alert, I walk around naked a lot of the time while I am getting dressed and when I am here by myself, so enjoy," I say with an edge to my voice.

"Alex, we aren't trying to be dirty, old perverts and see you naked. Honestly, all of us wish we did not have to watch this but it could be important," Carson says gently.

I look over at the three of them and I can feel the tears in my eyes. "I know, I am sorry. I am acting like a spoiled brat."

"No you aren't. I would be just as upset if I knew some hot women were about to watch me prance around and do yoga poses naked," Adam says trying to alleviate my stress.

I bust out laughing at him which was the reaction he was hoping for. "Plus, Carson and I have seen you in those tiny bikinis you wear at the beach. We pretty much know what you look like naked." I am back to blushing from the top of my head all the way to my toes.

We continue to watch the video and a few minutes later you see me come walking through the bedroom and I am taking off my shirt and going into my closet. Next time I am on the screen you see me walking towards the camera and I only have on my thong and I am standing there brushing my hair. I want to die at this point, I cannot believe I am sitting here in my living room watching a video of me half naked brushing my hair and Carson, Adam and Max are watching this.

I glance over to Carson to see his reaction and his expression almost takes my breath away. There is a look of desire burning brightly in his eyes, his jaw is clenched so tightly that I can see a little tick of the muscle on the side of his cheek. He can feel me looking at him and he glances my way. I feel like I am scorched by his eyes. I am so close to offering myself up to him before I remember there are other people in the room.

Mercifully, my hair brushing show comes to end and you see me turn and walk towards the bed. Now they are getting a full rear view and everyone knows for sure I wear thongs. "I did not take you for a girl who slept in her panties," Adam says mildly, he is really trying his hardest to make this seem like it is not big deal. I laugh, "Looks can be deceiving," and I watch all three of them just nod.

"I did not know you were having such bad nightmares, is that common?" Max asks me. This camera is motion-sensor activated and will continue to record for five minutes after it senses the last movement so it picked up on me thrashing about in bed during one of my nightmares.

"No. It just started after Peter and I broke up and I heard about Allison."

After seeing me get dressed and come in and out of the room for various reasons we get to last night. "So you sleep in pajamas when you have company Alex. That's disappointing for me tonight," Adam says picking at me.

"I try to be a good hostess," I remark back. I can feel Carson's eyes on me so I glance over at him and I try to suppress the shiver that runs over my body from the way his eyes are raking over me. I clear my throat, "I have another bad nightmare coming up soon. Carson actually tries to wake me up and you will get to see me give him a bloody nose."

This causes Adam to start laughing, "Oh man, I can't wait to see that."

It was truly funny to see that scene happen, I was trying hard not to laugh but I could not help myself. "I am so sorry again Carson," I should not be laughing but it is pretty funny.

"Laugh it up little one," Carson replies with a smile.

Adam and Max get quiet and I glance to see why they stopped laughing and realize it was because they see Carson getting into bed with me. "I asked him to lay there with me after my nightmare," I stammer out. I can imagine Max going back and telling my dad what he saw.

The worst part is coming up. The video clicks on but it was not when I was trying to move off Carson. It shows him lifting his head and looking down at me. Then he smiles when he sees that I am draped across him. The look on Carson's face is utter contentment at that moment. I realize my mouth has dropped open upon watching this.

I glance over at him but he is looking at the TV. Carson continues to look at the TV and is making it clear he has no intention of looking my way. I am getting giddy and butterflies in my stomach because this proves he is interested in me. I am blown away by the fact that Carson was awake before me and he seemed to be enjoying me laying all over him.

A few minutes later you see me trying to move off of him and then everyone gets an eyeful of Carson's blatant, magnificent arousal when he gets out of the bed. The room is filled with an extremely high amount of tension after this part of the video. Luckily my phone starts ringing so I use that as my excuse to get up and leave.

Chapter 15

I glance at my phone and sigh in disgust as I see it was Peter who is calling. There is no way I can go back into the living room right now after watching that. I get Carson was uncomfortable and given his outlook on relationships, I am aware enough to not push him or he will leave and never give us a chance.

I pick up the phone and call Catherine. Maybe she will want to come over and have dinner with Adam and I. She answers on the first ring, "Hey Alex, what are you up to?"

"Nothing much really. I am almost done with my regular secret service sweep and Max is talking with Adam and Carson. I think Adam pulled babysitting duty tonight. Do you want to come over here and eat dinner with us?"

I decide to start cooking since that will keep me busy and away from the living room. "Sure, what are you cooking?"

"Adam wants lasagna so I was going to make that with salad and garlic bread."

"Sounds good. I will come over shortly," she says as we hang up.

I begin getting all of the ingredients together to make the sauce for the lasagna. This is one of the few dishes I am happy to cook since I know it always tastes good. I can hear someone walk over to where I am at and I glance over my shoulder to see Carson is standing by the kitchen island.

"Alex, can we talk?" Carson says quietly. I smile at him and continue putting everything on the counter.

"Sure, what did you want to talk about?" I ask trying to keep my voice light.

"About this morning on the video- ", he begins, but I know where he is headed and I do not want to hear him finish his sentence so I stop him. "There is nothing to talk about then. It's fine. We are fine."

Carson stares at me for a minute. I am assuming he is trying to read my body language and determine if we are really fine. "Ok. Well Max and I are going to remove those cameras from those rooms and then you should be all set."

"Thank you for doing that. I will feel slightly better knowing I can have some privacy until this is over."

Carson and Max walk into my bedroom and begin doing their work while Adam walks over to where I am cooking. "You ok?" he asks me quietly.

I glance over at him and smile, "I'm fine. That was a little intense but cooking will help along with a glass of wine."

Adam clears his throat and I glance up at him. "Don't give up on him Alex. He does care for you, but I think he is scared to admit it. Now he is going to have work through that especially after what we all saw."

"I know. Which is why I did not want to talk about it with him just now." I take a deep breath; I figure I can be honest with Adam. "I like him. I can tell he has feelings for me but I know Carson has issues with our age gap. And then there is the mystery woman who he called off his engagement over, and probably a thousand other reasons he has come up with to make me untouchable."

Adam smiles, "He told you about the engagement? He never talks about that. As far as I know, I was the only person who he ever told that to."

"We had a pretty intense dinner conversation last night and he told me. I am crazy to think I can compete against some woman he has such intense feelings for. I think he's crazy for never telling her or trying to at least see what could happen between them." I glance over at him to see he is looking at me with a peculiar look.

"You are too wise for your own good, kitten. I think you will be surprised by the feelings that Carson has for you." That gets a laugh out of me because I am an idiot for even wanting to be with someone so soon after Peter.

"Can I ask you one more question?', Adam says lightly. I nod my head as I am beginning to cook on the stove. "If you have feelings for Carson then why are you going to meet that guy we saw at the store?"

I stop what I am doing and think about how I am going to answer that. "Truthfully, I do not know why. Maybe because I am realistic to know Carson may never come around to seeing what is in front of his face and I have to live my life."

"Ok, I will leave you alone. Thanks for being honest with me," Adam replies as he walks over to see how Carson and Max are coming along.

*****

I need to get out of here so I can think straight. The way Alex hightailed it out of the living room after seeing how I had been fake sleeping this morning, I am sure she is thinking I am a horny, old, pervert and that is how I feel.

"What the fuck was that on the video?', Max spits out at me when we get into Alex's bedroom. I look over at him and see the steel in his eyes. I know he has been on the team that has been watching over Alex for years and he is taking this personally.

"Nothing happened. She asked me to lay there with her and I feel asleep," I tell him even though we both know what he is really talking about. "Adam is going to take over watching her because I'm not able to stay objective around her," I add to put him at ease.

"You promised to keep her safe. Lusting after her is not part of the deal. I respect you Carson, and have always enjoyed having beers with you and consider you a close friend. Alex is not going to become another one of your flavor of the month or night," Max states bluntly. I nod my head in agreement. "If you break her heart, I will break your legs."

I hold my hand up to stop his threats. "Look Max, I care about her but I know I am too old for her and not good enough. So I am not even going there, back off me." Max stares at me for a few minutes then nods in head.

"Jesus, what the hell am I going to tell the Vice-President? He will be here tomorrow and I can't allow him to come over here with cameras everywhere." I think about this for a few minutes and realize we need to keep Alex out of here as much as possible.

"Can she go over to their hotel or can he come to her office?"

"I will get his updated schedule and make those changes and let you guys know." We continue to 'find' these three cameras and take them down.

When Max and I walk about of her room, I glance over to the kitchen and see Alex busy cooking. She glances over at me and gives me a little smile. After seeing her naked on that video and knowing she sleeps naked, all I want to do is take her in my arms and bury myself inside of her.

"We are almost done Alex. You should be able to take your shower in a few minutes," I tell her as I walk by.

A moment later Max verifies that the cameras are gone out of her bedroom. "Alex, you are good to go in those 3 rooms," Max tells her. "

Thanks Max and please do not tell my dad. This is going to worry him."

Max walks over and gives her a quick hug. "You know I have to report this Alex. It's protocol, but I will make sure he knows that Adam and Carson are here so they can answer to his yells."

I walk over to where they are standing and I know I need to leave. I lean over and rub her shoulder. "I have to go, little one. Adam will stay here with you and I will talk to you later," I tell her as I turn to leave. "Bye Carson," is all I hear from her. As I walk past Adam, he grabs my arm and pulls me back into Alex's bedroom.

"Dude, you are being a dick right now. You should be here with her," he whispers to me.

"Back off Adam. I am leaving and will text you later," I tell him as I start to push past him.

"You have it so bad for her you can't even think straight. The sooner you admit that to yourself the sooner you will have your real brain back," Adam states as I am walking out the door.

"Later", I tell him as I am out the front door. As I am walking down the hallway, Catherine steps out of the elevator.

"Hey big brother, you look like shit."

I give her a quick hug, "Thanks for the compliment," I tell her sarcastically.

"Where are you headed? Aren't you going to eat with us? Alex is making her world famous lasagna?"

"Sorry little sis, I have to go and finish working on this case. Adam will eat with you guys," I tell her as I am getting onto the elevator. Catherine stops the door from closing and eyes me.

"Carson, it is ok to like Alex. Maybe you should spend some time with her. You are what she needs."

"Catherine, stay out of it. This does not concern you. Alex and I are just friends and that is the way it is staying," I tell her firmly as she lets the door close.

Finally, some peace and quiet. I need to get home so I can think about the case and figure out how to catch this guy. Deep down I know Alex is going to be the key since he seems so fixated on her.

I need to see if the coroner found any useable DNA on this latest victim.

I should have known the Secret Service would conduct a check of her condo. At least it was not a thorough check with the other detective distracting the agent doing the search. Leave it to Detective Knight to have the agent go back through her bedroom again, I will miss seeing her getting ready. Alex has a delightful body to look at. At least my equipment is state-of-the-art and whatever sweeping devices the agent used did not pick up the tracker or other cameras.

*****

"Bye Max. Thanks for doing this and I will see you later this week," I tell him as I give him a quick kiss on the cheek.

"Are you bringing a date to the gala on Wednesday?" he asks me before he leaves.

"Well, I am not sure if it is really a date but Carson agreed to come with me," I tell him.

Max gives me a scowl, "You need to watch out for him," he says sharply.

Adam opens the door, "Time to leave, Max," he says as he frowns at Max's statement about Carson.

"Well, I love the service at your home Alex," Catherine says laughing as she walks in. She was about to ring the doorbell but Adam opened the door at the same time. "Hi Max. Nice to see you and stop bad mouthing my brother," she tells him as she sticks her tongue out at him playfully.

"Hey Catherine. See you on Wednesday as well," Max tells her as he leaves.

"How long before dinner is ready?" Catherine asks while she begins opening the bottle of wine she brought.

"The lasagna is in the oven and should be ready shortly."

"Anything fun and exciting happening over here that I missed?" Catherine asks us. I glance over at Adam because I am not sure how much, if anything I should tell her.

"Nope, pretty boring day. Alex did some yoga and your brother stopped by long enough to get himself worked up and leave," Adam tells her. I roll my eyes at the both of them, Carson is not a subject I want to discuss at this moment.

"I saw him as I was getting here and he looked frazzled to say the least," Catherine replies sending a smirk my way.

I decide it is time for a subject change. "By the way, everything is ready for the gala on Wednesday so we should have a pretty easy next two days at work," I tell her.

"That's good to hear. Also are you going out on your coffee date with that guy?" she asks.

"I told her not to go," Adam jumps in the conversation. "

I am probably going… that is if he calls. We ran into him at the grocery store and I thought Adam was going to eat him alive," I tell her laughing at Adam's face.

"That's weird," Catherine retorts.

"What's weird?" I ask her.

"Well, he ran into you at the coffee shop, then he runs into you and I and Eric while dress shopping and now he runs into you and Adam grocery shopping. I mean does the guy have a tracker on you?"

Whoa, when you put it that way, it does seem a little weird. I glance over at Adam because Catherine has no idea what occurred here earlier and the fact I do have a tracker sitting inside of my coat. "What do you know about this guy?" Adam asks me.

"Nothing really. I just met him. Besides the conversation at the coffee shop, I have always been around other people so we have not had a chance to talk."

Adam is picking up his phone and texting someone. I assume it is Carson. I hear the timer go off for the lasagna and I have never been so happy to eat.

Chapter 16

I am amazed that I was able to fall asleep last night. After I shower and get dressed for work I go into the kitchen to grab a cup of coffee and wake up Adam. I guess he is an early riser since he is sitting on one of my bar stools drinking coffee and reading something on his IPad.

"Good morning kitten. You make great coffee," he says with a smile and lifts his coffee cup up at me.

"Good morning. Did you sleep ok on the couch?" I ask him while I pour my coffee.

"I sure did. I'm a little disappointed that I didn't get to run into your bedroom and share your bed. Then again Carson would kill me if that had happened," he replies with a chuckle.

I shake my head at him, I guess this is what I can expect going forward. "Don't start with me so early. I haven't even had my coffee."

"I was going to take you to work and then Eric is going to swap with me," Adam tells me as I am putting my laptop and iPad into my purse for work.

"Sounds like a plan."

"Aren't your gorgeous legs going to be cold today?" Adam asks me while he is looking me up and down. I just shake my head at him, I am wearing a black pencil skirt with bright pink button down shirt. I love how I can dress conservatively, but he makes it sound like I am half naked.

I am a little disappointed because I hoped Carson would have drawn the short stick to watch me. Maybe he will come over tonight or at least call me. I shake my head because I need to stop acting like a lovesick teenager waiting for a boy to call. I gather all of my things and we are ready to leave for the day. "I feel like I need to give you guys a key to my place with how everyone keeps coming and going," I say to him as we walk down the hallway.

"Nah…Carson and the team have been working on this all night. We both think we can have this solved in a few days and be out of your hair," Adam says thoughtfully. I wonder what Carson and their team have been working on. I am not going to focus on the fact that once they solve this case then I will go back to only seeing Carson a few times a year. The thought makes my stomach hurt.

I glance over at my car to see if another note has been placed and thankfully the windshield is clean. "You are quiet Alex. Is everything ok?" Adam asks me as he is pulling out of the garage.

"I'm good. I have a lot going through my head with work and doing my mental to-do list right now."

We are pulling up to my building and I see Eric standing outside of the door. "Thanks for keeping me safe," I tell Adam as I get out of the car.

"Anytime kitten. Dinner was awesome so I may come over for more," he yells back with a wink.

"Good morning Eric. How are you?" He is standing there holding the door open for me.

"Hi. I brought some reading material so I will stay out of your way," he tells me as we get onto the elevator.

"I have a comfy couch in my office and there is a TV in there so you can make yourself comfortable. The noise will not bother me."

Eric gets settled in and I begin responding to emails and answering incoming calls regarding the gala for Senator Gregg. Catherine walks in to review our schedule. We have a standard Monday morning meeting to make sure we each knew who was doing what for the gala on Wednesday. This is how our business runs so seamlessly; we constantly communicate with each other so every detail is covered. "Hi Alex. Eric, you are the bodyguard today? Good to see you again."

Eric waves from the couch and tunes back to the sports channel. We are finishing our meeting when Shannon buzzes my phone, "Alex, sorry for the interruption but there is a David on the phone. He said you were expecting his call, but I don't have anything down so I was not sure if he should go into your voicemail or if you want to speak with him."

Catherine wiggles her eyebrows, "Well, well, looks like your coffee date is calling. I will leave you so you can make plans." I wave Catherine away. As she is about to leave my office she turns around and says, "Even though I think you should blow this David guy off and pursue Carson." Catherine is out the door with a laugh before I can even say anything back to her.

I turn back around and walk over to my desk and sit down. "Shannon, you can put the call through. Thank you." I glance over at Eric and I am pretty sure that while he looks enthralled watching sports, he is listening to everything Catherine and I just said. He will also hear my side of this call.

"This is Alexandria", I answer once my phone starts ringing. "Good Morning Alexandria. It's David from this weekend," David says in a deep voice. "Hi, how are you?"

"Good. Are you free to meet me this morning for coffee?"

I glance at my calendar and I see I am booked with meetings and phone calls all day but tomorrow I have some time at 10:30am that I could meet him for a quick cup.

"Today is an awful day for me. What about tomorrow at 10:30am for coffee? How does that sound?"

"That works for me. Is there a coffee shop near your office?" Catherine and I love this office building since there is a coffee shop downstairs in the building so we can always run down for a good caffeine fix. "There's one in my office building."

"Sure. What's the address?" I give him the address and we hang up and I throw the appointment into my calendar. I realize I just thought of this coffee date as an appointment. That should tell me I am not really interested in this guy but I already made the plans.

I glance over to Eric and can tell he just heard everything. "I kind of agree with Catherine. You should go after Carson. You would make him relax more," Eric states while still staring at the TV. That gets a laugh out of me.

After a long morning of reviewing menus, picking out wine and specialty drinks for the gala, Catherine stops in to see if we want to order lunch in for the office. "That sounds great. I know everyone is working hard getting everything ready for Wednesday," I tell her. We are trying to decide what to order when both Catherine and my phones go off from a text message. We glance down and it is from Darcy. She just got promoted at work and is expecting us all to be at the bar down from our office for a celebratory happy hour.

"That is great for her and it should be fun. I love the tavern she picked, they have great drinks and food," Catherine says excitedly.

"Eric, do you know who is watching me tonight?" I figure I need to give whoever will be with me the heads up so they know what they are in for.

"I think it may be Adam again but let me send a text and see. Why, what's up?"

"We got invited to a happy hour and I want to make sure that whoever will be with me is ok with it."

"Sure thing Alex, let me send the text now. Trust me, no matter who it is, they will not have a problem going with you," he tells me with a smile as he types out the text message. A few minutes later Eric glances up, "It looks like Adam and Carson both will be here."

Catherine starts laughing, "Man, my brother wants to stay away from you so bad but then he can't bring himself to actually do it. My mom told me to keep her posted on this thing between you two. It's like a soap opera." Ah hell, Catherine has told her mom which means her entire family probably knows I have a major crush on Carson and Catherine is trying to play match maker. All I can do is groan.

My phone beeps again with a text message and this one is from Carson, 'I will pick you up at your office at 4pm and we can walk over to the tavern'. I smile because even though I should not get my hopes up on a man who has serious relationship issues, I still love to see him. I type back a simple, 'see you then' and get back to work on the introduction speech I have to give for my father.

The rest of the day flies by and next thing I know Carson and Adam are standing in my doorway. "Thanks Eric, we will take her from here," Carson says has he pats Eric shoulder.

"Looks like a hard job the boy has, watching TV all day," Adam says jokily.

"Later guys, Alex have a good evening and I will see you tomorrow morning," Eric replies to them.

I smile over to Eric, "Thank you so much Eric. I know today was boring and you had to listen to me drone on all day."

Catherine walks in with her purse, "Are we ready to go?" I shut down my computer and grab my coat and purse and follow her out the door with Adam and Carson trailing behind us. We leave the building when I realize that I left my phone on my desk. "Shoot, I left my phone on my desk. I need to go back and get it. I will just meet you guys across the street."

"I'll go with you," Carson says while Catherine and Adam continue to walk down the block. As we are taking the elevator up to my office, I glance over at Carson and can see that he is clenching his jaw. "Is something the matter?"

"No, why?" he responds as he glances over at me. I watch him clench his fist right after he does that.

"Well, you seem a little tense or pissed off. Did I do something or is it because you have to keep changing your plans so you stay with me?" I ask him nervously.

"No, there is nothing wrong; I am just working through some things in my head," Carson replies as he reaches over to brush some of my hair back from my face. "If I did not want to be here with you right now, I would not be here."

I open my mouth to say something, anything but nothing comes to my mind. I just close my mouth and thankfully the elevator doors open and we walk down so I can grab my phone. As we leave the building for the second time I feel like something has changed between us. While I have always dreamed about what it would be like to kiss Carson, I am beginning to realize he may be out of my league. I do not have enough experience to probably even begin to know how to satisfy a man like him.

"Now you seem a little a tense, Alex," Carson says back to me with a smile on his face.

"I'm fine," I say softly as we walk over to meet our friends.

Just as we are walking up to the tavern I slip on some ice, and Carson is right there grabbing me by the waist to make sure I do not fall on my face. He pulls me up fast and close to him. I am pretty sure that I feel the very long, hard length of him against my back. I slowly turn around to face him and his eyes are dark and stormy looking and I can feel the tension vibrate between us. I can feel his erection pressing against my stomach, and I wish I was taller so it could press him against the ache between my thighs. I slowly drag my hands up his arms. I feel his strong biceps and finally I am at his shoulders and I start to pull him down towards me.

He does not fight me on this like I thought he would. We are frozen in time, just Carson and I standing there slowly inching towards each other. Right as we are about an inch away from our lips making contact, Carson slowly breathes out, "Alexandria. I have been dreaming about this for years."

I cannot even breathe. I just want him to close that inch and kiss me. I have never heard him call me Alexandria before. I hate people using my full name but when he says it, it sounds like a caress.

Just then the door to the tavern swings open and Adam is there, "Hey guys we saw you cross the street, what is taking so lo-oops. Sorry," when he realizes what he just interrupted.

Carson jumps so quickly that I am back to slipping on the ice and he is back to trying grab me before I go down. I cannot believe

Adam just interrupted our almost kiss! Thankfully I get my balance back and we finish walking up the steps while Adam is standing there laughing.

"Hey dude, I'm really sorry, but glad to see you are coming to your senses," Adam says still laughing.

"Shut up Adam and don't say another word about this. It's nothing", Carson barks out to him as he holds the door open for me to walk inside.

I guess maybe he wasn't as into our almost kiss as I was. Maybe I misunderstood what he said. 'It's nothing', well maybe I was the silly one who felt that chemistry. I need a drink and fast after that statement.

I walk quickly over to Darcy to give her a hug. "I am so happy for you."

"Thanks. This is so exciting. I wish Harrison wasn't out on a case so he could be here to celebrate." Her boyfriend is an undercover cop who works on drug cases and he just got knee deep into a case. I glance over to see Adam and Carson are headed our way so I turn towards the bar to order a drink while they talk to her.

As I am waiting for my drink I feel someone put their hand on my shoulder and I glance to see Carson is standing beside me. "Will you order me a beer if the bartender comes over to you before me?" he asks me. I nod my head. "You seem a little stressed Alex.

Why don't you let loose and enjoy yourself tonight? I will make sure you get home safely and tucked into bed."

I would love it if he would tuck me in my bed. I can visualize what it would be like to tug him down on top of me by his tie and slowly unbutton his dress shirt to reveal those rock hard abs. The tension between us begins to sizzle again and it is too easy to forget we are surrounded by all of our friends.

All of sudden I hear a squeal from Chelsi, "OMG. You guys totally look like a couple standing there together just staring at each. I swear that you guys are eye fucking each other!"

I jerk back from Carson and try to laugh off the situation while I am blushing from my head to toes. "Whatever Chelsi. We are talking and we are just friends," I tell her. I glance over at Carson to see how he is reacting and notice that Adam is by his side. They are talking to each other and it seems like I have been forgotten again.

The bartender hands me my drink and I see Carson is ordering his so I walk over to the table that Catherine is at. "Chelsi, I could kill you for saying that!", I hiss at her.

"What? We all know you have had a crush on him. Now you are single, enjoy it," Chelsi replies back with a huge smile.

Catherine leans over to me and says, "Carson really can't take his eyes off you. He is watching you from over there. In fact, there are quite a few boys in here that can't keep their eyes off you."

"Stop, he is just watching all of us. I am sure that Adam is doing the same thing." Just then someone bumps into me from behind and I fall into Catherine. "Hey, are you ok Catherine? Someone just bumped into me," I say to her making sure I did not spill anything on her.

"Sorry about that. This place is crowded. Are you ok?" a guy is saying to me and I as turn around to see who it is I recognize that is David.

"David! What are you doing here?" I exclaim when I realize who just almost made me spill my drink.

"Hi Alexandria. I'm here with some guys from work and it was my turn to get the next round. Sorry for bumping into you. I seem to do that a lot," David replies with a big smile. I glance at Catherine and can see she is eyeing him with a certain look I know too well. She thinks he is hot and she is about to start flirting.

"You remember my friend Catherine and this is Chelsi," I say as I introduce him to our friends.

"Hi David. We are here celebrating our friend's promotion. Are your friends single, if so then you guys should join us?" Catherine boldly states and I am pretty sure she just batted her eyelashes at this him. David is attractive but there is something about him that just seems off to me.

"Yeah, are they rocking the sexy, nerd thing like you are?" Chelsi adds. I am mortified by her lack of a filter when she speaks.

"Sorry David, Chelsi here just says anything," I tell him.

"It's not a problem Alexandria. You look great by the way," he says to me, looking me up and down. I do not even know what to say. I am not interested especially given everything that has been simmering between Carson and I tonight. Catherine nudges my side and just grins.

"I look forward to our coffee tomorrow and getting to know you better," he continues to say as he picks up his drinks. "Maybe me and my friends will come over here and join you guys and you can determine if they are sexy nerds," he adds to Chelsi.

I have no interest in David and I cannot think of a way to let him know he and his friends should stay at their table. Thankfully, I am saved from that because at that moment I see Carson and Adam walking over to where we are. Carson drapes his arm across my shoulder, eyeing David and asks, "Everything ok, Alex?".

"Yes, we are fine. This is David. He accidentally bumped into us and was just apologizing," I say hoping that David can pick up on the hint to leave.

"You seem to run into Alex a lot, David," Adam says with a sneer on his face.

"It's a small neighborhood. The last time I checked I was not speaking to you," David replies.

I glance over and see the pissed off looks on Carson and Adam's faces. This is reminding me of what happened at Catherine's the other night. "It was nice to see you again, David. Go enjoy your drinks with your co-workers," I tell him trying to diffuse the situation.

"Sorry again Alexandria and I will see you tomorrow. Catherine good to see you again, Chelsi nice to meet you. Have fun tonight," he says as he walks away. I am happy that David is smart enough to realize he would not be the winner in this situation.

"Well, he seemed a little pissed to get cock-blocked by us," Adam says laughing.

"You also cock-blocked Alex, you jerks," declares Catherine. Carson had just taken a sip of his beer and starts choking while Adam busted out laughing at the statement. "We are trying to get Alex laid. Unless you are going to take care of that, stop chasing boys from talking to her," Catherine says while Adam is doubled over from laughing so hard.

Carson is standing there looking dumbstruck by what she just said. I am turning a bright shade of red which I seem to be doing a lot of when he is around. I try to laugh off that statement and grab my drink and say, "I'm not trying to get laid. Catherine is trying to have me expand my experience. I am going to sit down and enjoy my drink."

As I am walking away I can hear Carson say to Adam, "Did I just hear that correctly? My little sister is trying to get Alex to have sex with someone tonight." I can only imagine what he thinks about that and of me.

I sit down and have to stop myself from finishing my drink in one big gulp. Catherine sits next to me and says, "Sorry, please don't me mad at me. I could not help myself. He is being so possessive of you and I want him to realize he is a moron if he does not ask you out." I can tell her heart is in the right place, but I can tell while Carson seems to be interested in me, there is no way I could satisfy someone like him.

"I'm not mad. I am embarrassed. Your brother is so hot and very much out of my league." I can tell Catherine is about to argue with me so I stop her before she can even begin. "Look, I don't have the same experience with guys like the rest of you do. I was so sheltered growing up. It took me close to a year before I would sleep with Peter and in all honestly we haven't had sex in close to eight months."

"Holy shit Alex!", Catherine exclaims. "What the hell have you guys been doing all these months?"

"We were only seeing each other on the weekends. We would go to some event and then he would drop me off at home and say he was tired. Plus, I was usually exhausted after spending an evening hearing Peter complain about everything and everybody. I should have realized that he had been cheating on me all this time but I guess I turned a blind eye to it."

"Well at least you have nothing holding you back now. Just have fun and do what you want."

"You girls look like you are in a serious discussion," states Adam as he sits down next to us, I glance up and see Carson in front of the table. "By the way it's getting late so this is the last drink so we can get you girls home and into bed."

"Adam and I have to work our case in the morning. We have some leads to review," Carson explains. Catherine and I both finish off our drinks and begin the long process of saying good night to our friends. As we are leaving, we are immediately blinded by flashes off of a ton of cameras. It looks like someone recognized me and called the press. Adam and Catherine are lucky because the press is not even bothering them so they are already walking down the block to cross the street back towards our office garage. Meanwhile,

Carson and I are being peppered with questions and pictures are being snapped repeatedly.

Carson grabs my hand and smiles at me, "Think you can run in those heels or should I make this front page material and carry you?"

I burst out laughing and shake my head. "I can run in these heels. Don't you dare pick me up."

We begin running to my office building as the photographers are behind us yelling out their questions, "What is your name, how long have you been seeing Alexandria, what do you do, are you guys getting married, are you guys sleeping together, are you the reason that she broke up with Peter King?" the questions are never ending. Luckily, Adam is holding open the lobby door for us and the security guard is there to stop the press from following us inside.

I am laughing so hard that I have tears in my eyes. "What's so funny?" Carson asks me.

"Nothing. Everything. Tonight was fun. All I could think about was what would it have looked like with you running down the sidewalk with me in your arms," I dissolve in another fit of giggles. "I am sorry guys. This does not happen often but every so often the press will show up and take pictures," I tell them.

"Don't worry about it. Catherine has mentioned it a few times. Our mom always gets a kick out if seeing her in the gossip section with you. Let's go Adam, before anyone has any time to figure out how to sneak in here. I will drive Alex home and you can meet us there," Carson says.

Once we are in his car, Carson is back to being quiet and serious again, I wonder what is going on in that brain of his. "Thank you for tonight," I tell him. He glances over at me and smiles. "I had fun. I also have had way too much to drink and I'm not sure I can walk straight when I get out of your car," I add.

"That's great you had had fun, and you can't walk straight when you are sober so nothing new there," he says laughing. He puts his hand on top of mine and gives it a quick squeeze. I am amazed at the elation I feel when he does these little gestures. I should really have my head examined and I need to be smart and back away from him. I can begin to feel the sizzle of our attraction in this small space and wonder if he can feel it too.

"You seem to be thinking pretty hard over there," Carson says interrupting me from my thoughts. I glance at him quickly. I wonder if he can tell that I am having an internal debate about how to end this night. I want to give in and see if his kisses and caresses are like what I have imagined. Then again, I am too frightened to go down that path. I realize I still have not answered him.

"Just thinking about everything I need to do for Wednesday." I hope he can't tell that I am lying.

We pull into my garage and I can see that Adam has already parked in the visitor space. Carson helps me get out of his car, he is still standing so close I am wedged between him and the car. "You know Alex, I really did have a good time tonight," he tells me as he brushes my hair off my face. I just stare at him.

He finally steps back so we can walk into my building. "Alex, I want to do a quick check to make sure everything is ok before I leave you with Adam," Carson says quietly as we are riding up the elevator.

Carson is back to clenching his jaw again. I know I have had too much to drink because before I can stop myself I am touching his jawline. "I am surprised you have not broken any of your teeth from how hard you clench them," I tell him as I softly stroke his jawline. I can tell that I have crossed a line with him because he has gone extremely still and barely looks like he is breathing.

Carson takes my hand in his and looks at me with his eyes burning like coals. "Careful little one. You are playing with fire," he tells me, his voice husky, filled with what I think is desire. Just when I think this may finally be the time I get to feel what it is like to kiss him. The elevator doors open and like Cinderella, the clock striking midnight, everything stops and he drops my hand and walks off.

We are walking down the hallway and I can see Adam is lounging against the wall next my door. "About time you guys got here," he says with a smile. I laugh and unlock the door and it is silent.

There is not the usual beep of my alarm. I walk past Carson and look at the alarm panel. "That's weird. I turned my alarm on. Why is it disarmed?" I ask him. Carson has gone deadly still. "Alex, I want you stand right here and don't move from this spot while Adam and I search your place."

I watch as Carson pulls out his gun from underneath his jacket. My eyes go wide. This is becoming a regular occurrence. I am starting to shake. WTF is happening? There is only one light on by the door so I cannot really make out what or where Carson is. A few minutes go by then Carson comes out of my room, "Alex, I think we are good. Why don't you take a look around and see if anything is missing or out of place?"

I am in disbelief. My home has always been sanctuary and I can feel that someone has been in here. "You ok?" Carson asks me as he walks back over to help me take off my coat.

"Do you think it was the guy who placed the cameras was in here again?" I am shaking and can't seem to stop. This week has been awful and I can tell that I am about breakdown.

"I'm not sure, but I know that you are diligent with your alarm so someone was in here."

"I'm fine," I say as my voice cracks and tears start spilling down my cheeks. Carson wraps his arms around me and begins stroking my hair. He places a kiss on the top of my head. I take a deep breath and step out of his arms while I try to wipe my eyes and make sure that I don't look horrible. "Thank you," I tell him as I turn away. Adam is standing by the kitchen silent and has a deadly look in his eye.

I begin looking around my living room and I don't really see anything out of place. We walk into my bedroom and I look around.

"Does Peter have a key and know your code?" Carson asks.

"Yes, he has a key. I have not gotten it back during this whole mess. I guess I should have the locks changed instead of trying to get my key back."

"I can help you with that tomorrow," Carson replies. They are both following me around as I walk to look in my bedroom.

"I am going to go get out of these heels," I tell them and walk into my closet. As I glance down to step out of them, I notice that all of my bras and lingerie are on the floor. I begin opening the drawers of my dresser looking to see if anything else has been moved and realize that someone has taken all of my panties. "Are you freaking kidding me!", I shout at the top of my voice.

"Alex, what is wrong!", Carson yells. Both him and Adam come running into my closet with their guns pulled. I turn around and look at them wide-eyed because I am not used to seeing armed men in my closet. I also realize I now have to explain what the problem is. I am mortified.

"I was stepping out of shoes and I noticed all of my bras are on the floor, and some of my lingerie. When I checked my drawers to see what else may have been moved, all of my panties are gone."

Carson and Adam both glance down to where my shoes are laying and see next to them are a bunch of my bras and lingerie. "Uh...how do you know what is missing? There are a ton of bras and other things on the floor," Adam asks trying to keep from smiling.

I groan and glance at Carson who is staring at me with the same passion that I have seen from him before. "This is so embarrassing!", I exclaim. I have a penchant for lingerie and I buy a ton of it. "I can't find one scrap of underwear in my closet except for what I am wearing right now. That is how I know what is missing. Plus, whoever the pervert that did this, they dumped everything on the floor and I also had this black lace teddy that I love and it's missing also."

"What the hell is a teddy and how can you be sure it's missing?" asks Carson. I open my mouth to begin explaining what it is and then I realize I can't describe it in the way that they would understand what it is.

I walk over to the pile of lingerie on the floor and pull out a red lace teddy that is similar to my black one and hold it up and state," It looks like this but in black. Can we please be done with looking at my lingerie?"

Adam slowly whistles and says, "Alex, I never knew you had it in you, you little sexy minx.". Carson is still just staring at me until he finally breaks eye contact and looks around the room. "Ok, so someone was in here and took your underwear and whatever that thing is in black. We can have some crime scene techs come over now to dust for fingerprints."

"Great, now everyone you work with gets to hear that someone did a panty raid on my place. It is probably Peter." I am standing there just shaking because I am so mad and upset.

Carson walks out of the room to call his crime scene techs to come over. Adam walks over to give me a quick hug. "Don't worry Alex. Everything will be alright. If we can't find your pretty black teddy thing, I will buy you a new one if Carson doesn't beat me to it," he says laughing as Carson walks back in the room.

"They will be over here shortly and work quickly so you can get to bed," Carson tells me as he is giving Adam a dirty look for his last comment.

"What the hell am I supposed to do tomorrow morning when I need to go to work?"

I can tell that my question has made Carson uncomfortable since he has an awkward look on his face and opens his mouth to answer my questions but shuts it quickly. Adam starts laughing and I glare at him. "Go commando until you can go buy more," Adam suggests. I huff off into the living room.

I know I am acting like a baby but who on earth steals someone's underwear? That is gross. I hear my doorbell ring and Adam answers it to let the crime scene tech into my condo and shows them the closet. About an hour later I hear them leave and Carson comes and sits next to me on the couch. "Are you going to be ok?" he asks me quietly.

"I will be fine. I'm just a little upset by this."

"Ok. I am going to leave, but Adam will stay with you. Call me if you need anything," he says as he gets up to leave.

"Carson, I know you do not want to be around me, but thank you for trying to keep me safe," I tell him gently.

He stops and looks at me, "Little one, it has nothing to do with me not wanting to be around you. I can't focus on the case when I am around you. I worry too much about you," he says softly and then leaves the room.

"Good night", I tell Adam as I head to my room to go to sleep, I am exhausted at this point and it looks like I will only get a few hours of sleep. I fall asleep into a dreamless slumber.

I am disappointed I cannot watch her reaction when she realizes her panties are gone but this is the fun part of the game. I wish I had time to replace those cameras. I need her to want to lean on a man for support. Too bad these detectives are constantly hovering but I will take them off her soon enough.

Chapter 17

I wake up and after spending too much time on what to do since I have no panties, I finally figure out commando is the best plan until I can run over to Victoria Secrets later this morning.

Adam and I have fallen into our morning routine of him drinking coffee and eating a bagel. As we are leaving my condo Adam looks me up and down, "I see you like those skirts and from the way it fits, you took my suggestion.". I roll my eyes but it lost its effect since I started laughing.

As we are driving to my office my phone starts ringing and I pull it out of my bag and glance at the number, Peter again. I decide to answer it and make it clear for him to stop calling me. "What do you want?" I glance over at Adam and see the surprised look on his face.

"Who is that?" Adam mouths to me. I put the call on speakerphone.

"Alex, why aren't you returning my calls?" Peter whines to me. I can already see where this call is headed and it has barely started.

"Peter, we broke up. In fact, you cheated on me with numerous women. Which is why I am not returning your calls," I tell him curtly.

"I have apologized for that and if you had been more responsive in bed and cared more about my needs, I would never have had to sleep with those other women."

I see red, literally red upon hearing him blame me for his cheating. "Peter, shut the fuck up and don't ever call me again, you ass! How dare you blame me for your cheating! And talk about caring about someone's needs, what about my needs? How about whenever we had sex, you could care less if I was enjoying it or if I even had an orgasm. In fact, I never had an orgasm with you. I would have to use my vibrator after the fact, and my vibrator was a much better bedmate than you ever were!"

"I will get you, you bitch. You think just because of who you are that you can jerk men around. I see the way you are prancing around town with Catherine's brother. Ever since we've been dating, I have known that you wanted him. Just wait until I get even," Peter yells back at me.

I have had enough of him. "Do not come near me or call me again," I tell him and then hang up on him.

"Wow, I have never seen you lose your temper before. It was kind of hot," Adam says and I bust out laughing.

"Oh my god. You just heard everything that I said. Please don't repeat any of it," I beg him. I am turning beet red because now

Adam knows that not only do I own a vibrator but I was using frequently since Peter never satisfied me.

"Do not worry about your hot, little secret. I will not blab it to the world," Adam tells me as he pats my hand.

Eric is out front of my office building again waiting for me to get out of Adam's car. "Thanks Adam, see you later," I tell him since I am assuming that he will stay with me again tonight. I wave to Eric as I approach.

"Good morning Alex."

"I hope you don't mind but I have a few errands to do today and one may be a little painful."

"Sure, what are they?"

I grimace, "I need to go to Victoria Secret when they open at 9am. Someone broke in my condo last night and stole all of my panties."

Eric face is priceless, his mouth drops in shock and I start laughing as we get on the elevator. I spend an hour responding to emails and finalizing the guest list for the gala tomorrow. Catherine is going to be in later which works out great since I need to run my errands and have coffee with David.

At 9am I interrupt Eric from watching whatever sports show he is into, "Do you mind walking around the corner with me to the store?" I ask him.

Eric blushes, "Sure."

At least I know I can be quick in there. When walk into the store, Eric stands off the side and looks at his phone. Guys are so funny when they get dragged into this store. "Eric, I will be very quick," I tell him as I walk over to the section with the panties that I love. After I pick out everything I want, I pay and we are back out the door.

"Let me drop this off in my office. If you don't mind waiting outside for a moment, I need to slip into one of these," I tell him as it is my turn to transform to a brilliant shade of red.

"Um...sure Alex, I will see how Catherine is," Eric stammers out.

After a quick change, I am ready to run back downstairs for my coffee with David. I stop by Catherine's office to say good morning and grab Eric. I have a little time to return some phone calls and make a few last minute changes to the gala for Senator Gregg. Before long my reminder goes off to meet David. I take a quick look at myself in the mirror to make sure I look ok and Eric and I head downstairs.

"Eric, do you think you can let me go in first by myself and then go in and sit down so you can see me?" I am nervous because I am unsure of how serious he has to take this or if this will work. "I just do not want to explain to someone who I do not know that well why I have you around."

"That's fine, but I have to be able to see you the entire time," he tells me seriously.

"Thank you," I tell him as I walk off the elevator first and head over to the coffee shop. As I get close to the entrance, I glance over my shoulder and sure enough Eric is a little way back but close enough if something happened he would be by my side in a matter of seconds. I walk into the coffee shop and David is standing right inside.

"Hi David. It's nice to see you again," I tell him with a smile.

"Alexandria, you look stunning."

I blush since I do not handle compliments well. "Thank you, but this is just a normal work day for me." We walk up to the counter to order, I get my usual and he orders a plain black coffee.

"The first time I saw you, you were in gym clothes and the other times it has been casual so you look different all dressed up for work. The color of your shirt really makes your eyes pop," David continues as we wait for our coffees.

We get our coffees and sit down in two chairs. I glance over and see Eric has gotten his coffee and has taken a seat near us pretending to read a newspaper. "Speaking of work, what do you do for a living?" I ask him.

"I am an IT security analyst."

"Ok, that is like someone who keeps people from hacking into things right?"

David smiles at me, "Something like that."

"Do you know for some reason I feel like I have seen you before but for the life of me I cannot figure out where."

David pauses for a moment before giving me a grin, it is a little crazy looking and gives me the creeps. "I would remember if we had met before Alexandria. You are unforgettable." He really does lay it on a little thick.

"I do not even know your last name, what is it?" I ask him trying to learn some information about him.

"My last name is Hall," he answers.

"My turn to ask questions. I heard on the news this morning that you are responsible for the big gala on Wednesday. Are you going to it with anyone?" David asks me.

The way he asks me raises the hair on the back of my neck because it is almost like he is trying to invite himself to go with me.

"Yes, I have plans to be there," I say hesitantly. I can already tell I do not have any chemistry with David. This will be the one and only time we have coffee. I think Carson may have ruined me for any other guy because the sexual tension between the two of us is out of this world.

"Are you dating anyone else that I have to compete with to see your beautiful eyes?" David asks me in a tone that is making me nervous. I glance down at my phone and decide it is time to end this.

"Thank you for the coffee David, but I need to get back to work. It is a busy week for me with the gala coming up," I tell him nicely and start to stand up.

David looks surprised I am about to leave. "Can we see each other again later this week when you are not so busy?" he asks me a little too eagerly.

"Probably not. Look David, you seem like you are really nice guy but I just got out of a three-year relationship last week. I am not looking to begin dating anyone so soon," I tell him trying to be nice.

He nods his head and smiles, "Sure Alexandria, I get it. Thanks for meeting me for coffee and maybe we will see each other around the neighborhood."

"Bye, David. Have a good rest of your day," I tell him as I walk out the door. I glance over my shoulder to make sure that Eric is following me and I look over at David. The look on his face causes me to stumble a little bit. He looks extremely angry and the hatred shining through his eyes seems to be zeroed in on me. I turn back around and walk quickly to the elevators.

When I get back into my office I walk over to my desk to sit down and try to calm myself down. Something about David really bothered me and for the life of me, I cannot figure out what it is. Eric comes running in and stops short when he sees me sitting there with my head in my hands.

"Alex, are you ok?" he asks urgently. "You took off out of the coffee shop so quickly. Then all but ran into the elevator. What happened? You are shaking really bad."

I look at my hands and they are shaking almost as bad as when I bumped into the guy in my building the same night Allison was murdered. And that is when everything clicks in my head. I start to have trouble breathing, "Eric, I think- ", that was all that I got out before I passed out and hit my head on the corner of my desk going down.

Chapter 18

That little bitch, who does she think she is blowing me off like that. I knew she was going to be a challenge. I was surprised when she said she thought we had met before. Alexandria is a lot smarter and more intuitive than the others. I have to get her eyes. They are a glorious shade of blue and apparently all knowing. I may not be able to wait until the next full moon; she may have figured out who I am before then.

*****

"Hey dude, how did you sleep?" Adam asks as he puts a cup of coffee by me and takes his seat.

"Fine, how is Alex?" Adam gets a funny look on his face and it takes a few minutes before he answers.

"She's good. She showed me a side of her I have never seen before until this morning. Our little kitten has some serious sharp claws that can come out when she pushed," he says with a laugh.

I am intrigued, I have never seen Alex get angry before. I have seen her frustrated and hurt but never actually angry. "What happened?" I ask wanting more details. Adam gives me his usual 'I am going to make your life hell' smile.

"Not sure I can tell you that. I did promise her not to repeat what was said." I roll my eyes at him. "Ok, for you, I will spill the beans and gossip," he says with a smirk and proceeds to tell me about Alex yelling at Peter and about how she never had an orgasm with him. "Dude, I told you she had a vibrator!", Adam says at the end of retelling me the story.

"You are such a pervert," I tell him. Meanwhile, the mental image I have of Alex using a vibrator on herself has me feeling like the pervert.

"I need to update you on the case. The medical examiner found some skin under the latest victim's fingernails. We are running that DNA through all the databases to see if we get a match. We also had the crime scene techs go back to all the past scenes to do a sweep for hidden cameras. We found them at all of them but the most recent murder that took place."

Adam lets out a whistle, "So he was spying on them. Learning their habits," he says. I nod my head in agreement.

"One thing has been bothering me. I think whoever placed the camera in Alex's bedroom was in her place the same time as the killer and had no clue. We need to figure out who the asshole is who placed the bedroom camera."

"My vote is for Peter. I am hoping we can pin this on him after we finish tracking down where the camera came from," Adam states.

"I have a few of the other guys working that angle. There is a serial number on it so we should have that information pretty soon."

Before we can continue to discuss the case my phone begins ringing, I glance down to see that it is Eric calling. I glance up at Adam, "Isn't Eric watching Alex?"

"He sure is," Adam replies while he is checking his emails.

"Knight," I answer.

"Carson, you need to get over here quickly. I have no idea what just happened to Alex, she passed out and hit her head on the table. I have called an ambulance and we are trying to get her to wake up," Eric stammers out.

"What the fuck happened? We will be right over. Call me the moment she wakes up," I yell in the phone at Eric. Adam, along with everyone, in the room is staring at me like a mad man.

"Dude, what's going on?"

"Grab your shit. We have to get to Alex's office. She passed out and hit her head on the corner of her desk and hasn't woken up yet. That's all Eric could tell me."

"I will drive," Adam states. I look over at him and see the concern in his eyes. I know I am coming undone at the thought of Alex being hurt.

This is the longest ten minutes of my life. Adam is driving as fast as he can and we finally get there. I see an ambulance is parked in front of the building so at least the EMTs have arrived. When we walk out onto the floor of her office the entire place looks like a madhouse. Adam and I push our way past the employees and stop when we get to the door of Alex's office.

I can see Alex is lying on the ground with a paramedic by her side examining her head while another one is checking her pulse. "How is she?" I ask the paramedic as I rush over to her side. Catherine is standing over her watching her with tears coming down her face. One of the paramedics glances up at me and smiles with recognition.

"Detective Knight, good to see you again. What are you doing here, it's not a crime scene?" she asks with confusion showing on her face. "Her pulse is strong and I think she is finally waking up."

"Alex, honey, can you hear me? Wake up, tell us what is wrong," I say to her gently.

I glance over to see Eric standing there looking pale. "Carson, I have no idea what happened. One minute she was shaking and pale and then she just fell over."

"Give her some space, she is waking up," the paramedic tells us all. I have never been so happy to see those blue eyes look up at me.

*****

"Carson, what happened? Why am I on the floor?" When I try to sit up my head feels like it is going to explode.

There is a paramedic next to me shining a light in my eyes. "I think she will be ok. You should probably come into the hospital to have some tests to determine why you fainted," she tells me.

Just then everything comes flooding back to me and I start shaking. "No, I am fine. I will come in later," I stammer out to the paramedic. I begin to have trouble breathing again because I am panicking.

"Ms. McNeil, you need to take some deep breaths and calm down. You are about to cause yourself to hyperventilate and maybe pass out again," the other paramedic says as he is trying to force me to lay back down on the carpet.

I shake my head no and try to shake the paramedic off me. I can feel myself getting more agitated and I look up at Carson hoping he can help me. "Samantha, can you guys leave her alone for a moment? Let me see if I can get her to calm down," Carson says to the paramedic. "Tell me what has you so upset sweetheart," Carson says to me gently.

"Ok, if she injures herself or has something else going on with her then it is on your head, not ours," Samantha replies back. Carson nods in acknowledgement. "She has a pretty nasty cut on her head but I think she will be fine. She probably will have a nasty bruise there tomorrow," Samantha continues as they are leaving the room.

Carson helps me up from the floor and it takes me a few moments since I am dizzy. Instead of giving me a minute to adjust to being vertical again, he bends over and scoops me up in his arms and carries me over to the couch and sets me down gently. I look up at him and smile, "I could have walked," I tell him.

"Little one, what happened?" Carson asks while he gently brushes my hair back so he can look at the cut on my head. I know I must have hit my head pretty hard because I am just staring at him and thinking about how much I love the pet name he has for me. "Alex, are you ok? What is going on?', Carson asks again since I never answered him.

I look at Carson and tell him, "I think I know who the killer is."

Everyone is silent for a few seconds before Carson says, "Why do you think you know who the killer is?" I know I sound crazy, but I know that it is David. "I'm pretty sure if you change the hair color on my sketch and add glasses. You would have the exact same guy I just had coffee with and who keeps running into me around my neighborhood."

"What are you talking about?" I can tell that Carson is having a hard time following me and then I realize that each time I have ran into David I have been with a different person. I begin telling Carson about how I met David and all the times he has just shown up and the comments he has made and finally what happened at the coffee shop.

"We were downstairs at the coffee shop just now. It was the guy from the bar last night, the one that you came up and ran off. I had made plans to meet him for a quick coffee and get to know him better. He was being a little too intense and it freaked me out. Which is why I got out of there fast," I explain to them.

"Eric, where the hell were you during this coffee date?" Carson growls out. I glance up and I can tell from Carson's face that is furious with me and Eric. "You were supposed to stay with Alex the entire time," he adds.

"Look, I asked Eric to hang back and not sit with us. I did not want David asking any questions about why I have someone guarding me," I continue hoping to calm Carson down. I look over at Eric and can see that he is nervous. "Eric, I am so sorry I didn't wait for you. It has been instilled in me that if I get a nervous or uncomfortable feeling around someone to get the heck away as fast as I can. Which is what I did."

"Alex, you did the right thing. I was about to come over there when I saw the guy was getting pissed off at you. Then you jumped up and left so quickly," Eric says gently to me. "Carson, man I am sorry. I know you told me to stick to her so if you want to kick off me the team, I get it."

"Eric, you aren't in trouble. Trust me I know Alex well enough if you did not hang back when she asked, she would have figured out a way to lose you just to protect her privacy," Carson says calmly. "Now Alex, what did this guy say to you that made you so nervous? Why did it make you think he was Allison's killer?"

"He made a comment about my eyes and he's made other comments about my eyes. I guess my intuition picked up on it and told me to get away from him fast." I feel silly because it does not even sound like they have any reason to believe me.

"You should always trust your gut Alex. It has saved Carson and I more times than you would believe," Adam says as he is pacing the room.

"Ok, let's get Kate over here and do a new sketch and compare the two," Carson states and I can tell he is reviewing this all in his head.

"What's the guy's last name?" Adam asks me.

"It is Hall or at least that is what he told me. He also said he was a computer security analyst, if that helps," I tell him.

Adam smiles at me, "That is perfect."

"Do you have his number so we can trace his phone?" Carson asks.

I frown, "No, I never got his number and I only gave him my office number so he called here yesterday morning."

Carson stands up and looks at Adam and I can tell that something passes between them without words. "We are leaving but Eric will be here to watch you. Either Adam or I will come pick you up," Carson says as they walk out the door. I wave to them both as they walk out the door.

Catherine walks over and sits down next to me, "Are you ok?" she asks with concern in her eyes.

"I'm fine. I am just trying to figure out how I ever got wrapped up into this mess and how much I miss my quiet life."

She brushes my hair back, "As long as you wear your hair down tomorrow, no one will know what happened," I smile back at her and start laughing because I do not have the energy to cry.

"Only you would think to say that to me," I tell her with tears of laughter going down my face. I dry my tears and look over at

Eric to see him staring at me with a worried look on his face. "I am so sorry, Eric. I promise I am fine. I'm going to get back to work and that will help me calm down," I tell him hoping to ease his worry.

Shannon buzzes on the speaker, "Alex, there are some flowers that just got delivered up here for you. Do you want me to bring them back?"

I look around my office and Catherine smiles and answers for me, "Shannon bring them back, we want to see who they are from." Catherine grabs the note off the flowers and frowns, 'Your eyes are mine and mine only, I will take them and stare at them for eternity. – P'. "What the hell kind of note is this?" Catherine demands. I shake my head and Eric is standing up and taking the note from Catherine with a tissue so he does not get his fingerprints on it. We watch as Eric picks up the phone to make a call, "Hey Kate, bring an evidence bag with you. We have another note," he tells her and then he is texting Carson.

The rest of the day goes by without any more incidences. Kate came by and did an updated sketch, and took the note back to the police station. When 4pm rolls around I hear a knock at the door and glance up to see Carson standing there. "I was not expecting you," I tell him with a smile.

"My evening was free. I figured Adam needed to spend some time with whichever lady friend he has his eye on for the week. Thanks for staying with her Eric. Enjoy your evening."

My phone begins ringing and I glance down to see it is my dad calling, I wave bye to Eric as I answer, "Hi daddy, how are you?".

"Good Alexandria, are you coming by for dinner tonight at the hotel?" he asks me. Shoot, I had forgotten he wanted to do dinner. I glance up at Carson and cover the phone, "Are you up for dinner with my dad? I forgot," I whisper to him. Carson nods his head in agreement.

"Sure daddy, I will leave the office in a few minutes. By the way, Carson will be with me since he has guard duty tonight."

"Good, I like him and would enjoy having dinner with him."

"See you shortly. Love you," I tell him as we hang up.

"Are you sure you don't mind?" I ask Carson. "Of course not, plus Max gave me the Vice-President's itinerary and I saw it and told Adam I would take you." I smile at him then finish up my last email and turn off my computer and gather my things.

As we are walking towards the front of the office, I hear a lady screaming at Shannon, "I know he is here and he is with that bitch!"

I glance at Carson, "I wonder what on earth is going on," I say to him not expecting a response.

We turn the corner and there is a women standing there and when she sees Carson and I, she storms over. "You bitch, you whore! How dare you think you can steal him away from me!", she screams in my face and throws a newspaper at me.

Carson puts himself between us and looks down at her. "Kristy, leave here now. Alexandria has nothing to do with my decision to not see you anymore. The way you act has everything to do with that," he says firmly.

My mouth drops open and I look around Carson, so this is Kristy. She could be pretty if her face was not so distorted with anger. I bend over to pick up the newspaper and see a picture of Carson and I smiling and laughing at each other. A photographer must have snapped that at the perfect moment; it is a great picture of the two of us.

"Carson, I am begging you. I know you love me. I love you. You can't leave me for her. Look at how young she is. There is no way you have anything in common like we do."

"You need to leave before Alexandria calls security and has you removed. We are done. Do not bother her again," Carson says coldly.

"You are such a jerk. How can you use me for sex and think you can throw me away!", she screams at him.

Carson looks at her with such a cold, hard look that I shiver. I hope I never see that side of him. "You made the decision to sleep with me. I was very clear that I was not interested in anything more than sex. Just because you deluded yourself into thinking the relationship was more, is your problem not mine," he states furiously.

Carson grabs my hand and we walk around her to the elevator, I glance at Shannon who looks stunned. "Call security if she does not leave," I tell her as we get on the elevator to go to Carson's car.

I can feel the anger vibrating off Carson. "Man, I hope I am never on your bad side," I tell him. He looks down at me quickly with a frown.

"I am sorry you had to see that Alex. She has been calling me nonstop since that photo was printed this morning. I had no clue she would show up here."

I smile up at him, "It was a great photo. If we were dating, I would call the photographer and buy the print from him." That gets the reaction I was hoping for, Carson begins laughing and as the elevator doors open we walk out and he puts his arm around my shoulders. I love the feel of him and I really wish we were dating.

We arrive at the hotel and after Carson has the valet take his car, we go inside to meet my dad and mom for dinner. When walk into the lobby of the hotel, I can see my father's secret service detail spaced out around the room. I nod my head to a few of them and when we get to my dad, he picks me up and gives me a huge hug. "Alexandria, princess, look at you. You are so tiny. Have you been eating?" he asks me as he sets me down.

"Hi daddy. Yes, I have been eating. I am still the same size I have always been." I look over and see my mom and give her a hug.

"Darling, you look wonderful and Carson is looking delightful as well," she whispers in my ear as she kisses my cheek. I look over and see my dad giving Carson a big hug and there is Max standing beside my father giving Carson the evil eye.

I give Max a look that says leave it alone and be nice. "Let's go eat dinner and talk about tomorrow," my dad says to us and we follow him into the restaurant. We are shown to their private dining room and after we place our order, my dad immediately begins grilling Carson on the case.

I am nervous since I do not want Carson sharing all the details with my parents. "Mr. Vice-President- ", Carson begins but my dad interrupts him, "Now son, I have told you to call me Ryan. We are all friends and I consider you part of the family."

"Ok, Ryan, we are getting close to solving the case. We have a potential name and another lead we have been working on today. Alex has not been in any immediate danger that we are aware of and we are keeping someone with her at all times."

My father is grinning at him, "Has she lost her bodyguard yet? There was a time in college when she and Catherine tricked them and went into a bar underage, remember that Max?" he begins telling Carson a really embarrassing story.

My mom pats my hand to get my attention. "Darling, what are you wearing tomorrow night and who is your date?" I clear my throat and describe my dress for her. "That sounds lovely even though the back may be a little risqué."

"Who is your date?" she inquires again.

"I am bringing Carson with me." My mom pauses and has a speculative gleam in her eye. "You seem to enjoy spending time with him. I saw the picture of the two of you in the paper today. I have not seen you that happy in, well forever," she states.

I glance over at Carson and realize that they have stopped speaking and were listening to what my mother was saying. "Yes, Alexandria, you do look extremely happy. How has everything been going at work?" my dad adds.

"Work has been good. We have been extremely busy with Senator Gregg's upcoming events and tomorrow will be exhausting.

I will be at the hotel all day making sure that everything is perfect for the evening."

My dad glances at Carson and smiles. "Carson, I'm glad to hear you will be accompanying Alexandria to the event tomorrow night. Did you know she's giving the speech to introduce me?" My dad loves to brag about me and I start turning red. "It is not really a speech but more of a very short introduction," I add.

Carson smiles at my dad, "Your daughter is very talented, sir. I have seen the way she interacts with her team and she is well respected."

My dad nods at Carson, "You make sure to keep her in line. She likes to push boundaries." I roll my eyes at them and thankfully our salads are placed in front of us so I am saved from any more embarrassing conversations.

"Max tells me you handled a security issue in Alexandria's condo. Is that resolved or do I need to have agents stay with her?" my dad asks Carson while I start choking on my water. "Dad, it is fine and I am not having agents stay with me!"

"Sir, we have handled the situation and someone from my team is with Alex at all times during the day and throughout the night," Carson adds.

I hear Max snicker and I give him a dirty look as my father glances over at him. Finally, our food arrives and we finish a great dinner without any more talk about me or my safety. Carson and my dad spent a ton of time talking about football. I am pretty sure my dad has a man crush on Carson.

We get up to leave and as we are walking out of the restaurant we can see the press standing outside trying to get pictures of all us. "That is the price that I pay. Let's walk you out and give them their photo opportunity and you kids can get on your way," my dad says as he steers us outside.

I glance over at Carson who has his hand on my back, "I am so sorry you are caught up in this," I tell him. He glances down and smiles, "Not a problem little one. Now smile for the all the cameras."

We give the press a few photos of the four of us while the valet is pulling up Carson's car. A photographer yells to my father, "Who is the guy with Alexandria, Mr. Vice-President?" my dad turns and grins at Carson and I. "A friend of my daughter's," he replies vaguely. "What's his name and are they dating?" another person yells out. "He is Detective Carson Knight and I don't know the answer to that," my mother replies which gets a laugh out of everyone.

We walk over to Carson's car to say good-bye while the cameras are keeping their distance out of respect for my father.

"Thanks for dinner daddy. I will see you both tomorrow night at the gala," I give them both hugs and kisses.

"Keep my baby safe Carson. We look forward to having dinner with you again tomorrow," my dad says as he is patting Carson on the back and my mom is giving him a hug.

"Sorry about that. I'm sure the last thing you need is Kristy flipping out again because there are more photos of us in the paper," I tell him as he is climbing into his car.

"It's no problem. Honestly Alex, if it bothered me, I would not have stood there," he replies with a smile as we drive towards my condo.

"Thank you for not mentioning everything that has happened the past few days to my dad."

"I know Max updated him on the camera situation. There is no reason to worry him about how you apparently went on a date with a suspected serial killer," he says sarcastically. I am pretty sure there is a hint of jealously in his tone but I am not sure.

"Please, like you haven't made your fare of dating mistakes. What about Kristy showing up screaming in my office about how you have taken advantage of her by sleeping with her?" I retort.

"Sheath your claws little one, I was only joking," Carson says lightly. Carson pulls his car into my visitor spot and walks around to open my door.

"Are you staying with me tonight or someone else coming to relieve you?" I ask him as we walk onto the elevator.

"You are stuck with me, Adam has his date and no one else was available. I need to finish working on some things for the case, can I use your office?" he asks as we are entering my place.

"Sure, make yourself at home."

"Sleep well Alex. I will see you in the morning," he says as he walks into my office and shuts the door.

Well, hell, I was hoping since he was here and we had a nice dinner that we could continue to flirt and banter with each other. It looks like Carson has gone back to the way things used to be with us. Me in one room, him in another. I get ready for bed and I am pretty sure there is no way that I will sleep. I am wrong and I have another great night of sleep.

Chapter 19

I wake up and get dressed. Since it is the day of the gala, I am in jeans and t-shirt and flats due to all the running around that will take place. Today is about making sure everything is perfect for tonight. I walk out of my room and see Carson making a cup of coffee. He looks fabulous in his suit and with his scruffy facial hair.

"Good morning. How did you sleep?" he asks me as he is pouring me a cup of coffee.

"Fine, and you?" I reply as I take a sip. I am amazed he can make the perfect cup of coffee.

"I was up late tracking down some things but I slept fine," he answers.

"Oh, today is different. I have to go to the hotel to make sure everything is set up for the gala. Is Eric going to meet me over there?" I ask as I begin gathering my things.

"Yes, Catherine mentioned that last night when I spoke with her so I sent him a quick text."

After Carson helps me with my coat, I am trying to juggle my coffee, purse, keys and set the alarm. "Give me something before you drop everything," he says exasperated after watching me. I hand him my purse and coffee. "What the hell do you have in your purse? It weighs fifty pounds," he states while looking at my bag.

"Stop over exaggerating. It has my lap top, iPad, phone and a pair of shoes in it," I tell him while I roll my eyes and we head towards his car. Carson holds the door open for me and as I am getting in I notice that our fingers brush against each other and linger for a moment. I look over at him to see if he noticed or felt the sizzle that rushed up my arm but he looks unfazed by the contact.

As we pull up to the hotel, I see Eric standing there waiting just as he does at my office. "Have a good day, Carson," I tell him as I get out.

"Hey Alex, what time do you want me to pick you up tonight?" Carson asks before I close the door.

"5pm should work. I plan on being done here by 3pm so I can be ready in time."

The day is frantic. We spend it running around making sure all of the details are covered. Everything from the types of chairs people will be sitting in, making sure we have enough bars evenly spaced throughout the room, flowers arranged perfectly and so on.

"I think we did it!", Catherine exclaims as we stand on the stage looking out at the ballroom.

"Yeah, this looks amazing. I think this may be one of the best designs we have done."

"So are you ready for your date this evening with my brother?" she asks with a laugh.

I roll my eyes at her. "Yes, I should be ready but it is not a date."

"I saw the pictures in the paper. You guys look like you are dating, and that is what the gossip columnists are all speculating. You could at least try to have sex with him."

"Catherine! This is your brother we are talking about. He is not interested in anything other than a casual relationship and I am not sure that is not my cup of tea," I tell her.

"Alex, are you ready to go?" Eric asks as he walks over.

"Sure, let me grab my things. Catherine see you later tonight," I tell her as I walk over to Eric. "Man this room looks great," he states as we walk out.

Once Eric and I are back at my condo, Eric settles in the living room while I begin getting dressed. I glance at the clock and see that Carson will be here in thirty minutes. My make up is minimal and I begin to curl my hair since I am going to wear it down to cover the cut from yesterday. The next thing I know I hear the doorbell. Well crap… he is early. I throw on my robe and run to the door.

"Eric, I will grab the door. It's Carson," I yell to Eric as I look out the peephole.

When I open the door I am stunned. I thought Carson looked hot in a suit and in a t-shirt and jeans but nothing compares to seeing him in a tuxedo. He is mouthwatering and I could eat him up. "You look amazing," I tell him as I blatantly look him up and down.

I glance back up at his face and see his smirk. "You shaved!", I exclaimed as I reach up to touch his smooth cheek.

Carson begins to blush, "Yes, I figured this is a pretty big event and sitting at the table with the Vice-President. I needed to clean up a little."

"Come on in. I am running a little behind but I just need to throw on my dress and we can go," I say ushering him through the door. "Do you want anything to drink while you wait?"

"No, I am good. Eric, I will take over from here."

"Ok. The TV remote is on the coffee table. Make yourself at home. I will just be a few minutes." I tell him as I run back to bedroom. "Bye, Eric. Thank you as always," I say as I close my door.

I go into my closet and begin putting on my gown. After spending a few minutes trying to see if any of my bras will work with this gown, I realize I will have to go without one. Luckily, my breasts are perky enough that they look amazing and the cleavage is perfect with the V-neck of the gown. Next, I need to find my very sexy black thong. Not that anyone will see it but at least I know underneath these clothes is some very sexy lingerie.

I look in the mirror and I think the back of the dress is more stunning than the front, it dips into a V all the way down to my lower back. I am struggling getting the clasp to hook at my waist. "Hey Carson, can you help me in here?" I yell from my closet.

"Where are you?" I hear him ask at my bedroom door. I stick my head out of the closet and motion for him to join me but he is standing there and actually looks afraid to enter my room.

"I'm in my closet. Come on, I need to finish getting dressed, but I cannot get this gown to clasp at the waist. Can you help a girl out and hook the clasp so my gown does not end up around my ankles tonight?" I ask him laughing.

He finally is standing in the doorway and I back up so he can come in. All of a sudden he stopped walking and I noticed he is staring at the floor. That's when I remembered I had laid out all my bras and thongs to see which ones would work with my outfit. I don't even know what to say but he seems mesmerized by the sight of lingerie.

I turn my back to him and say, "So here it is, you can see the hook and clasp. Just connect them together and then you can you help me pick out my shoes. I have it narrowed down to three pairs."

*****

Holy shit…what have I gotten myself into? Not only am I standing in Alex's bedroom closet but looking at those bras and thongs has gotten me so worked up that I can't even remember why she called me in here. Who would have thought sweet, little Alex had such a penchant for skimpy, lacey lingerie? I wonder what she is wearing now.

Alex finally helps me remember what I am supposed to be doing since staring at her lingerie is not why she called me in. Dear lord…her back is beautiful and this dress is sinful with how low the back dips to the small of her back. Who would have thought a back could make me even hornier? I take the hook and clasp and slowly connect them and when I make contact with her lower back, I see her shiver. I am not sure if I should be as excited about the reaction as I am. I know I need to leave her alone but I am not sure I will be able too.

Alex turns around, "Thank you. Now help me pick out my shoes."

I can only stare. This gown she is wearing is amazing. I am not sure I want her going outside in it, every male in a twenty-mile radius will be staring at her breasts. They are just sitting up there perky and begging for someone to touch, lick, I have got to stop this thinking.

"Shoes…um…sure, I thought you bought a pair already?" I manage to croak out. I am surprised she has not started screaming at me because I cannot seem to stop looking at breasts. This is going to be the longest night of my life.

*****

The last piece that will take me forever to figure out is my shoes.

"Yes, but now I cannot decide between these three. Which one do you think looks best?" I ask as I am trying on all three pairs for him. I am bending over and glance up and see that Carson is just staring down at me with his mouth open. I look down at where he is looking and realize that he is staring at my cleavage. He looks like he is about to drool over my perfectly, perky breasts. I give him a smirk, "Shoes, which ones?"

"Go with the second pair. I like those," he growls out. I grin at him while I put on a diamond necklace that my parents gave me for my college graduation.

"Sounds good. Do I look ok?" Carson looks stunned when I ask him that question and I hold breath waiting for his response.

Peter always had something critical to say about everything I wore so I am bracing myself for what may come out of Carson's mouth.

"You look better than ok. I really like your necklace," he says as he is trying very hard to not look at my breasts. My necklace is laying right above my breasts and apparently he really likes what he sees. I want to do my happy dance since I know he is looking at me not like a little sister right now.

"What about your coat?" Carson asks as I am picking up a small faux fur wrap.

I smile at him and wiggle the wrap at him, "This is my coat for the evening," I tell him with a smile.

"But your entire back is still showing."

I roll my eyes at him, "We are getting into a limo that is downstairs. We get out of a limo and walk inside; I can handle the two minutes of cold," I tell him sarcastically.

"I just want to make sure you are comfortable and taken care of," Carson replies as I turn on my alarm and we walk out the door.

"Really, you will take care of me?" I say with a teasing smile. "How exactly will you do that? Will you do everything that I ask you to do?". This may be a fun little experiment, Carson seems relaxed and he's smiling which I hardly ever see so I wonder will he flirt back.

"I guess you will just have to ask me and see if I take care of it for you," he says as he clears his throat. I am laughing as we get off the elevator and walk towards the door and the limo that is parked by the curb.

We both climb in and the driver pulls off and heads over to Catherine's house to pick her up and Adam. My phone begins ringing, I look down and see it is Peter calling again and I send it to voicemail. He is a major pain in the ass. When I go to put it back in my purse I notice Carson staring at me with a raised eyebrow.

"What?" I ask him.

"Nothing, I can see that Peter is still bothering you." Carson reaches over and puts his hand on top of mine and begins rubbing the back of my hand with his thumb. I never would have imagined that this one little innocent act could be so erotic. My nipples get tighter with each sweep of his thumb as I am imagining him doing that to my breasts. I hope that it is not noticeable that I am beginning to get flush from this contact.

We pull up to Catherine's and I move over in the limo to make room for them as they are climbing in. Carson moves closer to me and drapes his arm over the back of seat and pulls me into his side. "Catherine, you look great. Adam, you clean up nicely," I tell them as they get settled in the limo.

"Alex, that dress is to die for. I'm glad you bought it," she replies.

Catherine glances over at Carson and busts out laughing. "Seriously Carson, now I can tell mom what it will take for you to shave. A fancy party and Alex," she says teasing him.

"Can it Catherine. I shaved since we are sitting with the Vice-President," he mutters. "Plus mom would kill me if she found out that I was still scruffy at this event," he adds with a laugh.

We arrive at the gala and Adam starts laughing as he looks out the window, "Seriously a red carpet and photographers?"

I forgot about that and I look over to Carson, "Sorry, this is going to be three days straight that you are being photographed with me."

He just smiles, "It's not a problem."

We climb out of the limo and begin walking up towards the entrance. I am forced to stop a few times for pictures. To my surprise, some of the photographers request for Carson to be in the pictures with me. "You don't have to do this if you don't want to," I tell him as he walks over and puts his arm around me and pulls me close for the picture.

Carson looks down at me and smiles. "So this is what it is like to be on a date with a McNeil?" he says teasingly as he is stroking my bare lower back.

"I was not sure if this was a date since I kind of forced it on you," I tell him softly.

"This is a pretty good first date, Alex," he replies as we walk off to enter the gala.

Catherine and Adam are standing there and I am looking over everything to make sure it is just the way it is supposed to be. "I need to do one more walk-through of the ballroom before more people get here," I tell them.

"You are such a perfectionist Alex," Catherine states as I am walking off.

"Alex, wait up. Let me come with you," Carson says as he catches up with me. We walk inside the ballroom and it is perfect. Carson lets out a whistle. "Wow, Alex, this looks amazing. I cannot believe this is what you guys do," he says in awe.

"I am extremely proud of the parties we pull off. This is what the Senator asked for and I know without a doubt, we delivered."

"OK, let's get back out there for the cocktail hour and mingle," I tell him as I pull him away by the hand. When we return to Catherine and Adam, I see that my dad and mom are speaking with them. I glance over to see that my dad's secret service detail has spread out so they can reach him in seconds but not be so intrusive at this event.

"Hi mom, hi dad," I say as we walk up and I give them big hugs. I see that Max is right behind my dad, as usual. "Hi Max, you look nice in a tux," I tell him with a wink.

"Alexandria, you look beautiful darling. That dress is stunning," my mom says as she looks me up and down. "Carson, you clean up nicely. By the way we were peppered with questions about the two of you when we were walking up," my dad says as he is patting Carson on the back.

"Thank you, sir. I figured that you will be getting a lot of that," Carson replies with a smile.

I notice Max has moved closer to stand by all of us and he exchanges a look with my father. I look over to where my father is looking and see Peter's parents walking towards us. I groan out loud which causes Carson and Adam to look at me questioningly. "Peter's parents are walking over and they do not look to happy," I say them with a shrug.

"Margaret, Ryan, good to see you again," Peter's father, Brian King, says ha he shakes my father's hand and gives my mother a kiss on the cheek. Brian glances my way and nods his brusquely in my direction.

"It is nice to see you, Mr. King," I say with a fake smile on my face. Peter's mother, Sarah, has finished her greetings and moves closer to me. "Alexandria, I am sorry to hear that you and Peter have hit a slight rough patch in your relationship."

I can feel Carson has moved closer to my side and my father is keeping a close eye on the situation. I smile nicely to her, "Mrs. King, I wish it was that simple but we are simply not suited for each other any more," I tell her softly. I watch has her eyes grow hard like ice, so this must be where Peter gets it from.

"Maybe if you had been more attentive to his needs instead of focusing on all of this party stuff, you could have kept him his attention. I see that you have moved on to less suitable people," she replies coolly as she looks Carson up and down.

I take a deep breath since this is not the time or location for me to scream at this spiteful lady. I hear my father clear his throat, "Sarah, that is rude and unacceptable. If you cannot be polite to my daughter and her guest then you will have to leave this event," he says sternly.

I watch has she goes pale at the thought of being frosted out by someone like my parents. "Ryan, Alexandria, I am sorry. Sarah has been upset by Peter and Alexandria's split. Sarah, come now we have other people to greet," Brian says as he tries to smooth over the situation.

"Why would she think you are less suitable? She has no clue who your family is?" I say to Carson. I hear Adam and Catherine snicker as they walk away.

"Can you believe that women? You would think she would have better sense than to insult you in front of father," Catherine says shaking her head. She glances down at her watch, "It is time to start corralling everyone into the ballroom for the dinner."

I look over to the waiters and nod my head to signal them to open the doors and begin ushering people inside. Senator Gregg walks up to us and gives Catherine and I both big hugs. "Ladies, this is marvelous. Everyone is raving about this event. You have really outdone yourselves."

"Are you ready to go get seated?" Carson asks as he puts his hand on my back to lead us into the ballroom. I try to suppress the shiver it sends up spine but I know he notices; his eyes look like they are on fire. We walk into to the ballroom and it takes about ten minutes before we are finally at our table. I was stopped so many times by people and I can tell Carson is overwhelmed by the number of people I have introduced him to.

As we are sitting down, Carson and Adam both pull their phones out and read a text. I watch as they exchange a look and can feel a communication go between them. I know they have been partners for a long time but it is weird to watch them communicate without even speaking. They simply know what their looks mean to one another. "Is everything ok?" I ask them as Carson is putting his phone back in his jacket.

"Yes little one, nothing for you to worry about," he says vaguely.

I look at my watch and glance around the room to make sure everyone is seated before I get up to walk to the podium. As I stand up, Carson stands and leans over to my ear, "You look phenomenal. Have fun up there." I just stare at him then realize everyone is probably watching us and begin to walk to the stage.

I share a quick, funny story about my father and Senator Gregg from when I was younger before I wrap up my introduction of my father. As the room is applauding, I give my father a quick hug and kiss. As I am walking back to the table, I swear one of the waiters looks like David. It was enough that I paused while I was walking and do a double-take, but the waiter has turned away from me. When I take my seat, Carson leans over, "What was that about?" he asks. I look at him knowing nothing ever gets past his eyes.

"I thought one of the waiters looked like David but he moved away before I could get another look," I tell him with a frown.

"Stay close to me and let me know if you see him again." We finish listening to my father's speech about supporting the Senator's reelection campaign and now it is time for dinner. While we were eating, Carson and Adam receive another text message that they both read and frown at. I am waiting for Carson to tell me he has to leave.

I give him a look and he responds by tugging on my hair. "What is it little one?" he asks as he drapes his arm across my chair and is playing with a piece of my hair.

"I am waiting for you to tell me you have to leave since you keep getting text messages."

"Nah, you are stuck with me for the night," Carson replies with a smile. I look at him and his smile blows me away. That is, it, I am going to do it. I am going to seduce him.

The gala is finally over and after we drop Catherine and Adam off at her house. It is just the two of us in the limo again. Carson is sitting close to me and he takes my hand and he is rubbing his thumb along the inside of my palm and it is sending sensations through my body that something this innocent should never do.

I hear his phone beep again as another text message is coming and he breaks his contact with my hand to check it. "What is going on? You have been getting messages all night?" I ask him as he replies to the message.

"Don't worry about it Alex." We are pulling up to my building and he helps me out of the car.

After we are in my condo, Carson is responding to another text and I have no idea why it is driving me crazy. I know something is going on and it has to do with the case. I realize Carson has become so familiar with my habits and home because he is locking the door and turns on the alarm on. "So are you going to tell me what is going on?" I ask him since he failed to acknowledge my earlier question.

Carson looks at me and sighs, "Until we know more, I am not comfortable letting you know what I think is going on. It's unnecessary to get you worked up over something that may be nothing. Just trust me on this Alex.".

Just trust him, I think about it for a moment and realize I trust him wholeheartedly and if he is not ready to tell me then I can wait. As I am looking at him, I begin to be aware of the sexual tension that is back around us now that we are alone.

And alone is what we are. There is no one around to interrupt anything that may or could happen. I swallow because I have made my decision. "It looks like you are staying the night since you locked yourself in with me. Why don't you come help me get undressed?" I request as I turn around and walk towards my bedroom.

Chapter 20

I glance over my shoulder and Carson is frozen where he is standing. I can see the lust shimmering in his eyes as he has his own internal struggle on how to handle this situation. This will be the first time I can say I am actively attempting to seduce a man into bed with me and I am not sure if I am doing it right. "Carson, you had to help me get dressed earlier. This is nothing you haven't seen before," I say teasing him and hoping he will relax.

That must have worked because he shook his head and starts following me into my room. I keep walking and head into my bathroom so I can take off my jewelry. Carson is standing in the doorway looking around. "I still can't get over the size of this massive bathroom," he says looking around. "It's the size of my apartment."

"Like I said, a girl knows what she wants," I say smiling at him. This can have a dual meaning since I love my bathroom and I am loving the site of the man standing in front me. I begin taking off my jewelry and watch him in the mirror. Carson is just staring back at me and I can feel the heat of eyes raking over my body. I wonder if he can tell that my nipples are hardening in response to him.

"Come on over and unhook the waist of my gown so I can get it off me," I say to him casually. I am approaching this situation with him like he is a scared cat. Slowly trying to get him to relax and not bolt out the door.

He walks up behind me and I am amazed at our size difference in the mirror. Even with my heels on I am only eye level with his chest. He sweeps my hair over my right shoulder and begins to fumble with the clasp at my waist. I can feel his knuckles skimming over my back as he unhooks the clasp at my waist and I am not able to suppress the shiver that the contact brings. "There. All done," he whispers to me and we both are still staring at each other in the mirror.

I slowly turn around to face him. He is standing so still he could be a statue. I begin to pull down the straps of my ball gown until I am standing in front of him, brazenly exposing my aching, magnificent breasts. I watching him clench and unclench his jaw. I reach up and gently caress his cheek and he clears his throat.

"Alex, what do you think you are doing?" he asks me as he turns into my caress and kisses the palm of my hand.

"What does it look like I am doing?" He puts his hands on the counter so I am trapped between him and the counter and I can feel the heat emanating off of his body. I am aching to rub against him to feel his hardness against my center.

"I am not good for you," he replies as he leans in closer to me. "I can't give you what you deserve or need."

"Carson, just tonight then, no strings attached. I'm a big girl and I can handle this," I whisper close to his mouth. I am staring at him and notice how his eyes are glowing with an intensity I have never seen, like lava. I can feel the heat in his eyes.

"You have no idea how many times I have fanaticized about you," he whispers back. He angles my head just the way he wants it and finally closes the last inch and his lips and mine make contact.

Carson tries to be gentle with his kiss and pull back but I am on fire with passion and will not let him hold anything back. His lips are soft but demanding against my mouth. I breath in his smell and wish I could bottle it and sniff it whenever I pleased. He is so masculine and hard with his clean scent. I can feel his hands moving up my back and I arch into him. I feel his erection pressing against my stomach and wish I was taller so it would rub it against my aching core. I open my mouth to welcome the invasion of his tongue and good lord, the man can kiss. I am reeling from the sensations of his kisses and I slowly arch up against him again, making contact with the bulge that is straining against him. Carson's hands slowly move across my collar bone then move to my breasts. They are straining to be caressed by him and he begins to slowing pinch and pull my nipples, "Oh god, that feels wonderful," I moan in his mouth.

He lifts me up to the counter and begins kissing down my neck following the same trail that his hands have left. "You are so beautiful. Even more beautiful than I have imagined," he says against my throat. I am on the edge of the counter and I move against his erection that is now at the right height to make contact with my hot center, which elicits a groan from him. I can feel him looking at my bare breasts, "amazing", he breathes out. Carson leans over and captures one of my tightly beaded nipples in his mouth. "Ahh", I groan as he continued to suck my nipple into a tortured peak while pinching my other one into a tight bud. I am moving restlessly against his hard erection and wish these layers of clothes were not in the way. Not to show one breast favoritism over the other, he moves over to the other one and I am on fire. I swear if he keeps this up, I may explode from the sensation.

I move my hands through his hair and pull his head up to capture that delectable mouth of his. Carson tastes like mint and I want to lose myself in his taste. I begin working on the buttons of his tuxedo shirt and push the shirt off of his shoulders. He has worked me up to a fever pitch and I am becoming a madwoman. When he leans up so I can pull his undershirt off, I am in awe of his body. His skin is tan and it does not look like he has an ounce of fat; he is nothing but sculpted muscle.

My mouth has gone dry as I look at him, he is smooth all over with a small trail of hair leading down his abdomen and disappearing in his pants. I notice the very hard length pressing against his pants and can't wait to see it, "You are incredible. All muscle and Greek-god like," I tell him.

Carson leans down and takes my mouth again in another mind-blowing kiss. I pull away and begin kissing down his throat to his chest and move over to his nipples were I lightly flick them with my tongue. I am surprised by the groan it elicits and even more surprised when Carson jerks back from me and takes my mouth again in a passionate kiss. He grabs me by the waist and lifts me off the counter to stand in front him. I feel him working on pulling the ball gown off of me. Once he has my gown off, he steps back and just stares at me, "I have been dying to see what panties you are wearing all night", he murmurs.

"Do these work for you?" I ask him breathlessly as I am standing in front of him in my black, lace thong and stilettos.

He leans down and captures my mouth again and breathes against me, "More than you can imagine. I love the shoes as well," as he pulls my panties off, leaving my stilettos on. Carson lifts me back on the counter and spreads my legs to step in-between them. "I could spend all night kissing your breasts. They are so sensitive and your responses are driving me insane," he utters against my neck while he kissing a trail back to my aching, swollen breasts.

"Please Carson. I want you so bad," I moan as my head falls back against the mirror.

"Shh…Alexandria we have all night and I want this to be good for you," he murmurs back. I love him hearing use my full name since he only does it when he is in the heat of the moment. I slowly feel his hands trail down my sides to my hips and slowly move to the inside of my thighs. I spread my legs wider to accommodate his hand. My breath catches as he slowly circles around the soft petals of my womanhood. "You are so smooth, soft and wet. I can't get over how bare you are," Carson moans as he steps back to look at me again. I have to fight the urge to close my legs to cover myself. I raise up on my elbows so I can watch him as he slowly enters one finger into my tight depths. "So tight", he whispers as he looks at me with smoldering eyes. As his finger begins to move against me, I reach up to grab him for another passionate kiss and he slowly adds a second finger filling me.

I am moaning and moving my hips against his hand when he removes his fingers. "Carson, you are torturing me. I want you inside of me now!", I demand.

He chuckles at me and says, "Not yet Alexandria, I still have one more thing I have to do." Carson slowly drops to his knees and drapes my legs over his shoulders. I am holding my breath waiting for what I know will come next. He slowly peppers kisses along the inside of my thighs and I shiver in response. I think he is enjoying making me this hot and out of control. I can feel his breath on me as he gets closer to my center, "Alexandria, you should see yourself right now. So alive with passion. You are exquisite," he sighs against me as he takes his first taste of me.

I am on fire. I have never felt this type of raw animal passion with anyone before. He continues to worship my warm, wet center and I grow even more out of control. My hips are moving uncontrollably and just as I thought it could not get any better, Carson slowly adds his two fingers back into me as he manipulates my clitoris with his tongue. I see fireworks. I begin convulsing around his fingers and it takes all my might not to squeeze my legs together and hurt him. "Oh my god, Carson!", I yell as I have the most explosive climax of my life.

Carson slowly pulls his fingers out of me and kisses his way back up to my mouth. I can taste myself on him and it is such an erotic taste to mix me and him in that way. "That was amazing," I tell him breathlessly.

"Now you are ready for me," he replies as his eyes darken with passion.

He picks me up and carries me into my bedroom and puts me on the bed. I sit up on my knees near the edge of the bed and grab him by the belt loops to pull him close to me. I undo his belt and unbutton his pants. I can see the bulge pressing against the zipper and can only imagine how bad he must be aching. I slowly unzip his pants and push them down over his hips, "Alexandria, you are killing me going so slow," Carson groans out. I just smile at him and he groans again. I push down his boxers and I am greeted by his straining erection. It is magnificent just like Carson is, long, hot and extremely hard. I see a drop of pre-cum on the tip and lean over to lick it off. "Holy shit Alexandria!", Carson exclaims as I take his hard shaft into my mouth. I am awestruck that he gets even harder by me doing this.

Suddenly, he jerks me up and pushes me down on the bed and kisses me greedily. I begin moving against him. Without our clothes in the way, I can feel the pulsing of his hard erection against me and I want to feel him enter me. I begin shifting underneath Carson and beg, "Please Carson, I want you now."

"Do you have a condom?" he asks me trying to slow his breathing. I reach over into my nightstand and pull out an unopened box. He impatiently rips open the box and pulls out one to put on. I am memorized by the sight of him rolling the condom on his thick, pulsating erection.

Carson leans back over me and says, "Alexandria, are you sure you want to do this?"

"Yes!", I cry out and pull him down to my mouth for another crazed kiss. He slowly positions him just at my entrance and begins to slowly fill me.

"God, you are so wet and tight," he groans against my mouth.

All I can do is moan over how good the sensation feels of him filling me completely and slowly. I arch my hips upward to move against him and we both lose control. All I focus on is the hot, wet, abandoned movements and I soon realize that I will have my second orgasm in seconds. "Carson, I am going to come," I cry out.

Carson is meeting me thrust for thrust and gasps in my ear, "Come for me sweetheart." I begin to convulse around him and cry out with unabashed abandon. I can feel Carson begin to pulsate within me while he moans, "Alexandria."

We both stay still for a moment trying to catch our breaths. There is sheen of sweat over our bodies. Carson leans up on one arm and stares at me. "That was amazing Alexandria," he whispers and gives me a slow, sweet kiss.

"I agree," I tell him lazily. I could stay like this forever with me laying on his chest but I remember I promised him no-strings, that was my last thought as I slowly drift off to sleep.

Chapter 21

I wake up and see Carson is sleeping. I slide off of him and go to use the bathroom. I am pleasantly sore from our vigorous love making. As I ease back into bed, Carson rolls over and grabs me to pull me on top of him. He caresses my face and takes my lips in a sensual kiss that soon turns frantic.

The lust that shoots back and forth between us is not like anything I have ever felt before. It is breathtaking and should scare me. Instead I feel magnificent knowing I can cause him to hardened like he is. Just looking at him makes me wet. Carson breaks our kiss and lifts me up further on his chest so that my aching breasts are level with his mouth.

"Splendid," he says as I can feel my nipple stiffen as his lips close around it.

"Carson," I moan out as the sensation of him tugging my nipple gently with his mouth. This is heaven.

I pull back a little and lean down to relish in another passionate kiss that has both of moving restlessly against each other. I can feel his hard shaft against my entrance but before we lose ourselves, I want to truly taste him. I begin peppering kisses down his hard chest. I can feel the muscles beneath his warm skin rippling at the places that I am licking.

*****

She must be trying to kill me. My entire body is on fire from where her lips have placed those sweet licks. I suck in a deep breath as her tongue swirls around my belly button and she has moved in between my legs. Those wonderful breasts of hers are brushing against my balls and I am sure I am going to explode from the sensation.

"Alexandria, what are you doing?" I growl out as I can feel her move lower. I look down at her and I am captivated by the sight of her between my legs looking up at me with a devilish grin.

"You know what I am doing," she replies huskily and then she leans back to complete her quest.

She takes me into her mouth and begins to lick and suck with wild abandon. It takes all my strength not to thrust harder and further into her mouth. I brush her hair away from her face so I can have a better view of this torture. She is giving me the most mind-blowing blow job I have ever had. "Alexandria, you are amazing," I moan as I feel her caress my balls and I know I am getting close to the edge.

I want her too badly, I have to be inside of her. I sit up and grab her by the arms and pull her up to capture her mouth. I can tell I have surprised her. Her moment of shock turns to a moan as I plunder her mouth and slip a finger into her tight sheath to make sure she is ready for me. She is more than ready I can tell from her moans and the warm, wetness against my fingers.

Alex surprises me again by swatting away my hands. She takes my throbbing shaft and slowly encloses me with her tight, warm heat, I have never felt anything like this. "Shit, Alex. We need a condom," I tell her as my real brain kicks in at the last moment when I realize what the difference is between the first time and this time.

"I'm on the pill. Don't worry about it Carson," she says with a smile.

I am blown away by the image of her sitting astride me with her wild hair, just like my dreams. I grab her by the back of her neck and pull her down for a kiss. The hurricane of desire breaks loose between us.

She begins moving against me with wet, hot, abandoned movements. I grab her hips to meet her thrust for thrust. I can hear her moans in my ears or it may be mine. I am so far gone I can think of nothing but her. Her smell, the feel of her slick, wet, core tightening against my dick. "Carson," I hear her moan. I can tell that she is close. I lean up and capture one of her tightly beaded nipples between my lips. "Ahhhh," she moans out as I feel her core pulsing against me as she comes. That sends me over the edge as I begin to explode inside of her.

Alex is draped on top of me and I can hear us both trying to catch our breaths. She leans up to look at me and kisses my lips. "That was fantastic," she tells me with a satisfied smile. We are still connected to each other and I hug her tightly because I do not want to leave her warmth.

"Little one, you will kill me if we keep doing this," I tell her with a smile. I know tonight is the one night I will ever have with her and it is going to suck when I leave in the morning. I lift her off of me and pull her into my side. "We need to get some sleep," I tell her as I give her one last kiss.

"Carson, tonight has been fun," she replies and then I can feel her breathing slow down as she goes to sleep.

*****

I awake with a start, I hear music and then I realize that it is Carson's phone ringing. I look over to see him sitting up and turning on the lamp on the nightstand to grab his phone. "Knight", he answers then he glances over at me and smiles. I am sitting up and the sheet is around my waist so he is getting an eyeful of my nakedness.

I can tell that he must not be hearing good news because he has gone rigid. "I need someone to meet me at Alex's place before I can go anywhere," he tells whoever he is talking to. "Shit, ok, let me think. How about I call Max and see if he can help us out? Let me call him and I will call you when I am on my way. No one goes in without me there," he states as he hangs up his phone.

Carson turns towards me and smiles, "Little one, you should not be able to look so good in the middle of the morning like you do. Your breasts are perfect and so beautifully formed like a goddess. It's a shame I have to go," he murmurs as he leans over to give me a kiss and then quickly caresses each of my breasts. He has to stop as our kiss begins to take on an urgency I can tell he does not have time to fulfill.

"Do you mind if I call Max to come over?"

At this point I would agree to walk naked across the street if he asked me to. "I guess."

"I need everyone on my team with me. We have a huge break in the case and need to go execute a search warrant," he tells me as he stands up to get dressed.

"Will you let me know how everything goes after you are done?"

"Of course. Let me call Max and see if he can come over," he says as he picks up his phone.

*****

Holy shit, I cannot believe we may have finally caught a break or at least we may be able to nail Peter's sorry ass for stalking

Alex. I glance over at Alex sitting in the bed and I am blown away by how beautiful she looks with her swollen lips and messy hair. Peter was a moron to not know how to push her buttons to make her explode. Unresponsive my ass, she is one of the most responsive women I have ever been with.

In all honesty, no one even comes close to comparing to her. There are so many reasons why I love her. I freeze when I realize what I just thought in my head. I cannot love her. This was a one-time, we both wanted to get this out of our system, no-strings attached, crazy, mind-blowing sex.

I shake my head and need to focus, Max finally answers his phone and I can tell I woke him up. "Do you have any idea what time it is?" he asks me grumpily.

"Yes, it's 2:30am and I need a huge favor. Can you come over to Alex's and stay with her until we can get someone over here?"

"Sure, why?" Max replies, I can hear him moving around.

"We have a break and I need to be there for the search warrant"

"Give me ten minutes and I should be there," Max tells me and hangs up.

I have put my pants back on but cannot find my shirt for the life of me. I glance over at Alex and see her smiling at me. "You can't find your clothes, can you?" she asks with a smile on her face.

Dear lord, I love this woman and everything about her. She gets out of bed in her splendid, naked glory and walks into her bathroom. I am mesmerized by the the sight of her perfect, alabaster, round ass and the way her hips sway as she is walking. I am still in shock that Alex has everything waxed to a smooth perfection.

Alex walks back carrying my undershirt and dress shirt. "You left them in the bathroom with the rest of my clothes," she says with a smile as she hands me my clothes.

"Thank you", I give her a quick kiss on the lips and finish getting dressed. I need to be dressed so once Max arrives. He does not need to figure out that I spent the night in Alex's bed. He looks after her like a big brother and I do not have time to get into another argument about her.

"Look, Alex, do we need to talk about what happened between us? I mean you are my little sister's best friend and we will have to see each other at social functions, so are we good?" I feel like an ass for saying this. She deserves more than a one-night stand with me. I can see her body stiffen before she replies.

"No, Carson. I told you no-strings attached. I wanted this as much as you did and it was great, but I do not expect things from you that you are not ready to give me."

I watch her turn around and walk into her closet. Shit, I know I have hurt her but I have to focus on this case. Once it is over then I can stay away from her. I hear a knock on the door and I walk over to the closet door. "Alex, Max is here. I am going to let him in," I tell her as I walk away. I can feel my heart breaking as I walk away from her.

"Thanks for coming over so late Max," I tell him as he walks in. "I woke Alex and told her you were coming over so she is aware." I glance over to her bedroom door and see her standing there in a robe. I can feel my erection straining against my pants as I look at her. I glance over at Max and readjust myself so it is not as obvious.

Max clears his throat and I look over at him and see that my adjustment was not lost on him. Based off the eat shit look he is giving me; he has figured out that Alex has the 'I just had mind-blowing sex' look. "Alex, I'm going to stay with you until for the rest of the night and tomorrow. Your parents wanted to have breakfast with you so we can do that," Max explains to her while looking at me.

"Thanks Max. Alex, go back to bed. I will talk with you guys later," I say as I high-tail it out of there.

"Bye Carson", I hear Alex say as I am closing the door. I am such an asshole, probably a bigger one than Peter ever was to her.

Chapter 22

As I get into my car, I dial Adam. "Hey, I am leaving Alex's now. I will meet you in ten minutes."

Over the past two days we have been tracking down who purchased the camera in Alex's bedroom. It was traced back to Peter's credit card. The idiot, I cannot believe he used his own credit card to purchase that camera. In addition to that, we received a call on the tip line that is pointing towards Peter being our serial killer. My gut told me he was the one to focus on for the one camera, but I would be surprised if we find anything to link him to these murders. When Adam and I got the text last night that our team had pulled him in for questioning and he admitted to hiding the camera, it was all we needed for a search warrant.

I pull up to Peter's townhouse and Adam and the rest of our team are waiting outside. "Hey guys, are we ready to do this?" I ask them.

"The judge signed off on pulling this place apart. The moment he heard Peter had placed hidden cameras in the Vice-President's daughter home, he was onboard," Adam says dryly.

We start walking up to let ourselves in. At least Peter's attorney was smart enough to give us a key instead of us breaking the door down. Adam glances over at me and stops me, "Dude, is that lipstick on your collar?" he asks with an incredulous look.

"Don't start. It's nothing," I tell him as I continue to walk towards the door.

"Well, at least you got your head out of your ass and did something before these calls started," Adam says laughing as I shoot him a dirty look.

The crime scene techs have already begun their careful search of the house. We have our investigative team split up to carefully go through each room. We are all looking for anything that may connect Peter to the murders, as well as his stalking of Alex. Adam and I walk into the room that Peter uses as his office and look around.

"Whoa, he was really into Alex wasn't he," Adam says rhetorically. There are pictures of her everywhere, some pictures are of them together at parties, but most look like they were taken without her being aware.

"I wonder if she ever saw this room or was aware of this. I would think she would have been freaked out by this type of attention," I say as I am thinking out loud.

We are about to begin digging through his desk when Eric runs in. "Guys, you have to come see what we just found in his closet!", he exclaims. We go up to the second floor and walk into the bedroom and see a massive closet.

"Maybe this is what Peter and Alex had in common, a huge ass closet," Adam says as he is eyeballing this massive room.

I walk over to where the crime techs are and see that they have pulled back a false dresser. Behind it in the wall are little glasses filled with eyeballs. "Holy shit, is that what I think it is?" I say out loud.

"Detective Knight, we won't know for sure until we get the DNA back but I am assuming that these are all the missing eyes from the past seven victims," the tech replies.

"This does not make any sense. I never would have thought Peter fits the profile of the killer," I mutter to myself. I look over to Adam and he is just shaking his head.

"There is more. Either he has thing for women's underwear or these may be the ones that were stolen from Alex's place," Eric states as he shows us an open drawer in the closet. Adam and I look at what is in it and I am pretty sure some of those panties match the bras I have seen in Alex's closet.

"Let's go back to the office and keep looking around," I say to him as I walk out of the closet. Adam and I have returned to the office and I begin pulling out the desk drawers to see what is in them.

"Dude, you should be ecstatic. There is enough evidence upstairs to convict Peter for the sicko that he is."

I look at him and know I should be happy but this does not feel right to me. "What about the guy Alex ran into in the hallway? Don't you think she would have recognized him as Peter? Plus, the night of Allison's murder, Peter was at the event being held up by Catherine."

"Maybe the guy was really Allison's boyfriend and he went for a visit and freaked out and left." I am still in disbelief; my mind is telling me the evidence does not lie. But I also know what my gut says.

"Carson, I hate to say it but do you think your judgment is clouded because of Alex and your feelings for her? You should be happy about this because this means she is safe and we no longer need to keep her guarded 24/7. Or is that what the problem is?" Adam says gently.

Adam has a point and I have lost my focus on this case since Alex became involved. "Let's get back to going through all of his papers," I murmur. We spend a few minutes going through bills and from the looks of it, Peter was not as well off financially has he liked everyone to think. He was in massive debt. I open another folder and in it are a list of florist shops and at a quick glance, they seem to be the same florists that sent flowers to Allison's condo. I put that into a separate evidence bag.

"Hey man, look at these," Adam says. I look over and he is holding a stack of cards and I can see writing on them. "Looks like he had a bunch of these notes already written so he could stick them on Alex's and the other victim's windshields. Some of these are the same sayings we already have in evidence."

This case looks like it is about to be closed once we have the DNA confirmed on those eyeballs. Add that to these notes and I know that Peter stopped sleeping with Alex about eight months ago so the timing of everything makes sense. I just do not know what made him go off the deep end to do this.

His attorney is going to have a difficult time defending him. "At least this should be an easy interrogation. I am not sure what his attorney will be able to say," Adam says as we continue to bag evidence.

"This entire house is covered with evidence that links Peter to these murders. Have you ever seen a case that was this simple?" I ask him.

Chapter 23

I never went back to sleep after Carson left and the bags under my eyes reflect it. When I walk into my bathroom to get dressed, the images of what took place last night in this bathroom make me flush. I am not sure I will ever be able to get dressed in here without getting aroused from reliving those memories.

I finish adding concealer under my eyes and walk out to the kitchen. Max is in the living room watching the news. "Hey Max, do you want any coffee?" I ask him as I pour myself a cup.

"No thank you, Alex," he says as he glances over. I walk over to sit next to him on the couch.

"You okay?" He asks me as I plop down.

"Yes, just tired. I never really went back to sleep after Carson left. I guess it's a good thing Catherine and I took the day off after the gala."

"Speaking of the gala, it has been all over the news and everyone is saying what a great event it was," Max tells me as he passes me a paper to look at the write up that was done. I am reading over the paper and smiling over the rave reviews. I flip over the page to continue reading when I see a picture of Carson and I smiling on the red carpet together and my heart drops.

"Are you almost done with your coffee so we can head over to meet your parents before they have to leave?" Max asks pulling me out of my thoughts.

"Sure, let me put this in the sink and grab my bag."

I am rinsing out my coffee cup when I finally give in and ask Max the question I have been trying not to ask since I walked out of my room. "Max, have you heard from Carson? Is everything ok?" I ask him as he is walking over with his overnight bag.

"No sweetheart, I haven't heard from him, but I am sure everything is fine. He is just busy."

"Thanks. When we get into the car, I need to call Catherine to let her know about the great reviews and see what she is up to today," I tell him as we are leaving my condo. Max glances at me and stops me before we get into the elevator.

"Alex, do I need to beat the shit out of Carson for you?" he says seriously.

I look at him with a startled expression, "What are you talking about?"

Max shakes his head at me while he rubs his hand through his hair. "Listen, if he took advantage of you last night, I will break his legs."

I start laughing because I know Max obviously figured out what happened between us last night. "No, Max, believe it or not, it was me who started everything. Carson tried to stop me but I told him no-strings attached. He was very clear on what his limitations are with relationships."

"Ok, well the offer is out there. He is an even bigger idiot than I thought he was to pass you up," Max says as we walk onto the elevator.

"Max, please do not mention this to my dad."

"No worries sweetheart, this can stay between us."

*****

"Adam, this does not make any sense," I tell him for the millionth time. We just got the DNA results back from the lab and the eyes we found in Peter's house match the DNA of the previous victims.

"I hear you, Carson but the evidence is saying otherwise. You are going to have to deal with it."

He looks over at me and shakes his head, "Dude, you need to go home and shower and change your clothes, you look like hell." I am still in tux from last night and I can faintly smell Alex on me which could be one of the reasons I have not changed yet. I feel guilty as hell for the way I left things. "By the way, are you going to call Alex and her dad to let them know that we are making an arrest?" Adam asks as he finishes up the last of the paperwork on this case.

"I need to. I am putting it off because it is going to be hard as hell to tell them both what we found in Peter's house." This is going to be a media nightmare. Peter and his attorney have been screaming his innocence and how someone must have framed him because he has no clue who those women are. Peter is also insisting he never stole Alex's underwear and the only time he snuck into her condo was the night to hide the camera.

We have credit card transactions that prove otherwise and I am sure all of these women are the ones he was cheating on Alex with. "You know another thing that does not make any sense to me?" I say to Adam rhetorically. "Why would Alex's neighbor sleep with Peter? She would have seen him with Alex."

"Dude, give it up. I know you say it does not add up but it is adding up. You need to look at it objectively like everyone else is doing," Adam states sharply.

I glance up at him and nod, I get it, I am not being objective. "I get it, I am done."

"Are you going to continue to see Alex now that this case is done?" Adam asks me quietly so no one else can hear the question.

I already know the answer to that one, "No." Adam shakes his head at me. He throws a paper over to me and when I look at it, it is showing a picture of Alex and I taken at the gala. We look so happy together but then I read the article underneath it and there in print is one of the reasons why I know we cannot be together. 'Looks like someone is robbing the cradle, Alexandria McNeil's new flame is ten years her senior', reads the caption.

"Carson, your age difference is not the issue no matter how much you tell yourself that it is. You are the only one who has that issue. You have been in love with her for years and now is the time to give that a chance and be happy," Adam states as he gets up to leave.

On the way out the door he yells over to me, "You need to call her and take a shower!" Christ, how did I get myself into this mess. I pick up the phone to call the Vice-President but I cannot bring myself to make the call. I let the rest of our team know I am heading home to shower and I will be back shortly. I will call Alex and the Vice-President from my house.

*****

Max and I arrive at my parent's hotel room for breakfast. I am glad they opted to have breakfast in their room instead of a restaurant since it will be more causal and private. We walk into the suite and I see my dad standing by the window pacing while on the phone. He motions for us to come over.

"That is great news to hear Carson. While I am a little surprised by the outcome, I am happy to hear you have caught the killer. Alexandria and Max just walked in and I will share the news with them. Again, thank you so much for keeping her safe and I hope we see you soon," my father says as he hangs up his phone.

My father turns to me and gives me a big hug. "Alexandria, that was Carson. They just made an arrest so you should be safe again," he tells me with a huge smile.

"That is great daddy, so they found David?"

My dad gets a funny look on his face and clears his throat. "Well, sweetheart, this is the hard part, they received a tip and conducted a search and found enough evidence to convict the killer. It was not that guy David, it was Peter." I am shocked, there is no way Peter could be a killer. A jerk yes, but not a killer.

"Daddy, I cannot believe that. Peter is a lot of things but he is not a killer," I tell him shaking my head in disagreement.

"Honey, they found DNA evidence which links Peter to the murders. I know it is tough to hear, but we will need to come to terms with that," my dad says gently as he leads us to the dining room to sit down for breakfast. I do not think I can eat anything so I just grab a cup of coffee and a croissant to pick at.

Breakfast was a chore to participate in, I barely paid any attention to what we even talked about. All I can think about it is Peter and how none of this makes any sense. "Mr. Vice-President, I will drive Alexandria home then return so we can head to the airport," Max states as we are getting up from the table.

"Perfect Max. Alexandria, we love you and miss you. Your mother and I are both so proud of you and Catherine, your work is impeccable. We also hope to see more of Carson around with you. He brings a lightness to you that we have not seen in a long time," my dad says as he gives me a hug goodbye. I kiss my mom as we walk out the door.

"Alex, this is a good thing that Carson solved this case. You are not in danger anymore," Max says as we enter my building. I nod my head in agreement, I know it is good but it still a huge shock. When we get off the elevator, I see someone leaning against the wall down my door and recognize it is Carson.

My heart begins doing somersaults in my chest. I should not be feeling like a sixteen-year-old girl with her first crush. "I will take it from here Max," Carson tells Max as we approach him. I glance over and see the dirty look that Max is giving him.

"You and I need to have a long conversation," Max states bluntly to Carson.

I realize that Max is playing 'the big brother I never had role'. "Back off Max. There is nothing you and I need to talk about," Carson says coolly.

"I told you a few days ago what would happen if -", Max starts saying.

This has gone on long enough. "Thank you Max for staying with me and taking me to see my parents," I say as I give him a hug and kiss on the cheek. "You can go now. See you in a few weeks when I come to visit my parents," I tell him as he gives Carson one more nasty look and turns to leave.

"We are not done with this," Max says coldly to Carson.

I unlock my apartment and we walk in. There is an awkwardness in the air as we both try to figure out how to act around each other after last night. "I know you heard about Peter's arrest. There is a ton of evidence against him so there is no doubt in anyone's mind that he is guilty," Carson begins to explain. "You now will have your privacy back since he has been denied bail. There should be no issues with your safety. I need to grab all of the cameras out of here and bag them for evidence," Carson tells me as he begins pulling out everything he needs.

"Sure, I will stay over here until you are done." My eyes are roaming all over his body as he works. Carson has the best butt. Watching his pants hug him there brings back the memory of last night when I was grasping him by his firm buttocks and urging him to thrust deeper into me. I can feel myself getting turned on by the direction of my thoughts and this is not good. So much for me being able to handle a one-time thing.

I clear my throat and shake my head trying to get myself back into the present. "I still can't believe Peter would have done such horrible things. I know he was not the best person and could say hateful things, but he never did anything to show he was capable of murder."

"Alex, I know. I thought the same thing but again the evidence is too damning." He has finished removing all the cameras and I feel a huge sense of relief knowing no one is watching me. "Well, I just wanted to come over and tell you in person that the case is over. You may get called to testify if this goes to trial," Carson states as he looks around my place like he is lost.

"What about David, did you guys ever find him?" I ask. "I know I bumped into him before I saw Allison."

"We have not been able to locate him and I do not know what to tell you about it." I can tell by his tone this is the part where he says goodbye and leaves my life. I am not going to act like Kristy.

I told him the life-altering, earth shattering sex we had last night was a one-time thing and I could handle it.

"Alex, are we good?" he asks me. I look at him and do not even pretend to not know what he is referring to. I reach up and stroke his cheek and feel the now day old scruff that has begun to grow again.

"Yes, Carson, we are good. I told you last night it was a one-time thing," I tell him with a smile even though my heart is breaking.

"Ok, I guess I will see you around then. Maybe around the holidays if you are with Catherine," Carson says with a certain level of detachment in his voice.

He leans over to kiss my cheek and whispers in my ear, "You are the best, Alexandria." With that statement he is walking towards my door and I am trying to not cry until I know he is gone.

Once he is out my front door, I walk over to lock it and then I break down crying. It is like a dam has broken open and a flood of tears come flowing. I am crying for so many things, the stress of the past week, the loss of Carson and for what Peter has done.

Chapter 24

I feel awful as I am walking out of Alex's building. I am good enough at reading people to know while she said she was fine, I crushed something inside of her but it is for the best. I get into my car and call Catherine. "Hey, oldest and favorite brother, how are you?" she answers the phone.

I smile since she is always so happy. I know Alex is going to need her after what I just did. "Hey, you are not going think I am your favorite after this conversation," I warn her.

"What's going on?" she asks with wariness in her voice. I update her on the case and let her know that we have arrested Peter for the murders and Alex is safe.

"I need you to give Alex a call and make sure she is ok. And there is more I need to tell you." I take a deep breath because this will be the hard part. "Last night, Alex and I slept together. She said she knew it was a one-time thing, but when I left I could tell she was upset," I blurt out.

"You did what?!", Catherine exclaims. "Are you a fucking idiot!?" she continues to yell at me. "Why on earth did you do that and why on earth are you walking away from her? Don't you realize she is the best thing for you and you are crazy about her?"

"Catherine, this is the best thing for the both of us. I am way too old for her and we barely have anything in common." I can hear her sputtering over the phone.

"Carson, you are the biggest idiot that I have ever spoken to. You guys are perfect for each other and spending time with her for the past week should have made you realize you have more in common than you think. Get your old head out of your ass!", Catherine yells and then hangs up on me.

This conversation went about as well as I expected. I head back to the police station to get ready for the press conference where Chief Anderson will tell the world we caught the killer. My phone starts ringing and I glance down to see Adam is calling.

"Hey, what's going on?"

"Just calling to see where you are," he replies. "I am leaving Alex's so I should be at the station in about ten minutes."

"How did that go? I'm assuming you are walking away from her,"

"It went about as well as I thought. She said she was fine, we are fine. I told her I would see her around," I tell him as it makes me feel even worse repeating it again.

"Sounds like that was painful for the both of you."

"It was not fun. I called Catherine so she will check on Alex and make sure she is good. I will be at the station shortly."

"Well, since you sound so chipper. How about tonight you have dinner with me and Samantha and her friend, Kami?"

Dinner sounds like a nightmare and I have no desire to go on a date with anyone other than Alex. But I have told everyone and myself, I am not going to go down that path. "Dude, how about it? At least you can get drinks and food. I will pay," Adam adds.

"Fine but I'm not interested in a relationship so I hope this Kami chick doesn't get any ideas," I reply.

"She will have as many ideas about a relationship as Samantha does. Which is fun in the sack and that is all," Adam retorts.

"Ok, I will see you in a few minutes," I reply as I disconnect the call. I cannot believe I had the most amazing sex with a woman I, without a doubt, love and now I am going out on a date with a complete stranger. What the hell is wrong with me?

*****

I hear my cell phone ringing and I get up off the floor by the door and dry my tears. I see it is Catherine calling so I might as well get it over with and tell her what happened. "Hey Catherine. What are you up to?" I ask her not even trying to hide the fact I have been crying.

"Oh my gosh Alex, you sound awful. What is going on?"

"I am just having a rough day. Carson solved his case and apparently Peter is the killer."

"Wow, that is heavy. Do you want any company?" Catherine asks with concern in her voice.

"Sure, how about you come over here since I look like death warmed over."

"Sounds good, see you shortly," she replies.

I walk into my bathroom to wash my face and retouch my make up. As I am standing at the counter, I realize I may have to have my bathroom renovated so I am not thinking about all the wonderful things Carson and I did in this room. Hell, if I am honest, I might as well move since I am not sure if I can sleep in my bedroom either without dreaming about last night.

Ok, enough of my pity party. I was the one who made the decision and took the initiative with Carson so I need to live with the consequences. I will not allow myself to wallow in my misery. It is so quiet in my condo now that I do not have anyone in my space and I am surprised at how quickly I had adjusted to having the extra noise. I walk into my living and turn on the TV and the first thing I see is Carson and Adam standing beside the Chief of Police at a press conference.

Carson looks amazing on camera as he does in person and I realize at this moment I am in love with him. How the hell did that happen? I start laughing because leave it to me to fall in love with a man who has no desire to be in a relationship with a woman other than to have sex. I hear my doorbell ring and go to let Catherine inside.

"How are you?" she asks as she gives me a big hug.

"I am upset but I will be fine," I tell her honestly. "I slept with Carson last night," I blurt out. "That is what I am really having a hard time with. I thought it was incredible and I got the impression he thought it was mind-blowing as well and it was more than just a one-night stand but I was wrong."

"What an ass. He called me and told me the same thing as well. He is worried about you which tells me that it meant more than a one-night stand to him. I may have yelled at him as well on your behalf," she adds with a smile.

"Thank you," I respond and then start laughing at the craziness of this entire scenario.

"I guess I should be happy this entire thing is over and I no longer have any babysitters," I say with a shrug.

"True, so do you want to grab a bite to eat and celebrate your freedom and drink away your sorrows?" Catherine asks.

"Sure, how about we try the tapas place down the block," I suggest.

"Can I borrow a nicer shirt? When I came into your building I noticed that some press people are already standing outside. I'm assuming they are waiting to get a statement from you about Peter", Catherine asks since she is wearing a plain t-shirt.

Great, I was hoping the press would leave me alone since we had broken up last week. "Ugh…Let me make a quick call to my dad's press secretary for a statement to memorize really quick," I tell her shaking my head.

After a quick call, I have the email with the short statement I will repeat if there are any questions direct my way about Peter. "Ok, let's go play dress up. Hopefully the press is gone by the time we are done picking out clothes," I tell her laughing as we walk into my bedroom.

Chapter 25

"Well, that wasn't too painful," Catherine remarks as we leave my building. I gave my quick statement. Let the photographers take a couple of pictures and then Catherine and I left for the tapas bar which is down the block from my building.

"It wasn't too bad. It was hard not to tell them I thought he was innocent," I agree with her.

As we are standing there waiting for the hostess to seat us, Catherine begins looking around. "Holy shit. This can't be happening," she utters.

I glance over at her sharply. "What?"

"Don't look, but over there in the corner are Adam and Carson with some girls."

It takes all my strength not give myself a whiplash and look. I cannot believe it. It has not been twenty-four hours, and he is out with someone else. So much for me being the 'best one'.

The hostess walks us to our table. Just my luck, we are headed over to the same area where Carson and Adam are sitting. "Do you want me to see if they have another table or we can go some where else?" Catherine asks me.

I shake my head. "No, I will have to get used to seeing him with other women in social settings so it's fine."

As we are approaching the table, I see Adam has spotted us and is nudging Carson. I watch as Carson's head whips up and he makes eye contact with me. I can feel the electricity in the air as our eyes lock onto each other. It is like a massive thunderstorm is about to begin. The hostess stops to seat us at the table directly across from them. I am unable to suppress my groan. I look around the restaurant to see if there are any open tables we can move to, but the place is packed.

I see the grin on Adam's face. I hope he will not torture me or Carson in front of the two women they are with. "Hi Catherine, Alex. What are you girls doing here?" Adam asks as we are about to sit down.

Catherine glances over at them and makes a face at Carson. "We came to have dinner and drinks since Alex had a rough day," she replies as she cuts Carson another dirty look.

"Ladies, this is Catherine. Carson's younger sister and Alex, her best friend. Catherine, Alex, this is Samantha and Kami", Adam says as he does the introductions. I smile and nod trying to be friendly, but not wanting to intrude. Carson is still staring at me and has yet to say anything.

"OMG, you are Alexandria McNeil. I absolutely adore you and follow your fashion style in the gossip section," Kami says.

"Thank you," I reply as I try to sit down.

"Wait a minute, crap. Now I know where I recognize you from Carson!", Kami squeals. "I saw those pictures of the two of you at the gala. Your dress was amazing, Alexandria. I assumed you two were dating just based on the way you were looking at each other in the photos."

This is getting very awkward. I look over at Carson and see an unreadable expression on his face. He does not look like he will to try to offer any explanation to his date. "We went as good friends," I reply hoping we can end the conversation and sit down.

"Wow. I'm on a date with a guy who knows Alexandria McNeil well enough to go to events with her. Amazing!", Kami says.

I fight the urge to roll my eyes at her. Carson claims to have issues with my age, but this girl has to be four years younger than me. I look at Catherine with a plea of get me out of this. "Ok, it was nice to see you guys. We will let you get back to your date," Catherine says as she sits down.

"Thank you," I tell her when I am seated. "I thought I was going to punch her for being so excited to be on a date with Carson."

"Well, she shouldn't be too excited about her date because all Carson is doing is staring at you."

I glance over and make eye contact with Carson. The emotions that fly between our eyes are so intense. I am surprised we have not caused this restaurant to burn down. "I'm going to go use the restroom. I will be back in a minute. Order me a vodka cranberry when the waiter comes for our drink order," I tell Catherine as I stand up. I need to get some space from Carson.

"Are you ok?" Catherine asks with concern in her voice.

"I'm fine. I need to use the restroom," I tell her with a relaxed smile. Or what I hope is a relaxed smile.

I go the restroom and I glance in the mirror. I am happy to see while I am a mess inside, I look great on the outside. I just need to keep up the appearance of everything being fine until Carson leaves. As I am walking out the bathroom, someone steps out and grabs my arm. I jump and then recognize Carson.

"Alex, I am so sorry. I had no idea you and Catherine would be here tonight," he begins.

"Carson, there is nothing for you to apologize for. You made it clear what last night meant to you," I tell him and try to walk away, but he pulls me further down the hallway.

"No, listen. Adam pulled me into this dinner at the last minute."

"We are fine," I tell him again. This is killing me. I believe he wants more from me. For us, but Carson is struggling with making it happen. I want to get past him, but he has me blocked with his arm.

"Alex. I. I don't actually know what I am trying to say," he says with a sad laugh.

I look up at him and see him clenching his jaw again. The intensity in his eyes tells me what he wants. I reach up and stroke his cheek. "You know I really like the scruffiness on your face," I tell him. Carson looks surprised and then he turns into my hand and kisses the palm of my hand like he did last night. I can feel a shiver run through me. It is like a bolt of lightening goes from my hand to my core. I can feel myself begin to get wet from the passion this one little move as elicited. "Carson, what are you doing?" I whisper to him as I gaze into his eyes.

"What I have been dying to do all day since I woke up and saw you sitting there naked in your bed." Carson begins to lower his head towards mine. My body is screaming in anticipation of his kiss. "Alexandria", he breathes out as his lips make contact with mine. My world explodes in this moment. The passion is flowing between us becomes frenzied. I can feel him pushing me up against the wall as his tongue begins its quest of my mouth. I can hear myself moaning into his mouth as his hands begin to move restlessly over my body. I grab Carson by his shirt and pull his body closer to mine. I feel the evidence of his hard arousal against my stomach. Once I again I wish I was taller so I could feel that hardness against my center.

I am aware of his hands slipping under my shirt and moving up towards my breasts. "I want you so bad Alexandria," he groans out against my ear has he nips at my earlobe.

Just then a flash a goes off which startles the heck out of the both of us. "What the hell?" Carson utters as we both look over. I see a photographer standing there with a huge smile on his face as he realizes what he just caught on camera.

"I thought I recognized the two of you when you each headed back here. This will make a great story in The Post, considering he is here with someone else," the photographer says with glee as he turns around and walks off.

"Oh my god. What were we thinking? You are here with a date and I am making out with you," I groan while I frantically push Carson's hands from underneath my shirt. "Plus, it will create a scandal for my family if that story is printed," I continue. I can feel myself getting panicked.

"Alex, calm down. I will take care of it," Carson says gently.

"How can you tell me to calm down?" I hiss at him. "We will be in every gossip section in this city. All because I find you too damn attractive and can't think straight when I am near you!"

"You think I'm too damn attractive?"

I look up at him and he is smiling like an idiot. "This is what you're worried about? My world may come crashing down on me, and you are smiling because I said I find you attractive. What the hell is wrong with you? Are you drunk?" I demand.

"Little one, I will take care of this for the both of us. I am sorry for what just happened. I should not have kissed you and let it get out of control so quickly," he replies. "Go back to your table and enjoy your dinner with Catherine." Just as he is about to walk away from me, he turns back and kisses me one last time on the lips and walks away.

I walk back to our table and ask the waiter for our check even though Catherine and I have only ordered a drink. "Let's go eat somewhere else or sit at the bar," I tell Catherine as I take a huge sip of my drink. "I can't sit here with them so close to us."

Catherine gives me a funny look. "What?" I ask her.

She smiles at me and glances over at Carson, who is returning to his seat. "Your lipstick is a little smeared. I also find that highly suspect since Carson followed you to the bathroom," she replies with a smirk. I groan and turn red.

I glance over at Carson and Adam and see they are whispering back and forth to each other. I watch as Adam gets up and makes a phone call away from the table. "So, spill the beans Alex. What just happened?" Catherine prods.

I sigh out loud, "Your brother followed me and things got a little out of hand between the two of us. A photographer took a picture of us making out."

At that moment the waiter returns but without our check. "Ms. McNeill, someone has picked up your check," he tells us. "Who?" Catherine asks. "The gentlemen at the table across from you paid for your drinks," he says with a smile.

"Of course he did," I say rolling my eyes.

Catherine and I grab our purses and walk over to sit at the bar. "This is better," I tell her now that I cannot see Carson and we are enjoying our drinks. "I'm sorry that my brother is a pain in the ass."

"It's not your fault. He says one thing but then does another. I feel like a slut since I just made out with someone who is on a date with another woman. I honestly would have let the entire thing get way out of hand if the photographer had not distracted us."

I feel a tug on my hair and glance behind me to see Adam standing there smiling at us. "Why did you guys move over here?" he asks trying to sound innocent.

"You know why," I tell him.

"Adam, why the hell did you bring Carson out on a double date? Don't you realize that I am trying to set him and Alex up?" Catherine demands.

"Calm down Catherine. I did it because I want Carson to become conscious of the fact he is head over heels for Alex," Adam says with a smile. "We are on the same team. Based off how he came back from the bathroom, I can see you worked him up nicely."

"Thanks guys, except Carson does not want to be on any team so please leave me out of it," I tell them.

"Alex, I came over here to let you know that I have taken care of the photographer," Adam states.

"What, how?" I ask him amazed.

"The editor at The Post owes me a favor, and I called it in. Also, your dad may have to give them an exclusive in exchange for not printing such a 'juicy story'," Adams says laughing.

"Thank you. I don't know how I can ever repay you."

"For starters, keep making out with Carson. You guys are good for each other," he says as he walks back to their table.

Catherine and I order some tapas and have another drink. We are beginning to enjoy the evening, and as usual men are coming to flirt with us. I am sitting there listening to a guy give Catherine the lamest pick up line when Carson and Adam and their dates walk over to say bye.

"Alexandria, it was awesome meeting you," Kami gushes.

"Nice to meet the both of you," I reply to both girls. I notice Kami is trying to hold one of Carson's hands but he moves his hands to his pockets to discourage her. I glance up at him and give him a look.

"Alex, have a good night with Catherine. Try to not stay out all night," Carson says as he leans over to kiss my cheek. Before he pulls away from me he whispers, "I am sorry about tonight little one. I never meant for any of this to happen."

"It's ok," I tell him as he pulls away. "I will see you guys around," I tell the both of them. In reality, I am not sure when I will see either of them again and my heart breaks a little at the thought.

"Are you ok?" Catherine asks me after we watch them leave. "I am fine. Just frustrated with your brother. Let's finish our drinks and call it a night. I know it's only 9pm but we do have work tomorrow."

As we are walking into my building, I notice someone leaving the stairwell and heading into the garage. He reminds me of David but I shake it off since Carson said he was not a suspect. I need to get over my paranoia now that everything is back to normal.

"Are you sure you don't want any company?" Catherine asks me for the twentieth time as we are headed towards the elevators.

"No, I am good. Go ahead and head home that way you do not have to ride the elevator up." We give each other hugs and I watch Catherine go into the garage.

I take the elevator upstairs and I am sure it is going to feel weird to be alone in my condo. I hope it does not take long for me to get used to the silence again. As I get off on my floor, I begin digging through my purse for my keys. When I glance up and see Carson leaning against the wall outside of my door.

"What are you doing here?" I ask him uneasily as I unlock my door.

"I'm not sure why I am here," Carson replies. I glance over my shoulder and see he cannot seem to make up his mind on whether he wants to come inside or not.

"You can come in, if you would like," I tell him as I put my keys and purse on the table and begin taking off my coat. He walks in and I want to laugh because he looks so miserable. I walk into my bedroom to put my shoes away. This may give Carson the time he needs to get his thoughts together.

Part of me is excited to see him standing in my house but the other part of me is hurt from the way he walked out earlier. I walk out of my room and see that he is standing by the kitchen island. "Do you want something to drink?" I ask him as I walk into the kitchen to fix a glass of water.

"No, I am good." As I am drinking my water, I stare at him waiting to see if he is going to tell me why he is here.

"Carson, what's wrong? If it is about tonight, I already told you it is not a big deal. We obviously have a serious case of lust between ourselves, but I am not going to be the woman on the side."

I can feel our sexual chemistry begins to simmer while we are looking at each. How is it possible for Carson to look at me with his dark eyes and cause my body to react? My nipples harden in response to his gaze and he slowly walks over to where I am standing. We are like two magnets that cannot seem to stay away from each other.

"Alex, I should go," he says as he sweeps my hair away from my cheek. I look into his eyes and can see the war that is waging behind those beautiful eyes.

"Then go," I whisper to him.

It feels like an eternity before either of us moves. I am not sure which one of us made the first move. All I know is we are locked in a mind-numbing, passionate kiss. I forget about all the reasons I should not be kissing Carson right now. All I can focus on is the feel of him against me.

I begin undoing his tie and then move to the buttons of his shirt. I feel his hands move down my back and then to my delight he begins pushing me backwards towards my bedroom. I feel my bed behind my knees Carson pushes down on the bed. He pushes my legs aside so he is settled between my thighs and I am thrilled by the feel of his hard arousal against my core.

I can feel him unbuttoning my shirt and I moan the moment he caresses my breast. Carson breaks our kiss and I can see he is panting like I am. "Alex, I am sorry. I should leave," he stammers out. "I can't think straight when I am around you," he groans as he stands up over me and starts buttoning up his shirt.

My mind is still hazy with passion. "Carson, stop. Come here," I say as I reach for his tie to pull him back to me on the bed.

"I never should have come by. I need to stay away from you," he says as he ignores me reaching for him.

I jump up form the bed and grab his face. "Stop fighting me. Stop fighting us. You can feel the attraction we both share. I have never felt anything this strong with anyone before and I would like to give it a chance," I tell him honestly.

I can see the panic in his eyes after I tell him how I feel. "Alex, I can't do this. I am sorry, I never should have let things get out of control last night and tonight. You are too young for me and I am not able to give you the things you need. I should have known with your age you would mistake great sex for something more. I really came here tonight thinking we could have another night of great sex, but you are reading too much into things", he says harshly.

I hear myself gasp at his harsh words. I can feel my heart breaking, I knew I was deluding myself into thinking he cared about me. I can feel tears pooling in my eyes and I am trying my damnedest to not let them fall in front of him. I watch through watery eyes as he finishes getting dressed and walks towards the door.

"Sorry," I hear him say as the door closes and I lose it. I cry myself to sleep.

Chapter 26

I wake up and feel awful. My eyes are swollen and sore from crying. It also feels like I did not sleep at all. After I have my cup of coffee, I feel slightly better and realize I need to get myself down to the gym. A long run on the treadmill is what I need to relieve the stress from last night.

As I head down to the gym, I hear my phone beep with a text message. I glance down and see it is from Carson, 'Sorry I was harsh last night, hope you are well'. He has got to be kidding me. Sorry for being harsh, he threw what I thought was the best night of my life back in my face and made me feel like a stupid teenager with a crush.

I jump on the treadmill and have the best run of my life. I am exhausted after I am done. After running six miles, I feel like a new person and I have a new outlook on life. I am not going to let anyone make me feel bad about myself. Including Carson!

I glance at my work calendar to make sure there are no meetings scheduled and I am happy to see that my day is clear. I grab a pair of jeans, white shirt and pink blazer and decide my leopard print shoes are perfect for this outfit. As I leave for the office, it is a great feeling to know I can drive my car again and not worry about notes, killers or stalkers.

After I arrive at the office, I make a quick detour to the coffee shop and grab Shannon, Catherine and I our favorite caffeinated beverages. "Good morning Shannon. I got you a little treat," I tell her as I place the coffee in front of her.

"Oh, you are the best, Alex. This is just what I need this morning," she replies with a smile.

"It's Friday. You should be happy and I think we may close up early today."

"Wow, I like this Alex that showed up this morning!", she exclaims. I walk away laughing, my goal today is to stay positive and happy.

I am humming a song that is stuck in my head as I turn into Catherine's office. "Good morning Sunshine. I brought you a surprise," I announce as I walk through her door.

"Well, well, well, it looks a kitten may have gotten some cream. She seems happy," Adam says laughing as I come to a dead stop.

Standing in Catherine's office is Carson and Adam. "Sorry, I did not realize that anyone was in here this early. Catherine, here is a coffee. I have some calls to jump on," I tell them as I set her coffee on desk and turn around to leave. As I am walking out the door I can hear Adam say, "That is weird, I have never seen Alex act like that."

I am not going to let Carson rattle me. I will stay in my happy place. I keep repeating that phrase in my head as I close my office door and go sit at my desk. I wonder how long they will be in Catherine's office. Today is a light work day and I was planning on spending time gossiping with her. I finish replying to my emails and I am bored.

I hear a knock on my door. "Come in," I say. Carson sticks his head in. Great just what I need is Carson in here.

"Alex, are you ok?" I look up and give him a big smile.

"Of course Carson, why wouldn't I be ok?" I can see he is not sure what to make of my tone. "You did not reply to my text this morning."

"I was not aware I needed to reply to it. You made it clear last night we are nothing to each other," I tell him coldly.

"Alex, that is not- ", Carson begins. I am not going through this again with him.

I rudely interrupt him, "Carson, I have a conference call to jump on so I need to get back to work."

I pick up my phone and put my ear piece in and pretend to dial a number. This is immature but I am not going to let him see upset over him again. "Ok, well, see you around," he says as he closes the door. I blow out a breath that I did not even realize I was holding when I hear the door close.

I text Catherine, 'Let me know when they are gone.' She replies, 'What the hell is going on with you two? He showed up here wanting to know where you were and if you are ok. You looked happy when you first walked in before you knew he was here. He just stomped back in here looking furious'

Good, I am glad he can feel something, I just wished it was something nicer towards me. Ten minutes later my phone beeps, 'they are gone'. I get up and rush over to Catherine's office. "I'm sorry that I was rude this morning," I tell Catherine as I walk in.

"What the heck is going on between you guys? Carson seems all in knots about you,"

"I find that funny since last night he told me I was taking what happened between us too seriously. All he wanted to do 'is have another go at it' and because I am so young I can't handle myself," I tell her angrily.

"My brother is an ass. Tonight sounds like a girl's night out. Darcy called me this morning and she and Harrison are having problems. So let's go out and let loose," Catherine says as she begins a group text to make plans.

The day is quiet so we reward our team with a half day off work on us and we close the office early. Catherine and I are walking down to the garage and when we get off the elevator I get the sensation someone is looking at us and I glance around. "What is wrong?" Catherine asks me when she realizes that I have stopped walking.

"I must be losing it. I swear I just saw David standing over there," I tell her as I point over to one of the columns by the door.

"Weird. Ok, I will pick you up tonight at 7pm," Catherine says as we walk to our cars.

Her intuition is uncanny. That was close, she almost saw me. It has been so easy to read her emails and her routine is like clockwork. The only issue has been Detective Knight showing up to see her. Tonight will be the night I finally get her. I will continue to watch her since I thought last night was the night until that pain in the ass detective showed up at her building. He thinks he is so smart finding and taking down those cameras. I am glad to see that he is not aware of the tracking device I have on her coat.

Knowing today was a slow day, I was lucky enough to get an appointment for a massage and a facial at the spa. It is a mild day so the walk down the block was enjoyable. This will be a nice distraction to keep my mind off of Carson. I want to apologize for the way I acted with him this morning, but I cannot bring myself to do it.

Two hours later I am walking into my building and I feel so relaxed. I have the perfect outfit planned for tonight and it has a been a while since we have had a true girl's night out so it should be fun.

My phone beeps with a text and I glance down to see the text is from Adam. 'Hey kitten, are you ok? You seemed a little off this morning.'

I smile at his concern. 'Hi, yes, I am fine. Carson and I had a slight difference of opinion last night so it was more to do with him.', I reply back. I can see that he is writing a text back so I wait for the smart ass reply. 'He can be a jerk sometimes. What are you doing tonight?'.

If I tell Adam what our plans are, then I can almost guarantee his meddling ass will figure out a way to get Carson near me. 'Not sure. It's a girl's night out so no boy's allowed.', is all I type back. Either way if Adam wants to play matchmaker, I know he will call Catherine.

After a quick shower, I put on my make-up and decide to let my hair air dry into it's natural waviness. I pull out my black leather skinny pants I hardly wear and pair it with a great BCBG top. This top is a sleeveless, ivory shell that has a big V-neck keyhole cutout so my cleavage looks phenomenal in it and it has the right amount of edginess with it.

I keep my jewelry simple with a fun, funky ring and my shoes are my favorite pair of Jimmy Choo's stilettos. I check myself out in the mirror and figure if Carson should see me tonight, I look damn good. I switch out my purse for a black cross-body purse so I can dance and not worry about the strap falling down all night. It is perfect timing, my phone begins to ring and I see Catherine is on time like usual.

"Hey, are you downstairs?" I ask her before I walk out the door.

"I hope you have your party pants on. I am down here and I hired a limo to pick us all up and drive us around tonight!", Catherine exclaims.

"So fun, I will be right down," I tell her as I grab my coat and leave.

Catherine is in a party mood tonight. As I climb into the limo and see I am the last one to get picked up. Darcy passes me a glass of champagne with a splash of cranberry juice in it. This is our favorite girl's night drink. "Yummy and cheers!", I say as I get settled.

"Where are we eating dinner?" I ask Catherine since she is the one who always seems to arranges everything for us. "

I know you all need food and I thought since it was Friday, let's eat Mexican and then we can dance the food off."

It is only four of us tonight so getting a table at the restaurant was easy. After we order a pitcher of margaritas, Chelsi begins the gossiping. "So Alex, what the heck is going on with you and Carson? I saw the pictures in the paper and you guys looked serious about each other."

"We are friends, nothing else."

"No way, I do not believe it. The way he looks at you, he's into you," she replies back shaking her head in disbelief.

"The truth, we slept together the night of the gala but I told him it was no-strings attached and a one-time event since he is not looking for a relationship. I also made it clear the one-time event was the most amazing event in my life and he ran away as fast as he could from me," I finish telling them. Darcy and Chelsi look stunned.

"Catherine, what the hell is wrong with your brother?" Darcy says shaking her head.

"That is rough, sorry Alex. At least you finally slept with a guy on a first date," Chelsi says trying to point out the positive. I bust out laughing because at the end of the day, that was what I had been trying to accomplish.

"That is so true," I tell them as we are all laughing. Our food arrives and we dig in and finish our margarita's. I see Catherine glance down at her phone and frown at the message she received. "What?" I ask her. She looks up at me and smiles.

"The idiot is wanting to know what we are doing. While he runs from you, he cannot stop himself from trying to see you. He needs to get his shit together", she replies.

"Oooh…Alex, you could totally booty call Carson later tonight. I bet he would run over to your place," Chelsi says laughing.

"Stop it, I did the one-night stand. I am not going to start booty-calling men," I tell her laughing.

*****

"What is going on with you and Alex? She told me you guys had a difference of opinions," Adam says as we sit down for dinner. At least she is talking to Adam.

"I really do not want to go into it with you," I tell him.

"She looked pretty upset today when she saw us in Catherine's office. She also would not tell me where they were going tonight." I run my hands through my hair and wish I could shake this feeling of dread I have felt all day.

"I went by her place last night after we left that tapas place," I state.

"You did what?", Adam exclaims.

"I was waiting for her when she got back to her place. I do not know what I was thinking. Actually, I do know what I was thinking. I wanted to continue what we had started in the hallway at the restaurant."

"Dude, you are a glutton for punishment. How did that go?"

"She makes me lose my head. One minute we were standing by her kitchen; the next minute I am on top of her in her bed."

"That's awesome Carson. I am glad to see you decided to stop torturing yourself and jumped in the deep end with Alex."

"Alex has no desire to see me after what I said to her last night. I freaked out and stopped what we had been doing. She is smart enough to know I am holding back and so she told me how she felt. I threw everything back in her face to push her away. It is for the best," I tell him.

"Dude, you have it so bad you are blind to how much you love her."

I look up at him and shake my head. "I'm not blind. I know how much I love her," I tell him quietly. The look on Adam's face is priceless. His mouth is hanging open and for once he does not have a smart ass remark.

"What! If you love her then why are you trying to fuck everything up with her?"

"Honestly, I think I am scared shitless of what if she does not share the feelings that I have. She is ten years younger than me and while I know how I feel. This could be a passing romance for her. That and the fact she deserves someone who can be there every night for her, wake up in the mornings with her, not run the risk of being shot at on the job."

"She doesn't have an issue with your job," Adam says bluntly. "You are the one who seems to have all the issues. She has never said a word about the age difference. The only thing that puts her off is the mystery girl who happens to be her," he adds.

"Text Catherine and see if she will tell you where they are at. I have been texting her all night and she is not replying to me. She is pissed off because of what I did to Alex." Adam rolls his eyes at me.

"I hate to say this but you sound like a stalker. If I find out where they are tonight, what good will it do?" Adam states as he sends Catherine a text.

"I will torture myself until I give in and go see her."

"You are insane. You are my partner and I have your back, let me see if Catherine will tell me where they are. I think we should finish our food and beers and call it a night though."

I wish Alex would respond to my text. I can't stop myself from wanting to see her, hear her, talk to her. "I know where she is," Adam states pulling me from my thoughts.

*****

We are having the best time. The music is great; we have a VIP table close to the dance floor so we can jump up whenever we hear a song worth dancing to.

My feet are killing me so I take a break and sit down on the couch by our table. I pull my phone out and see I have a missed text from Carson, 'call me if you need a ride home tonight. I want you to be safe'. I cannot help myself but smile at his text, he is still the most thoughtful man I know. I begin to reply to him then stop myself. I know I have had too much to drink because instead of texting him, I hit his number to call. Thankfully, my brain kicks in and I hang up before it rings. The last thing I need is another night arguing with him and me crying.

"Are you having a good time?" Catherine asks me as she plops down next to me. I put my phone back in my purse.

"Yes. It has been a while since we did this."

"Are you going to be mad at me if I told Adam where we are?" she inquires.

"So Carson is having Adam do his dirty work?" I say sarcastically.

"Alex, I don't even know what is going on in my brother's mind. He has feelings for you, no matter what he says."

"I'm not mad at you. I do not want to have a repeat of last night with Carson. If he shows up, I will ignore him and dance and drink," I tell her with a smile. "Come on, let's get back to dancing with Darcy and Chelsi," I say as I grab her hand to stand up.

The music is great and we are all hot and sweaty from dancing. "Time for a drink break," Darcy says as she pulls us off the dance floor. We walk over to our table and when we get closer I can see two guys sitting there.

"Looks like someone found out where you are, Alex," Chelsi says laughing. Great, Carson and Adam are sitting there and I have no idea how long they have been there.

"Hey guys, I see you got a drink," Catherine says as she sits down next to Carson. The waitress stops by to get our drink order and I sit on the couch across from Carson.

"Are you girls having fun?" Adams yells over the music.

"We have been having a great time. I hope you two do not plan on putting a stop to our flirting and dancing with boys," Darcy states.

"Where is Harrison? And what would he think about you flirting and dancing with other guys?" Carson asks her.

"We are not in a good place right now. He wants to think about us," Darcy says frowning at him for asking. The waitress has great timing as she appears with our round of drinks. I stand up to grab mine but Carson has beat me to it.

"Here you go Alex," he says softly as he passes me my vodka cranberry. Our fingers touch briefly and I ignore the electricity that passes between us. I am not going there; I keep telling myself.

"Thank you," I say briefly and sit back down next to Darcy.

"Kitten, you look great in those leather pants. You keep surprising me. I never took you for a rocker chick," Adam says.

"Thanks Adam," I reply. I can feel Carson's eyes raking over my body and I need to get away from him. "Girls, are you ready to hit the dance floor again?" I ask them as I stand up. I glance at Catherine and she has amused expression on her face as I drink my drink in one huge gulp.

Darcy grabs my hand and the two of us head out to the dance floor. "Thanks Darcy. I needed to get away from Carson," I tell her as we start dancing.

"No worries Alex. He was eyeing you like he wanted to eat you up. I think it was driving him crazy that you would not look at him."

I can still feel Carson's gaze on me. I glance over my shoulder and sure enough, he is staring right at me watching me dance. I am not sure how much longer I can take being around him. I feel someone tug my arm and see Catherine and Chelsi have joined us. I lean over to Catherine, "When are they leaving?".

She starts laughing and shrugs her shoulders. "Alex, I am not sure. Carson has barely said anything. All he is doing is staring at you. I think Adam is about to strangle him."

"Why is he doing this to me?" I groan out.

"Girls, lets dance and forget about those boys over there!", Chelsi yells over the music to us. After thirty more minutes of dancing, we decide to call it a night. Carson and Adam are still at the table when we walk up to close out tab.

I am pulling out my wallet when I hear Carson in my ear, "Do you need a ride home?"

I look up at him and see the pain in his eyes. I want to ask him why is he torturing us but instead I reply, "No, Catherine got us a limo so I am fine."

"Ok. By the way, you look beautiful tonight. I am glad that I got to see you," Carson says quietly. I am so confused by him.

"Carson, you need to make up your fucking mind. You throw in my face how I am too young and I took things out of context between us. And here you are acting like you want more from me," I snap at him.

"Alex, I can explain – ", Carson begins.

I interrupt him, "You know what, I am done with you. I have no desire to hear what you have to say." I look over and see that everyone is listening to us.

Catherine clears her throat, "The limo is outside, let's go." I look back at Carson and see the sadness in his eyes. I love him so much, a part of me wants to suck up my pride and take what little he can give me. I know myself well enough to know I could never be happy knowing he is only interested in sex and nothing else.

"Bye Carson. Bye Adam," I say to the both of them and turn around and leave.

"Sorry about that," I tell them as we pile back into the limo.

"No worries. Carson has to stop sending the mix signals. I know him well enough that he will have it figured out by Monday," Catherine replies.

We are all getting dropped off at our respective houses. "Ladies, thank you for the best evening! I needed this more than I knew," I tell them before I get out.

"You can still make that booty call!", Chelsi screams out the door.

"You go make one!", I yell back at her as I walk towards my building.

Chapter 27

As I am walking down the hallway digging for my keys I realize if I had a smaller purse this would be easier. I grab my phone and then find my keys, finally. I cannot believe I am going to be alone again this evening. I am not going to get upset about Carson. He owes me nothing I tell myself as I unlock my door.

When I walk in I become conscious of the fact that my alarm is not beeping which means it is turned off. All of the lights are turned on throughout my place, as well. Shit, this is not good. I slide the bar on my phone and glance down and see the first person to dial is Carson from when I called him earlier and hung up before it rang. I hit his name and hold my phone in my hand while I am standing there shaking.

I see movement in my living room and it is David. "Alexandria, darling, so nice of you to finally come home. I have been waiting here for you," he says with sneer. "Now don't try to run because I would hate to have to shoot you," he adds as I see a gun pointing at me. I can hear Carson has picked up his phone and is saying my name so I need him to understand what is going on.

"David, what are you doing in my house and how did you get in?" I ask him loudly. I make a production of putting my purse and keys down and I leave my front door cracked.

He begins to laugh, a very deep, disturbing laugh. "I have my ways of getting into places."

"Please leave, I did not invite you here."

"Oh, my beautiful blue-eyed princess, of course you did not invite me. You saw right through me and spurned my advances, unlike those other women that were before you."

"What are you talking about, what women?" I ask him even though I know the answer. I need him to keep talking since I have no idea where Carson is and this may be the only thing to keep me alive.

"Don't try to be coy, Alexandria. You know exactly what other women. I realized you recognized me when we had coffee, so I knew I would not be able to woo you and get you to trust me like the others. But your eyes, they are always seeing," he says with excitement.

"Why are you doing this? Why me?"

"I knew it the moment you bumped into me in the hallway. You saw who I truly was and I knew I had to have you. I just did not realize you would be so closely protected and so intuitive."

I can see the anger building in David as he is speaking. I need to figure out a way to keep him calm and talking. "Plus, I had to get rid of my trophies in order to frame your ex-boyfriend. I have been extremely upset about that," he adds.

"Why would you want to frame Peter? He was never involved in any of this." I knew that while Peter was a little crazy about me, killing women for fun was not something he could ever do.

"I could tell Detective Knight was not going to leave you alone until his little case was solved. I needed him to think they had the killer so you would be left alone again for me to come after. I also did not like having to compete for your attention with the detective. I made good use of my computer hacking skills and set up the credit card trail to make it look like Peter knew those girls. I even stole all of your panties and placed them in his house."

"Did you hide the cameras that they found in my house?"

"Of course I did. Peter placed the cheap one in your bedroom the same night I was placing mine. That's how I got the idea to set him up to take the fall," David tells me gleefully.

"I almost had you last night, you know. I was going to come up while you were gone. As I came out of the stairwell on this floor I saw your stupid detective leaning against the wall checking his phone and waiting for you. He would have caught me if he had not been so busy on his phone," David continues. I am shocked by the admission and thankful Carson had been here last night.

David begins walking towards me and I move around into the kitchen, "Come now, Alexandria. I just want to share a glass of wine with you. Get to know you a little better," he says with a gleam in his eye.

"Please no. Please leave me alone David. You are sick and need help," I tell him as I am looking around for anything that can help me.

"I have had it with how difficult you have been Alexandria! Nothing has gone the way it should. I want it to be like the others," he states as he lunges for my arm. My fight/flight instincts finally kicked in and the self defense moves Max taught me before going off to college come back in a flash. As David grabs my arm, I punch him with the heel of my hand in his nose and he stumbles back.

He looks at me with fury in his eyes. "Usually I strangle my women first before I cut out their eyes but with you, I am taking your eyes first so I can hear you scream and suffer. Just like I have been since you seem to not follow my rules," he yells as he grabs my arm.

This time he was ready for me and blocks my hit and smacks me in the face. I am stunned for a minute and can tell my lip has split open. I manage to kick his knee and throw my elbow into his face which forces him to let me go. "You bitch. It will be a pleasure to hear you scream in pain!", he screams as he comes after me again.

I run out the other side of my kitchen to try to get to the front door. David tackles me to the floor. He rolls me over onto my back and is trying to pin my arms. I bring my knee up and try to knee him in his balls but miss the mark. Unfortunately for me, he returns the favor and punches my face in anger. I cry out in pain and can taste the coppery taste of blood in my mouth.

"Now that is the sound I love to hear," he says looking excited now that he has me. I realize while he has my upper body pinned down with his legs, he is going to have to shift his weight in order to get his knife to cut out my eyes. I can feel one of my high heels laying by my right hand so I grab it.

I keep moving my lower body trying to get his weight to shift to give me any kind of leverage. I know he is getting pissed. "Hey asshole, now that you have me trapped. How exactly are you going to cut out my eyes? The moment you shift your weight, you know I am going to kick your ass," I say to him in an arrogant tone. If I am going to save myself, I need to mess with his confidence and take him down a few pegs. Plus, if I am going to die, I am going to die fighting.

"Don't you worry about that Alexandria. We are about to have some fun," David sneers at me and he begins squeezing my throat. I try to throw him off of me but he is too heavy and I am getting dizzy since he is cutting off my oxygen. I see my phone by my head and figure this may be the only time that I can tell Carson how I feel. I do not want to die with him thinking I hate him.

"Carson, I love you," I say hopefully loud enough for him to hear before everything goes black.

*****

I am heading back to Adam's apartment to drop him off when I glance down at my phone. "Who is it?" Adam asks as he sees me frowning at my phone.

"It's Alex. I wonder what she wants," I say and I hit the button on my Bluetooth so the call comes over my speakers in my car.

I do not hear anything at first. "Maybe she butt dialed you," Adam comments. I am about to hang up when I hear her voice.

"Alex, Alex, are you there?" We still do not hear anything then all of a sudden she is yelling that the guy David is in her house. "Holy shit, someone is in her house. We need to get over there," I say as I take a quick right turn to head over to her building.

"Dude, we are about five minutes away. I'm calling in for backup to see if anyone is closer," Adam states calmly as he pulls out his phone. I glance down at my phone and we can hear the conversation taking place between Alex and David and bless her smart head, she is trying to keep him talking.

"Adam, hit the record function on my phone. We need to get this on tape," I tell him as we begin to hear David admit to setting up Peter. Part of me wants say 'I told you so' since my gut kept saying Peter was innocent of those murders, but all I can do is focus on getting to Alex before anything happens to her.

"They are sending everyone under the sun over to her place now," Adam adds while he is texting with our Chief. This is about to be a shit storm.

As we turn onto her street we can hear a struggle taking place over the phone. "See, I told you the little kitten has some claws. It sounds like she got him pretty good," Adam says. Even in a serious time like this, he can find some humor.

"Adam, I can't fucking lose her."

"Carson, she is a fighter. We will get there in time," he replies trying to give me hope.

I am frantic as we hear her scream, my blood turns to ice when I hear him hit her. My hands are shaking as we hear David is on top of her. I have to get to her and fast. I pull up in front of her building as we listen to the struggle take a turn for the worse.

I hear the one thing that should make me ecstatic, Alex just said she loved me. Her saying those words sends me into a panic because I know that means she thinks she is going to die.

I take off running with Adam behind me. She lives on the fourth floor and I am running up the stairs as fast as I can. All I can think about is what an idiot I am. I may lose her and I never told her what she means to me. I left her thinking I cared nothing for her. I will kill that fucker the moment I see him for touching her.

I burst through the stairway door and can hear Adam right behind me. "Carson, you have no idea what you are walking into. You need to slow down and assess the situation," Adam yells behind me. I know what he is saying is true but I cannot wait. Adam grabs me as we get to the door, I see that it is cracked. "Dude, just take a peek. He could have a gun; you do not want her getting shot do you?"

I glance in and all I can see is this guy on top of Alex with a knife coming close to her eye. I kick the door open to surprise him and when he glances up, I aim to fire but see Alex shift from under him, "Take that asshole!", she screams and to my amazement, a high heel stiletto goes flying into his eye. She is crawling on the floor trying to get away from him.

He is on the ground screaming while Adam runs over to arrest him. I run over to grab Alex and get her out of the way. Just then we hear more feet running towards her condo and we are surrounded by police officers. "Holy shit Alex, you single-white femaled his ass!", exclaims Adam while he standing over David with his gun on him in case he tries to come after her again.

Alex begins shaking and I look at her face as tears are streaming down it. "Calm down little one, you are safe. You are amazing and kept yourself safe," I tell her as I lean down to kiss her. Two seconds after I kiss her, she passes out.

"Dude, you have a way with women," Adam says dryly and yells for a paramedic to come look at her.

"Adam, look at her throat," I tell him hoarsely as I see the marks from where David had apparently been choking her. I pick her up and carry her into her bedroom to get her away from all the noise and chaos until the paramedics can look at her.

We hear yelling at the door as someone is trying to get inside but the police will not let them thru. "Adam, go see what's going on," I tell him since I am not leaving Alex's side. When Adam leaves the room, I am amazed at how beautiful she she even with a bruised cheek and split lip. "I love you little one," I whisper to her as I gently kiss her forehead.

I hear someone clear their throat and glance over to see Max is standing there with Adam. "Holy shit, Carson, what happened?" he asks as he walks over to look at Alex. "I got a call from Chief Anderson that something had happened at Alex's condo and I told the Vice-President I would call him immediately with an update."

"She is fine, I think. The killer was the guy David she kept saying was the killer. He broke in here and she stalled him long enough until we got here. In all honesty, she saved herself," I tell him.

"I kind of gathered that when I walked in and saw the paramedics and police escorting a guy on a stretcher with a high heel stuck in his eye," Max says grimly.

We all turn when we hear a knock on the door and see another paramedic team is here to look at Alex. "What happened to her?" they ask.

"We aren't sure. She has marks on her throat so I am assuming he strangled her. She was awake when we came through the door. I think everything overwhelmed her and she passed out," I reply. The paramedics take her vitals and look at her throat.

"We are going to take her to the hospital for a full check to make sure there is nothing more serious going on internally. She looks like she has been through hell," the paramedic tells us as they begin loading her on a stretcher.

I realize I am holding onto her hand like a life vest and cannot seem to make myself let her go. "Stay with her Carson. I will handle everything here and we can finish up at the hospital," Adam tells me.

"I will meet you over there. I will update the Vice-President on my way over," Max adds.

Chapter 28

I wake up and have no clue where I am. I glance around the room and realize I must be in a hospital. I look over and see my mom sleeping in a chair next to the bed I am in. "Mom," I croak out. My throat is so sore and feels like I swallowed a million razor blades. She awakes with a start.

"Oh honey, how are you?" she asks as she takes my hand. "Ryan, she is awake," she yells loud enough for whoever is outside with my dad can hear.

"My throat hurts, what happened, why am I here?" I look over at the door as my dad, Max and Catherine come in.

"Alexandria, how are you feeling?" my dad asks repeating the same thing my mom just said.

"Ryan, her throat hurts. Call the doctor to help our baby," my mom tells him sternly.

I look over at Catherine who is standing there chewing her lip nervously. "Hey, can someone tell me what happened?" I ask her or really anyone in the room.

"You don't remember last night?" Catherine asks me. I think for a minute and then everything from last night comes flooding back into my memory. David, him admitting to those murders.

Setting up Peter, chasing me, choking me until I passed out and then finally, me hitting him in the eye with heel of my Jimmy Choos.

"Oh god, did that really happen?" I ask hoarsely. "Did they catch David? Is Peter being released?" I realize I am asking all of these questions without giving anyone time to answer.

"Alexandria, Peter will still be in trouble for placing the hidden camera in your bedroom but they did drop the murder charges," my dad replies.

"You made us proud defending yourself the way you did," Max adds with a smile.

"Yes, I am glad Max did teach you girls those self defense moves back in college. Based off the phone recording Carson let me hear, you saved yourself," my father adds.

"What phone recording?" I ask him. I remember calling Carson when I realized something was wrong when I walked into my house last night.

"You were brilliant in calling Carson. Once he and Adam knew what was going on, they recorded David's confession so he will be jail for the rest of his life," my father says has he sits besides me on the bed.

I look up as I hear a knock on the door and see Adam is standing there. "Hi, what are you doing here?" I croak.

"I just came by to check and see how you are doing," he replies. My parents walk over and give Adam a huge hug.

"Thank you for saving our baby," my mom tells him as she kisses his cheek.

"She saved herself. All Carson and I did was distract the guy long enough for Alex to make us look bad," he says with a laugh.

"Where is Carson?" I ask him. I am surprised that if Adam and Catherine are here why he is not with them.

"I don't know where he is," Adam says vaguely. I can tell he is uncomfortable with me asking.

"When can I go home?" I ask my dad.

"Max, go get the doctor and let's see if we can Alexandria home and get her settled," my dad replies to Max.

"By the way Alex, your shoe will be tied up in evidence for quite a while so I hope those weren't a favorite pair," Adam says with a laugh.

"How can you even joke about that Adam!", Catherine exclaims.

"It was one of my favorite pairs, but I am pretty sure I will never be able to wear them again," I reply.

Max returns with the doctor who after checking my vitals and asking me a ton of questions finally say I can go home. "Thank you Adam for getting to my house so quickly last night. I am pretty sure I would not be here if it wasn't for you and Carson," I tell him before he leaves.

"Alex, you scared the crap out of us. It was not pretty to listen to but you are a feisty little kitten." I can see everyone is waiting for us so we can leave.

"Why isn't Carson here?" I ask him again. Adam looks at me with a sad smile.

"Listen, I have never seen him so frantic and crazy as he was last night. Carson would not want me to tell you this but he was here all night with you and left earlier this morning after your parents arrived. I am not sure where he is. All he said was he needed some space and time to think."

"Thanks Adam. Um, did you guys hear what I said to him when David was straggling me?" I ask wondering if Carson heard.

"Yes kitten, he heard what you said," he replies softly. Deep down I was hoping Carson felt something for me. If he heard me say I loved him and he made the choice to not be here with me then that tells me everything I need to know.

"Hey Alex, don't give up on him. I think he will come around but you are good for him," he adds as I am walking towards my family.

My parents and Max drive me home. As we are walking down the hallway towards my condo, I start shaking. I am not sure I will be able to walk inside of my house. "Alexandria, it is ok. We are all here with you," my mother tells me softly.

We walk inside and someone has cleaned up the mess that was made by the struggle with David. My parents and Max stop in the foyer and I glance back at them wondering why they are not coming in behind me. "Alexandria, we are going to leave the two of you alone. Call us later and let us know how you are doing," my father says.

"The two of us?" I ask him.

I look over my shoulder and I see Carson is standing in my living room. My heart stops for a moment. I have never been so happy and so unsure of someone as I am right now staring at him. I hear the door close behind us but neither of us have moved. We both are staring at each other. I can feel tears forming in my eyes.

"How are you feeling?" Carson asks quietly breaking the silence. My throat is dry so I walk into my kitchen to get some water.

"I am fine," I tell him as I grab a glass. Carson is walking into the kitchen to join me. I can sense the heat coming off of his body as he is standing next to me.

"Little one, you had me so scared," he whispers as he leans over and picks me up and puts me on the counter. I look up at his face and I can see the tension etched in the lines and the little tick from him clenching his jaw so tight.

"I was scared too," I tell him. Not being sure what to do or what he is thinking, I smooth my fingers over his jawline. "But I am fine now."

"You were brilliant and brave," he says as he shifts my legs apart so he can stand in between them. I breathe in his scent and I can feel the heat simmer between us.

"Carson, why are you here?" He looks at me and I am holding breath waiting for his response.

"I am here because I love you Alexandria. I loved you for a long time and did not think I was the right person for you which is why I have tried to stay way from you."

It takes a me a moment to react to his statement. "I love you too," I reply with tears falling down my face. Carson wipes my tears away and leans down to give me a kiss. The moment our lips connect I can feel a shock of electricity and then we deepen the kiss.

Carson pulls back from me and takes a deep breath. "Alexandria, you make me forget myself so easily. I have more to tell you." We are both breathing heavily as he takes a step back from me.

"Carson, I will make this easy for you. I am not the type of girl who can just have sex with a guy and that is all. If you want to be with me, it has to be all in or nothing." He looks stunned by what I said.

"Alex, the past eight years and the relationships I had during that time were only sex because from the moment I laid eyes you, I have compared every girl to you. You are the girl I was talking about meeting when I called off my engagement. I know I am too old for you, my work is crazy and you deserve someone who can give you the world. But know this, it started with you, it has always been you, I want it to end with you, I want you. I love you."

About the Author

Melissa Alexander grew up in South Carolina and holds a BA in Liberal Arts from the University of South Carolina. She met her husband while in college and after living in Columbia, South Carolina, Chicago, Illinois and London, Ontario. Melissa and her husband, their two children and two dogs finally settled in Atlanta, Georgia. Melissa has always enjoyed reading and after a co-worker brought over some books for her to read while on maternity leave, she was hooked on romance novels. When Melissa is not busy with her family, she enjoys running, reading and working on her next book.

Melissa loves to hear from her readers. You can find her on Facebook or follow her on Twitter (@mzalexanderbook).

Printed in Great Britain
by Amazon